Praise for

The Sound of My Voice

"The sometimes not-so-subtle struggle between art and faith finds eloquent expression in the story of Jordon, a young novelist, and her pastor-father, Peter. For a brief moment they are brought together by the only force that ever really joins them: human suffering and need."

—MICHAEL CARD, award-winning musician,
author, and teacher

"In a nice shift of perspective, the child goes away from home to follow God's call, while her father, who remains at home, is the prodigal. *The Sound of My Voice* explores lostness not in location but in the soul."

—VINITA HAMPTON WRIGHT, author of *Velma Still Cooks in Leeway* and *The Winter Seeking*

"Jo Kadlecek's novel is a reminder that life isn't always tidy and predictable. Often it's downright messy. It's what we do with the messiness that determines who we are and how we live. Do we forgive and heal? Or do we hold onto our hurt and pride and find ourselves worlds apart from the ones we love? The characters in *The Sound of My Voice* are loving and generous and damaged and prideful and stubborn and insist on learning their lessons the hard way. What they learn is that sometimes we must go to a place of suffering to discover healing and redemption. In other words, they're just like us."

—LEIF PETERSON, author of *Catherine Wheels*

"Jo Kadlecek's first novel is cause for celebration. Lyrical and compelling, it evokes a New York City so enticing, so colorful, so alive with artistic energy that it was all I could do not to hop on the next flight there. More important, though, *The Sound of My Voice* is a story of faith and forgiveness, of reconciliation and being willing to take risks—a beautiful and never simplistic exploration of what it means to follow a God-given creative calling.

—JOY JORDAN-LAKE, author of *Grit and Grace*
and *Whitewashing Uncle Tom's Cabin*

THE SOUND OF MY VOICE

OTHER WORKS
BY JO KADLECEK

Fear: A Spiritual Navigation
Reckless Faith: Passionate Living for Imperfect Christians
Feast of Life: Spiritual Food for Balanced Living

THE SOUND
OF
MY VOICE

A NOVEL

JO KADLECEK

WATERBROOK
PRESS

THE SOUND OF MY VOICE
PUBLISHED BY WATERBROOK PRESS
2375 Telstar Drive, Suite 160
Colorado Springs, Colorado 80920
A division of Random House, Inc.

ISBN 1-57856-858-7

Library of Congress Cataloging-in-Publication Data
Kadlecek, Jo.
    The sound of my voice / Jo Kadlecek.— 1st ed.
    p. cm.
    ISBN 1-57856-858-7
    1. Conflict of generations—Fiction. 2. Parent and adult child—Fiction. 3. Fathers
and daughters—Fiction. 4. Children of clergy—Fiction. 5. Women dramatists—
Fiction. 6. New York (N.Y.)—Fiction. 7. Clergy—Fiction. I. Title.

    PS3611.A33S68 2005
    813'.6—dc22

                                                    2004027716

Printed in the United States of America
2005—First Edition

10 9 8 7 6 5 4 3 2 1

To Luci Shaw,
whose poetic voice and pastoral mission
have inspired many artists and clergy.

PROLOGUE

She didn't mean to drop the dish.

After all, it was one of her favorites, a wide, blue ceramic bowl with tiny flowers on the sides that curled up. She'd bought it years ago at the mall and used it for Christmas suppers, birthdays, and other special occasions...like this.

Her daughter was leaving tomorrow, moving across the country, and she wanted to give her a nice send-off. So she cooked her favorite dinner—spaghetti with homemade sauce and mushrooms—put the pasta in the dish, and set it in the center of the kitchen table. She struck a match and lit two tall candles on either side of the bowl. Then she sat down beside her husband, across from their daughter, and they began to eat. In silence.

Her daughter glanced up from her plate—light sparkling off her thick lashes. Her auburn hair hung neatly over her shoulders, and her mother couldn't help but wonder at how quickly she'd grown into such a woman. She smiled at her mother before she turned her head and looked at her father.

"I don't suppose you'd be interested in loaning me a few extra—" she said. But she did not have time to finish her question.

"I don't suppose I would," he interrupted, picking up his glass of sweet tea and gulping it so that his Adam's apple bulged in his throat. When he finished he set down the glass with a thud that seemed to threaten the young woman if she said anything more. He tossed his fork into his noodles, twirled them over and over against a big spoon, and then stopped, studying the pasta with the intensity of a scientist. Without moving his eyes he tried one more time.

"I do not for the life of me understand why…you…want to go…*there.*"

A sigh spilled out across the table.

"You know exactly why I want to, have to, go. You just don't like that it's not your idea of—"

"As far as I'm concerned, you're wasting your time as well as the money I already spent on your education. I don't know why you think you—"

The young woman erupted. So did her father.

"You're being irresponsible!"

"You don't understand art!"

"How can you ignore the values I've taught you?"

"How can you be so closed-minded?"

"Who do you think you are?"

"How could you say that?"

"What do you know anyway?"

Spaghetti and pieces of blue ceramic went everywhere. And father and daughter suddenly found a reason for a cease-fire as they scrambled to clean up the mess. They knew how hard this woman worked for both of them. They knew how much she needed them to stop.

Still, she hadn't really meant to drop the dish. It was one of her favorites.

ONE

Jordan Riddle was having a rebellious day. Instead of dropping off her rent check to Mrs. Gonzales in 1B, she pushed it deeper into her bag as she walked out of the apartment building and onto a busy First Avenue. If she wanted to hang on to $850 for another twenty-four hours, then no one—not even a motherly Spanish woman—would tell her otherwise. Besides, Jordan reasoned with herself, there was nothing wrong with feeling a little bit rich every now and then.

She hadn't cared about picking up the phone that morning either. Yes, she had heard the nasal drone of the temp agency lady on the answering machine, but Jordan decided this was not a day to work. It was not a day to squeeze her way into a pair of nylons or ride an elevator through a stuffy office building. It was not a day to push green buttons on copy machines or lick envelopes. It was, however, a day to watch the city walk by, a day to sip mochas and think about words, characters, and plots in a play. Today was for reveling.

Jordan was feeling a few inches prouder—and taller than her usual five-foot-four status—as she turned the corner in the East Village neighborhood where she lived. Horns honked at the red light on the corner, as if honking would make it change colors. She smiled at the pause, the muscles in her cheeks filling out her face. Jordan closed her eyes for a moment, took in a breath, and caught the charcoal smell of the hot pretzel stand a few feet away. She reached into her front pocket and found a dollar she must have stuffed in the last time she wore these jeans.

"I'll take the fattest one you've got, sir," Jordan's southern accent was easy, sliding over the horns of urban life. The pretzel vendor—a tall Indian man with hair as dark as his skin—turned over all the pretzels on the fire as if they were fish frying until he found one that looked as chubby and fresh as any. He plopped it on a napkin and held it out to the twenty-eight-year-old woman standing before him.

"This fattest one, lady. Just for you," he smiled in solidarity.

Jordan laughed at his kindness, grabbed the mustard, and squirted it all over the pretzel. And then some. She handed her new friend the surprise dollar and nodded at his pretzels.

"Have a fine, fat day!" she said as she bit into the soft-baked dough. He nodded, his eyes bright from the exchange.

The light was still red, so Jordan strolled as slowly as she could across the street, parading her proud self and hot pretzel like a

Broadway star at curtain call. She threw each leg out in front of the other—slow-motionlike—pretending they were the long thin limbs of a dancer instead of the short compact legs they really were. Legs just like her mama's. And her mama before her. Toned, full, the kind that once worked the land and needed all the strength they could find to hold up equally compact torsos and arms.

When Jordan's solid little body was halfway to the other side of the street, the light turned green. One man stuck his head out the window of his yellow taxi and screamed for her to "move it, move it!" Instead, Jordan smiled at him, her eyes turning up into moon slivers under her forehead. Then she stopped right smack where she was, took a dainty bite of her pretzel, wiped the corner of her mouth with equal daintiness, and closed her eyes. She was not about to hurry.

Once she swallowed she decided this was as good a time as any to start moving again and so she did. Mr. Window Head sped around her, a truck driver whistled at her, a bicycle messenger cursed her, and a homeless man standing on the opposite corner cheered her.

How could she *not* love New York City?

Two blocks later—revolution still floating in the air—Jordan studied the sign in a small storefront: "Sid's Body Art Shoppe—Y'all Come in and Get Painted!" Ever since she was sixteen, she'd wanted to get a tattoo. Not like a teenager wants her own phone or anything, but enough to know that the very act of carving some colorful design on her flesh was one her parents would not have understood—then in 1983 or now in 1995.

"Hmm, that's a dadgum interesting idea," Jordan said to herself as she looked at the sign. She finished her pretzel, scrounged in her bag for a few extra dollars, and walked down the steps to Sid's.

"Hey," she hollered as she pushed open the door, "what kind of paintin' do y'all do on a good girl's body, and how much is it gonna cost me?"

A small red-haired man in tie-dyed overalls stopped what he was doing and tilted his head at her. Then he put out his hand and said, "Well, well. What part of Mississippi you from? Me, I'm from Oxford—Faulkner Country—and I'm Sid."

Jordan couldn't have created a better scene in all the plays she'd written since she moved north: here in the middle of New York City—eight million people and counting—the small-town Mississippi heroine meets a tattoo artist who happens to be from her home state. She laughed at the coincidence. And when she told him, "Heck, our daddies were probably neighbors growing up," Sid threw his arms around her and exclaimed, "It ain't every day I meet a friend from the greatest state in the union!"

A few minutes later, he began to tattoo a tiny red-and-blue bell on the palest part of her elbow. Jordan bit her lip when the needle pierced her skin. "Ow! Can't you make it pretty without hurting?"

"Nice idea, hon, but you know what they say: all great art requires a little suffering," Sid answered dramatically. He laughed as he said it, but his face just as quickly turned serious again. He moved his head closer to her arm and concentrated on the design with such focus that Jordan noticed a slight whistle in his breathing. Like she did when she visited the dentist, she decided she'd better look away and stare at a spot on the wall so she wouldn't notice the pain.

When Sid finally finished Jordan exhaled a bit of relief, chuckled when she looked at her elbow, and shook it as if she expected to hear the bell ring.

Sid grinned at the gesture. "No charge," he whispered into her ear so his other customers wouldn't hear. He winked at her. "It's a Mississippi thing."

Her lips—the fullest part of her face—turned slightly upward at the sounds back on the street. She took the clip out of her hair, grabbed the long auburn strands, twirled them around her finger, and put the clip back in, keeping the hair off her neck. The blueness of the sky and Sid's hug suddenly surprised her with teary nostalgia for home. She stared up at the buildings and the clouds for a long minute. She took off her red wire-framed glasses, wiped the lenses with her shirttail and her eyes with her sleeve. She sniffed back the emotions. Then, with glasses resting back on her nose, Jordan strolled again.

She needed to forget, to make forgetting a habit. She trained herself in these moments—like an actor in this city prepared for a role—to believe that living in New York was better than anything she had given up back home. It had to be.

No matter what her father had said.

Jordan spent the rest of the afternoon at The Pink Teacup, waltzing her way through two mochas, one scone, and a lot of distractions from the scene she was supposed to have revised for her 4:00 p.m. playwriting workshop. She pushed her glasses closer to her eyes with her index finger as she tried to work out what exactly motivated Tamara, her main character, to stay in her mixed-up relationship with her man. She loved him, but why? She needed him, but how much? She wanted him, but at what cost?

Jordan scribbled the questions on a napkin, but today even the answers rebelled. And no amount of caffeine seemed to convince the young playwright otherwise, so she tossed her manuscript in her bag, gulped the last of her mocha, and walked toward the five-story building in Union Square where her class met. The place where theater dreams wandered in and out of reality's mean grip. The place where she met Vinnie.

"Like I said before *you* have to know what your character wants, so *he* will know what he wants. Then maybe—and it's a big maybe— your audience will know what your characters want." Vinnie Vanzetti was speaking this afternoon as he always did: like a preacher, tossing his hands in the air to punctuate each point. His black hair didn't move, though, for all the animation. It remained neatly gelled atop his head, perfectly placed, like the perfectly worn jeans and the perfectly starched, black denim shirt he wore that Jordan couldn't help but notice. *A beautiful man,* she thought every time she saw him. Probably twice her age but beautiful nonetheless.

From the time she arrived in New York, Jordan had heard Vinnie Vanzetti was the best to learn from. It was true too: he was a playwright's playwright, a master teacher who understood plays and stories and dramas better than anyone Jordan had ever met in her entire life, which she guessed, when all was said and done, wasn't that hard, because most people she'd known didn't know a thing about theater. Ask them about catfish or grits, kudzu or magnolias, or who was up to what at Second Baptist, and you'd get an earful until Christmas. But the strange world of theater? You might as well be asking them about Tasmania.

In fact, before she had picked up her life in Jackson, kissed her mama good-bye, and dropped her books and laptop computer in lower Manhattan, right beside Tompkins Square Park and Ray's Famous Pizza, the only two people in her world who knew a lick of anything about plays were her English professor, Dr. Mildred Mason, at Bellreed College—who made her read *all* of Shakespeare, Shaw, and O'Neill—and her Aunt Cynthia Sue, who took Jordan to her first play when she was thirteen.

Jordan remembered that night like she remembered her first prayer and her first kiss—and truth be told she still couldn't decide which of the three was most life-changing. She had worn last year's Easter dress, pressed it until the yellow-and-white pattern almost steamed off the board, and then braided her hair like she would for church. Her mama even let her put a little black mascara on her eyelashes—not that she needed to. Her lashes were the kind that curled upward naturally, dark brown and thick, the kind most women would kill for. People said it was the first thing they noticed about her.

Auntie Cyn picked up her niece in her sea-green Lincoln, drove through downtown Jackson, and escorted her to the fourth row of the Mississippi Stage Auditorium. The lights dimmed and young Jordan Anne Riddle's entire soul was transported into another world, one full of glory and wonder and hallelujahs. *Selah*.

It was more than a spiritual experience, she'd tell people, though it was a conversion of sorts. But the magic of the theater for her was far better than any church service she'd been to, with all due respect.

For two transcendent hours she sat beside Auntie Cyn, smelling her Avon perfume and watching the characters in Tennessee Williams's play, *The Glass Menagerie*, lament about their lives. Jordan felt every single feeling that walked across that stage. She was sad with Laura about her limp, mad that Amanda would be so mean to her daughter, and of course, confused about whether Jim, the gentleman caller, would fall in love with Laura or not. She stared hard, listened harder.

"The child did not move throughout the entire show," Auntie Cyn declared later that night to her family. "Why, I began to worry that she was bored out of her little mind. That is until I tried to get her home and all she wanted to do was sit in the theater and talk her fool head off. She just could not get enough!"

Auntie Cyn was right: the lights, the actors' faces, the words, the furniture set on the wood floor, the audience surrounding her, every part of the theatrical production was heaven to Jordan. She was captivated by the experience, like a girl who just got her first crush. Only hers never wore off.

This was not necessarily good news to Cynthia Sue's younger brother—Jordan's daddy—who scratched his head any time his daughter talked about plays from that day forward. It was an attraction he did not understand.

"Who could take it seriously?" he asked her, though he never expected an answer. "Who'd spend good money on *that?*" To him, theater was an impolite, even silly, distraction from the things in life that mattered most: family, church, and Jesus. He didn't mind saying so, and he could not be convinced otherwise. No matter how hard his daughter tried to convince him. Her new love for theater was proof to him that Jordan was born defiant.

She all but put her fingers in her ears every time he criticized her new devotion. No amount of sermonizing about the foolishness of theater and art could bring her back, let alone keep her from saving every dollar of her allowance for any show that opened at the Stage Auditorium the next year. In fact, she spent the months after *The Glass Menagerie* at the Eudora Welty Public Library in downtown Jackson devouring each edition of *America's Greatest Plays*. Six years later, when she arrived at Bellreed College, the first thing she did after joining the Thespians Club was sign up for the college's annual spring break "Week in New York" to attend four Broadway shows. She didn't care that she would have to work overtime at the Sirloin Stockade, refilling the salad bar and clearing dirty plates from the tables, just to pay for the trip. It was what she had to do, especially since there was no way her daddy could—or would—pay for a trip like that.

Something had happened the night Auntie Cyn took her niece to the theater, something akin to what a missionary might feel about a place or a group of people. Folks at Second Baptist even had a name for it: *calling*. In this case, though, calling did not apply to girls who loved the theater. There was another name for them altogether.

"Whatever," Jordan whispered at the same time she rolled her eyes thinking about it. Her elbow stung where the bell had been tattooed.

"Riddle?" Vinnie was asking to hear her comment. She didn't realize how far from class she'd just gone in her head. Jordan shook her head apologetically, and the teacher kept talking about character development. *This* was why she'd come to New York: to learn from playwrights like Vinnie about the magic of the stage. *This* was what she knew she wanted the first time she walked down Forty-second Street in Times Square on that college trip. She knew someday she'd call this place home. No matter what anybody said, especially her daddy, no matter how she did it. This city was where she belonged.

She scribbled *N-E-W-Y-O-R-K* on her notes, shading in each letter while her instructor kept talking.

She thought about the countless workshops, staged readings, and nonexistent opening nights (save the stuff of fantasy) that had transpired over the three years and seven months since she had moved here. She told herself she was following not the calling but the dream—though she was never quite sure there was much of a difference between the two. She didn't mind the dull office temp work or the weekend nights at the Dream Time Tavern on West Seventy-fifth where she waited tables. It was all fodder for her writing.

She formed the word *fodder* on her paper, using squiggly lines on the top of each letter, as she thought about the dozens of shows she'd watched in standing room only—as an usher in exchange for a free ticket—ever more thankful for her sturdy legs. She had managed to keep despair, as well as her daddy, at bay the past few years, so she could focus on her writing. All for the hope. The proverbial artist's quest. The adventure of words and stages and lights, the hope of opening night.

This place kept her blood moving. This place fed her faith…or her rebellion, as folks back home probably saw it.

She didn't care. She loved every inch of this city. She loved that she could get a huge slice of pizza for two bucks. She loved that she could wear anything she wanted, and that unlike her southern girlfriends, who always had to wear lipstick and rouge just to go to the grocery store, she never had to dab on any makeup if she didn't feel like it, because anything was "in" in New York. Mostly, she loved that she never had to get in a car to go anywhere, because the subways would take her from one end of Manhattan to the other any time of the day. Between Central Park and experimental theater in the Village, the tourist-driven blockbusters of Broadway and playwriting workshops, the restaurants, the museums, and the people who crammed New York's streets with color, quirkiness, and culture, Jordan knew a writer never had to look far for inspiration in this town.

But she especially cherished the divine moments, as she liked to call them, those times when the unexpected dropped into an otherwise ordinary day in the Big Apple—if there was such a thing. Like today at Sid's. Or the day the man in a three-piece suit dropped his wallet on Fifth Avenue during rush hour. And the teen in baggy jeans and gold chains walking behind him picked it up, handed it to the man, and said, "Uh, excuse me, sir. You dropped this." Jordan watched.

And scribbled.

Or the night Charlie—who owned Ray's Famous Pizza—saw her digging through her backpack for any money at all, her glasses slipping off her nose, and told her in his thick Brooklyn accent, "Aw, forget about it." He knew she was good for it. "Enjoy," he said as he handed her a slice of pepperoni, smiled, and turned to the next customer. Jordan couldn't remember pizza tasting so good.

Or the early mornings at her laptop, rewriting a scene until it sounded authentic to her, sipping Earl Grey or cold coffee (whichever was most accessible) while deliberating over each word that each character would say. She'd look up from the computer, at the bathtub in the middle of her studio apartment, at the photos on the walls her neighbor Barry had helped her hang, at the books stacked to the ceiling. Then she'd get that feeling you get when you know you're more alive than you've ever been in all your life. You're suddenly glad for every single thing that fills your senses, because each one stirs up a joy so deep in your bones that you know something like your first night at the theater—or your first kiss—is happening all over again.

Jordan clung to the moments, to the utter connection she felt with her characters and her one-room apartment. She hung tight to the glorious contentment she felt for her New York friends and the stories she watched every day on the street. God, this was worth it.

Besides, they helped her forget.

Jordan suddenly looked up at Vinnie again. His mouth moved faster, his lips up and down like waves, and she realized she still hadn't heard a single sound that had come from it during these last few hours. Now she was trying hard to reenter reality and decipher the language that escaped from that firm beautiful jaw across the table.

There was no question his workshops were the best in town. Jordan couldn't help but respect the black-haired playwriting mentor. Sometimes she found herself amazed just to be a student in his workshops, just to sit across the table each week from a human being so sure of what he was born for. Vinnie was the kind of person who looked you so deep in the eye, you felt both comforted and vulnerable; who listened so carefully to the emotion behind each sentence in a conversation, you knew you had no choice but to be honest. Self-assurance was an easy way of life for Vinnie, and he made writing plays seem like the most natural—and the most important—task in all the world. To him, theater was a sanctuary, and these workshops were the pulpit he used to mold his disciples. They guided Jordan.

They were also the cheapest. And for the little girl from Mississippi, Jordan Riddle needed cheap from the start. She'd almost exhausted her savings account to get here in the first place, when she stuffed a U-Haul rental truck and drove across country. Even the graduation money Auntie Cyn had given her was gone, and the last thing she'd do was ask her daddy for any money.

She tried it once. She hadn't been back home since.

Jordan pushed the memory of their last argument out of her head as she looked out the classroom window.

Focus, forget, move on, she told herself. *For heaven's sake, move on.* It was time to grow up.

Vinnie was talking about story structure.

"Oh, he *so* gets stories, you know," Barry had told her as he stood at the door to his apartment across the hall from hers. Barry's slender fingers danced to the rhythm of his own words each time he spoke about Vinnie, and Jordan couldn't help but see in him the face of an adolescent admiring his hero.

Her neighbor was right, too. Jordan marveled again at how Vinnie pulled every theatrical device imaginable from his sleeve to make a scene work today. He referred to this play by Shaw, that work by O'Neill, how certain events needed to happen to move the plot forward. As she listened, Jordan vowed to write Dr. Mason a thank-you note for her reading requirements in college and jotted her professor's name in her notes as a reminder. It went without saying—though everyone said it anyway—that taking a class from Vinnie was a sure investment in your future. It certainly didn't hurt, either, that the teacher knew just about every person who had had the guts to jump off the deep end and into the magical—but murky—waters of New York theater. Vinnie knew those who managed to swim to the top.

For all his knowledge, passion, and charm, Jordan couldn't help but wonder some days how such a striking man of the theater could be named *Vinnie* of all things. In her studies of American and British drama at Bellreed, she could not recall a single Vinnie. Vincent perhaps. Like Vincent Price of the old horror flicks she watched as a kid when her parents didn't know. Maybe even Vince. But Vinnie? It was just too straight-outta-Brooklyn-mob to take him too seriously—though of course she had to. He was, in spite of the name, good.

Nonetheless, names mattered to Jordan Riddle.

She'd always been proud of hers, for instance. It was funny to her how many New Yorkers assumed she'd changed her name for her career rather than believe her when she'd tell them she came "from a long line of Riddles." She took great delight in the double meaning it held, that it conveyed both complex mystery and child's play in a single six-letter word. She also didn't mind defending its British roots, since England boasted some of the world's greatest playwrights. Riddle was a name no one dared put into a box.

She wrote it on her notepad as she listened to the class interact with Vinnie. Then she wrote her first name like she was signing an autograph.

It was this name she particularly cherished. She smiled as she looked at it, remembering all the times it took people to the famous river—as her righteous daddy intended when he named his only daughter—and they would say, "Oh, the Jordan where Joshua and the Israelites passed through!" She'd nod and recall her Sunday-school days. She loved the story as a child, especially the part about how the water piled into huge heaps on both sides of the wide dry path the people hurried across. She imagined the high motionless walls of water—like enormous fish tanks—and laughed at the excitement of it all. Even now, living in a city where the only talk of supernatural phenomenon was usually associated with Wall Street, she marveled at the wonder and awe of the Hebrew story. And the name. *That* Jordan had power, complexity, and adventure in it, all the elements of great drama. *That* Jordan had miracles.

Today, though, she thought of herself more closely linked to F. Scott Fitzgerald's Jordan in *The Great Gatsby*. No, she wasn't as cynical or as shallow as Gatsby's Jordan, but she identified with her flapper-style independence, her tenacity, and her powers of observation, a secondary character to the more charismatic, larger-than-life protagonists, who roamed both Fitzgerald's book world and modern New York City streets. *This* Jordan did a lot of watching lately, caught under the spell of the world capital and its professional stage. *This* Jordan listened to the city's sounds and furies, and especially to the voices of beautiful Broadway veterans...like Vinnie.

"If you don't know, how will they ever have a clue?" Vinnie's voice brought Jordan back to the real world of her Tuesday afternoon workshop. As usual what he said was just as right as how he said it, and Jordan knew it: the main character in her play had nagged Jordan for days. She mulled it over while washing mugs at the Tavern, and though she knew that her protagonist *should* want to make her life better, well, this character seemed to have a mind of her own.

Sounded familiar. Words thrown at her four years ago.

Never mind. Keep going. Jordan scribbled her name and some more notes in the margins of her script and glanced at the clock on the yellow wall. Vinnie was assigning readers for next week, passing back scenes with his comments written on them, and chatting with the dozen or so students around the table. As she crammed her notebook into her bag, she saw her rent check and decided to give it up that night. There was no shame in being a starving artist, she told herself. Maybe someday if she worked hard enough...

"Nice stuff, Riddle. But I'm still wondering about this girl," Vinnie interrupted her dreaming and held out a few pages to her.

"I am too," Jordan broke in. "It's been bothering me all week. I'll figure it out."

Vinnie's gray eyes pierced her, and he rubbed that perfectly shaped chin as if it helped his thinking. He paused before offering her that voice again. "You're almost there, love. Almost there. Don't rush it. It will happen," Vinnie was passionate again, and Jordan felt the red in her cheeks rise and fall. She glanced toward the window.

He was making her a believer.

TWO

Sunlight streamed through the colored windows, thick and steady beams that reached across the room to warm each person in their path. With eyes forward and shoulders pressed against each other, couples and children, grandmas and neighbors let the shine of the Sunday morning sun soothe their souls. Together they sang heavenly choruses. Together they listened to sacred words. And together they invoked the power of their Maker to refresh them, guide them, and use them for purposes grander than their own. Like children at the beach, they reveled in the good news from the pulpit and held tightly to the joy it offered. A gray-haired man remained engrossed in his pew by the organ's melody. Two young women wept quietly at the altar. For almost two straight hours this congregation basked in the presence of a light everlasting. It was holy ground.

When the noonday clouds gathered outside the windows, the

organ hummed its last note and people shifted in their seats. They gathered up jackets, purses, Bibles and notes, turned to one another, and offered spirited smiles and hugs as fuel for the road. Some laughed as they embraced. Others simply extended a hand. And when they were sure there were no more hymns to sing or friends to greet, they strolled out of the sanctuary like regulars from a favorite restaurant: content, grateful, nourished. They exchanged sentences with each other as they walked outside, verbal memories of a morning they would relish for a long time.

Yes, they would talk about this service, tell their cousins across town and friends around the corner, even the kids' coaches. They'd hear about it through the grapevine too, at the barbershop or the grocery store, about the sincere pastor and his brave new approach to worship that had everyone excited about coming to church. This was a morning they could not forget, a message and service they would come back to time and again, with verses and prayers and lyrics they'd hide in their hearts for a day when the sun refused to shine.

Peter Riddle felt a slap of cold air around his neck, forcing his attention back on the saintly man across the table who had been talking—apparently—for some time. Peter sat up straighter in his chair, picked up his pen, and scribbled on the tablet in front of him, as if that would help him catch up with what the man had been saying. He was annoyed with himself for allowing his mind to wander, for entertaining the idea again of having his own church. He knew such ambitions became distractions from what he should be focusing on: his role at Second Baptist as assistant pastor. But he couldn't help it; the image of him in his own pulpit nagged him every day. He lifted his head back and squeezed the pen in his fist, determined to refocus.

"And if you make known your requests to God, ah, he hears. He hears. And maybe he will lead us into them, and maybe he will not. In his goodness he knows our wants. And in our frailty he wants our good." Dr. Stately spoke, as he always did, with assured conviction and gentle guidance, a deep smooth voice that wrapped dignity around each long Mississippi syllable.

Peter stared at his boss and noticed the reverend's eyes waltz as he spoke of God, even his tired crow's-feet turned upward at the mention. Years of cheerful sacrifice and honest living lined his face, one that signaled no regrets. To Peter, Dr. Stately always seemed as relaxed as a summer's day. He believed what he said and lived what he believed, which, to folks in these parts, was a pretty good quality for a preacher to have.

Peter, however, could not remember a time in his own life when regrets did not press the muscles of his neck and shoulders before he fell asleep at night. He exhaled in disgust with himself for daydreaming again during staff meeting. His foot started to tap in a steady beat as if an old song had just come over the radio, though of course there was no radio in this conference room. Peter had never been good at focusing on one thing in particular, but that didn't stop him each day from wishing he were. He sighed. Then he picked up his pen again—foot still tapping—and drew a skinny vertical line, curved it at the top, and filled out a few dropping shapes so a palm tree began to appear on the paper. Peter smiled at his creation, admired the tree, and planted it beside a sandy beach.

But instinctively his eyebrows pressed downward in concentration while his fingers redirected the lines into a to-do list across the top of the page, on down to the bottom:

1. *Pick up flowers for Miss Mary at Cherry Blossom Center.*

2. *Study 1 Timothy; prepare notes for prison worship service.*

3. *Call Douglas about youth camp.*

4. *Write debriefing letters to missions team.*

5. *Pay bills.*

6. *Organize drivers for Senior Sunday.*

7. *Call doctor for Jeanie.*

Peter glanced at his watch—10:45—took off his glasses, set them on his tablet, and rubbed his eyes with the palms of his hands. His broad shoulders lifted up and down as he breathed in new air and out old. He picked up the thin wire glasses—the kind his daughter once said reminded her of a professor's—and began to chew on the end of them as he studied the list below him. These were the priorities for the day, once the staff meeting was over. Tomorrow would present another list altogether.

"I'm heading over to the center this afternoon, y'all, if anyone wants to join me," he blurted out. Heads turned toward him. Bodies shifted uncomfortably in their chairs.

"Sorry, Peter, got some calls to make…"

"Wish I could, Pastor, but I'm planning the youth camp…"

"My son's got piano lessons, otherwise…"

Peter nodded at his colleagues and returned to his list. He didn't mind going alone to the senior center. He'd gotten used to it. It was easier than sitting at his desk with too much time on his hands. Those were the dangerous moments. A busy life was a fruitful one, he'd trained himself to believe, and he had grown accustomed to it.

He picked up his pen again:

8. Write agenda for community meeting next week.

"Sorry about that folks. I had to take that call." Dr. Stately apologized to the half-dozen people sitting around the mahogany table. Peter nodded his head as if he understood the pastor's contrition and didn't want him to worry about it, though it was actually the first time Peter realized the elder had left the meeting for a phone call, noticing neither the exit nor the entrance. He gripped his pen and wrote five deliberate letters: *F-O-C-U-S.*

Only if he concentrated could he accomplish each item on his list. There was so much to get done, so many needs he was responsible for meeting. His stomach tightened and his foot found a quicker pace.

"Now, where were we?" Dr. Stately asked, and one of the

deacons began reporting on the budget. The reverend's composure challenged Peter. It always had and was one of the reasons Peter moved his family back to Jackson; he knew if anyone could inspire him anew, it would be someone like Dr. Stately.

When Peter had asked around after a few weeks back in town, he discovered the "Doc" was still senior pastor at Second Baptist. He was still reciting from memory each week the scriptures on which his sermon was based, still the only minister in town who could talk to both Bellreed College professors and farmers in the delta like he was one of them. If anyone wanted to learn how to run a church and teach the Bible, well, Peter knew you didn't get much better than Dr. Stately. Sure, he was getting to be about as old as Moses, some folks said. And sometimes his hearing wasn't as sharp as it used to be. But Dr. Stately was still the faithful Christian parson (in the old sense of the word) he'd been for almost forty-seven years now, if you included those six months he took off to recover from his hip replacement surgery at Ike Lewis's beach house on the Gulf.

Peter himself had been changed by the reverend's words, and he wasn't afraid to say so. Even now, he could recall it like he could his first baseball game and his first girlfriend—but of course it was the one event that set all others in motion for him.

He was twelve years old when he and his older sister were riding bikes one April day after school. They had only until suppertime, so they rode to the huge church parking lot a few blocks away on Chestnut Street, their favorite place to ride. They liked to pretend the sidewalks leading into the church were motorcycle jumps. They'd dodge in and out of the few parked cars with "4 Sale" signs in the windows, get up speed from circling figure eights, and then go off the sidewalks like they were daredevil motorcycle riders.

Cynthia Sue would flick back her head and let out a laugh at the sheer exhilaration of being airborne, a laugh that would shame any fire engine in downtown Jackson. Peter, of course—who "came into this world way too serious," according to his sister— would stare straight ahead of him, his long curly eyelashes flickering up and down, and squeeze his handlebars tighter. Then a tentative but gurgling laugh would tumble from his lips, more from the terror he felt in his stomach than the excitement of flying through the air on his bike. But when he'd land, he would flash a victorious smile to his sister, and they'd do the whole routine all over again.

Anyway, this particular night when the children flew into the parking lot, they suddenly back-pedaled their brakes to a squealed stop at the sight in front of them: every inch of the blacktop was packed—with cars no less.

"Somethin' must be happenin' at the church," Cynthia Sue said. And then in the same breath, she shrugged her shoulders and added, "Shucks. Well, let's ride over to the ditch and throw rocks." But Peter, too disappointed to change his plans so quickly, parked his bike up against a Ford pickup, ignored his sister, and walked straight into the sanctuary. He had to find out what in the Sam Hill was going on, why all these cars were parked here, interrupting their bike ride.

He sat down in the last row, crossed his arms, and watched. He didn't know what to expect, but he didn't think it would be nearly as interesting as jumping off sidewalks.

That was the first time he heard it: the sound of the deep smooth voice that fell over the congregation with confidence and grace. Peter's entire body froze when he heard it: a voice so comforting and engaging that it slipped around the boy like a flannel blanket on a cold night. The words pierced him. Enormous stained-glass windows reflected the glory in the room, and young Peter Andrew Riddle's heart was captured by the sounds of holiness, salvation, and angelic choruses.

"It was that simple," he told people. It was his moment of faith. And no amount of worldly fortunes or human experiences could ever compare with what happened for him that night when "Jesus saved me."

For the rest of that Wednesday evening service at Second Baptist, Peter watched every move Dr. Stately made. With each story and each illustration in the preacher's sermon, something crystallized in Peter's mind. He felt happier than he ever had and safer than he'd ever been. And somewhere in his belly he felt a feeling he'd hardly felt before, let alone recognized, one he'd return to for a long time to come: affection. And the boy whose bike was outside, whose sister was off riding along a ditch for all he knew, wanted nothing more than to love back.

So he did. After the last amen he walked right down front to the minister and told him he wanted to give speeches like that, the kind that helped people see past this world and into the next. He wanted to stand up in a room like that forever and hear the people sing those songs and look at the light in the windows. He wanted to tell everyone about this nice, safe feeling he had. Even if it meant going halfway around the world to do it, he would. And Dr. Stately—who knew what such a proclamation could cost him— looked into the boy's face, put his hand on his shoulder, and simply said, "Well, Son, pray."

This was not necessarily good news to the boy's sister, who felt she'd forever lost her riding partner that night. Nor was it to their mama and daddy, whose only experience in a church had been visiting the food closet at the Catholic cathedral across town a few months back when they couldn't quite make ends meet. They didn't much understand this new devotion their son had. Still, anytime Peter wanted to go back to the sanctuary of Second Baptist instead of the parking lot, his parents would shrug their shoulders and nod their heads. Since the country was going through so many changes, what with civil rights and rock 'n' roll, they reckoned it couldn't hurt a teenaged boy to be in church. They figured he'd probably grow out of it.

He never did. Peter spent the next summer at Vacation Bible School, cutting out crosses from construction paper and singing songs about Joshua and Daniel. Within a few years he graduated to something the folks at Second Baptist called "Youth Crusaders," and soon he was working at the Jitney Jungle grocery store to help pay for summer mission trips, one to an orphanage in Mexico and another to an Indian reservation in Colorado. From the first time he felt the dirt floor at that Mexican school, Peter knew he would live like this someday. Folks at the church figured he had a special "anointing," and he believed them, which is why a few years later he enrolled at Jackson Baptist Bible College so he could someday lead his own church. In those days Peter didn't care what it took as long as he could "go into all the world" to preach about Jesus and to help people.

Nothing else mattered.

Twelve years after he graduated from Bible college—with two years of seminary and seven years on the mission field in-between—Peter's dream was flimsy at best. The last thing he expected when he went looking for Dr. Stately was to be offered a job. He only wanted to talk with the pastor who'd first inspired him. Maybe, he had told himself, if he returned to the place where he first heard Dr. Stately's voice and message, the memories of the last seven years would go away. Maybe something new would take over.

Maybe that feeling would come back.

He couldn't have known the doctor had been looking for an

associate pastor who could direct their missions department and charity work throughout Jackson. Who better to do that than someone who'd come to faith in this very church? Better still, a local boy who'd traveled the world and now was coming back home? They shook on it.

That made Peter Riddle the official associate pastor of the second biggest Baptist church in the capital of the state of Mississippi. It also put him back on the road toward his goal. And every Wednesday morning for more than a decade now, he'd join Dr. Stately and his secretary, Loretta (who'd been typing the minister's sermons for him as long as he'd been giving them), a few Sunday-school teachers, Jimmy, the Crusaders' leader, and whichever elders and deacons could get off work for these church updates and pastoral devotionals.

No one seemed to mind the weekly meetings; they helped the staff keep abreast of one another's work. Besides, they felt a little like personal instruction with the master teacher himself. But to Dr. Stately these meetings were coveted time with his spiritual family, as he liked to call the church staff, opportunities to remember their purpose and return again to their source of inspiration. He did not like being interrupted for phone calls. Wednesday morning staff meetings were as normal to Peter as Mississippi humidity. They forced him to sit still at least once a week. He admired his pastor's discipline and ability to stay centered on Scripture.

"Why, that man *wrote* the Bible!" Cynthia Sue liked to tease whenever she attended her brother's church, which usually was only for Christmas and Easter services when she visited the family. Though his sister wasn't much interested in Peter's religion, they agreed about one thing. Second Baptist's senior pastor knew just about everything there was to know about all things religious: martyrs through the ages, saints, revivals, spiritual gifts, denominations, and of course, human nature.

Peter studied the elder minister like a businessman studies the market. What got people buying? What made them let go? What helped bring them in? Somehow Dr. Stately had long ago figured it out and helped, it seemed to Peter anyway, almost every Baptist, Pentecostal, and Methodist leader in the state who was also trying to understand it. After all these years, Second Baptist's associate pastor was hoping that same wisdom might lead him in the same direction, where he would someday also be a senior pastor of a thriving church. That, Peter thought, would be his ultimate way of loving back.

If he could just concentrate.

"We're plannin' on takin' a bunch of kids to the Catfish Festival downtown as clean-up patrol," Jimmy announced when Dr. Stately finished his study and asked for staff updates. Peter rubbed his eyes as he tried to listen. The youth group volunteered each fall while the parade roamed past the Old Capitol toward the governor's mansion. Though it was a small city compared to others across the South, Jackson was the biggest in Mississippi and a town that loved its celebrations as much as the things it was known for, like catfish, blues, and grits.

"We're takin' about fifteen boys with garbage bags to pick up trash," Jimmy continued.

"Lord knows they're gonna need it! Tsk, tsk, the mess they make at that parade each year," Loretta said. She poked the bun in her hair with her pencil and shook her head.

"I'll go with you if you need an extra adult, Jimmy," Peter said. He wrote down *Festival* in his notebook.

"Remember the time they got stuck behind the horses?" one of the deacons chimed in.

"Next year was tough recruitin' any more kids!" Jimmy said. The group broke into laughter and more spontaneous stories, and a slight grin crossed Peter's face at the hubbub.

Though he'd moved his family around the world, Jackson was the place Peter had always referred to as home. He'd grown up here, and a man got used to the streets he saw every day during his childhood. It was a place where the local high school band marched through downtown in annual parades. Where clerks at the post office talked with you for fifteen minutes about the types of birds featured on the stamps you just bought. Where every time you went to the Jitney Jungle to pick up milk—even years after you worked there—you still bumped into an old friend or saw a familiar face. And where even the health clinic in West Jackson—the one Second Baptist partnered with—sent handwritten notes to patients to remind them of their next checkup. He was relieved to be around such familiarity again, where life was what you expected it to be: busy, predictable, safe. Packed each year with festivals and potluck dinners and church services.

Not a lot changed in Jackson. Here you could hold on to things without the fear of losing them. Most of the time.

While Jimmy, Loretta, and the deacons kept their parade stories going, Peter stared out the window and considered how much easier life was in Jackson than it had been on the mission field. From the paved roads and the massive shopping malls to the baseball diamonds and the school buses, it didn't take his family long to settle back into southern life. It was nice to be back in a town where he didn't have to worry about where he'd buy gas for his car or if he'd run out getting there. Though he was much too polite to tell anyone, he was also glad to be back in a house where he knew the toilet would flush when he used it. The little things helped get him through the transition. They were part of the reason they'd come home.

Peter swallowed and glanced back at his list. But he also knew being back had not resurrected the joy he'd lost a thousand miles away.

~‹❦›~

"How's the family?" Dr. Stately's voice penetrated his ears again, though this time Peter wasn't sure what he'd heard. Peter's eyelashes picked up speed. The pastor spotted the drifter. So did his colleagues.

"It's your turn, Peter. Everyone else has given an update. So how's *your* family? Jeanie? How's your daughter?" The smoothness in his voice drifted slightly out of that last question. The first two Peter could handle.

"Well, my sister is fine, though feisty as ever and still won't budge about matters of faith, bless her heart," Peter said. He had obviously missed what the others communicated about their families. He forced a smile and rattled off the rest of his answer like it was a grocery list: "Mama and Daddy sold the house and are moving down to Hattiesburg to be closer to the coast. Jeanie's still hard at work with her fourth graders at Harriet Tubman Elementary School, although she's fightin' some sort of flu bug. Oh, and she's been thinking about taking a trip up north."

A dozen eyes stared quietly at Peter. Heads nodded to signal they were listening, waiting for more. His face felt hot.

"And how's that girl of yours, Peter?" Dr. Stately asked firmly, expectantly. It was a question Peter could not find on his list of answers. Give the associate pastor inmates to teach or seniors to visit or even Sunday-school children to sing with. Send him into the jungles of South America with thirty junior high students for ten days or recruit him to play shortstop for the church slow-pitch softball league. These pursuits he could manage, enjoy even. Most he had mastered with some level of comfort and competence, and he'd be happy to report on *them*.

But throw him a question about his daughter, and he'd press his eyebrows together, squeeze whatever pen or coffee cup was in his hand, and let out one of those gurgly laughs that said more about his discomfort than about anything funny.

"Grr-ugh, fine thanks" were the only sounds that slid together and formed pseudowords in Peter's mouth.

He simply could not bring himself to tell the man he respected most on this planet that his only daughter was wasting her life. How she ever came to think that the artist's life, as she called it, was something she wanted to pursue, he would never know. Playwriting? Theater? Peter had no idea what—or why—she wanted either, and unless she came home where she belonged, he did not feel compelled to do any more for her. He'd let her go four years ago and hadn't seen her since. His stomach tightened again when he thought of her in a city like New York, and he cleared his throat in a quick, guttural cough. He was convinced: the elder would not approve. Though everyone around the table already knew.

Thankfully, Loretta intervened. "Surprise! The Ladies Fellowship wanted y'all to know how much they ah-ppre-ci-ate you," she declared. "Lunch is ready!"

"Meeting adjourned," the minister announced. Jimmy and the deacons did not need a second invitation for food. They moved their chairs back and started talking about chicken and macaroni, parades and baseball as they made their way into the large room that doubled as a kitchen and a basketball court. Peter pushed his glasses toward his eyes, exhaled, and examined the to-do list in front of him.

"I need to be out of town a few Sundays next month." The senior pastor was talking again, and this time Peter realized there was no one else in the room but him. Peter nodded as he looked Dr. Stately in the eye.

"Would you mind filling in for me in the pulpit? They'll be back-to-back Sundays so you could preach a series if that's how you're compelled." Peter felt the red fill his face at the minister's confidence in him. He responded with something about being glad to and smiled at the man before him.

Like old friends, the pastors walked toward the kitchen/basketball court. But when Peter noticed the clock, he knew he wouldn't have time for lunch. He excused himself and hurried to his office instead. He glanced at his notes and added in all caps:

10. PREPARE SERMON SERIES.

He underlined the three words. Then he picked up his car keys and drove first to the flower shop and then to the Cherry Blossom Center.

Number one on his list could be crossed off.

THREE

Jordan dropped her token in the subway turnstile and hurried toward the platform of the number 2 train. She was still thinking about Vinnie's comments, how her characters needed more motivation, when she glanced around at the passengers waiting for their rides. Times Square subway station still held its spell on her. Thousands of people passed through this underground world every day for a thousand different reasons: they were going to work, exploring the city's tourist attractions, hurrying to the theater, hustling a few bucks, catching another train to head home, you name it. Some were lost and trying to find their way back to their hotels while others were simply hoping to be discovered in a city where dreams came and went as frequently as the subway.

Jordan loved to watch the faces. She could always spot the tired ones, those weary from being in the city too long or those exhausted from the excitement of cramming too much of New York into only a few days. She listened to the languages: Chinese, Russian, Spanish, and many she couldn't recognize. She studied the countless expressions on the faces of construction workers, tourists, Wall Street suits, teen mothers—all of whom made Forty-second Street/Times Square one of Jordan's favorite places to observe the human sea of motion that gave Gotham its charm. Stories were everywhere.

Each time she wandered into New York's underworld, she marveled at the diversity of the creativity she encountered. The eyes, the shapes, the sounds, the colors, the voices, all of them—together and separate—couldn't help but remind her of the extraordinarily creative artist who had made them, one whose work was surely transcendent. Genius even.

God, she had thought for many years, was enormously artistic if he was anything. She believed that with certainty.

The train screamed to a halt as the playwright plugged her ears with her index fingers to soften the noise. The doors opened and she rushed to find a seat. Too crowded. Jordan didn't mind standing, though, since she'd be at her stop soon enough. She held on to a cold steel pole and smiled at the gray-haired Chinese woman who elbowed her way through the crowd, determined to sit down even if it meant squeezing in between two people. Jordan pushed her red thin glasses close to her eyes and read the advertisement above the passengers' heads. She glanced at the shapes of the faces around her and planted her feet as the train picked up speed.

She wondered what Barry would say about these passengers and chuckled at the thought. Sometimes when she and her neighbor would usher together at a show, they would size up the subway crowd on their way and create stories about some of the characters sitting around them: who they were, where they were going, what they did for a living. It kept their imaginations jumping and their wit fresh. It was great exercise for creative types "like us," Barry would say to his friend.

"That guy over there," Barry pointed with his big brown eyes one night and whispered to Jordan, "he's the son of a funeral director. Had to get out of the family business because it was a little too dull for him, if you know what I mean."

"So what's he do now?" Jordan whispered back, trying not to laugh.

"Manicures and pedicures," he said with as straight a face as he could muster. Jordan, nearing the edge of hysteria, bounced up and stood a few feet from Barry so as not to give away their secret. They were like two disobedient students in a class who had to be separated so as not to disturb the other kids. Besides, they understood the first rule of the subway-story game: never let your subject know you're talking about him. This was New York, after all, and you never knew who might or, worse, might not like your underground fiction.

Rule number two: split up if you're about to break rule number one. Then regroup.

"That woman over there?" Jordan mumbled to Barry who'd followed her into the next car. Jordan stood six inches shorter than her friend and nodded toward the woman. "The one in the yellow power suit?"

Barry glanced toward the woman and grinned to his accomplice, waiting for the punch line until he could no longer contain himself.

"Let me guess," he said. "President of the Daughters of the American Revolution?"

"Oh, please," Jordan retorted, looking away from the woman as if she *weren't* talking about her. "That's way too small. That woman runs the world."

"Wow, I always wondered what the head of the Republican Party looked like. She is evil and must be destroyed," Barry used his best extraterrestrial voice, and Jordan could no longer contain her laughter. She exploded into such a howl that every muscle on her compact body jiggled. Almost everyone in the train glanced at her and, in a typical New York second, just as quickly went back to their newspapers or magazines. Some, though, did not bother with Jordan or Barry at all. New Yorkers were not easily surprised.

The people-watching game, of course, would end the minute the two friends left the subway and entered the theater to help people find their seats. They'd hand out programs and lead visitors up and down steps, checking tickets and pointing to cushioned seats. Without fail the theater became especially hectic a few minutes before the curtain went up. Dinner crowds would rush in, show the ushers their tickets, and demand to be seated before curtain. Jordan would peer at them over her glasses, which by now had slipped to the end of her nose, exposing both her glorious lashes and her easy gaze. She'd smile.

"Y'all don't need to worry about a thing," she'd say gently, showing the latecomers to their seats and diffusing their anxiety. "Make yourself comfortable and enjoy the show!"

Their faces and attitudes would melt into a polite expectancy as they sat down and thanked Jordan. This was the theater after all, a place that invited thoughtfulness, celebration, and above all, respect.

When their jobs were finished and the lights had dimmed, Jordan and Barry would rendezvous in the back of the orchestra section, lean against the wall, and get lost in the story on the stage. At intermission they'd dissect the play's strengths and weaknesses, which actors were "on" that night, and how the audience was responding. Anyone could volunteer to usher in exchange for a chance to see a Broadway or off-Broadway show for free. But for Jordan this was more than a free night on the town; it was part of her education. It was why she lived here.

New York theater was the best and most influential in the country. People would travel from places like Denver or Tokyo,

Des Moines or Toronto just to see a play or a musical here. They'd order tickets months in advance or spend hours standing in the half-price ticket line to buy one. If Jordan could write for *this* stage, she knew she could affect many, many lives.

In spite of what her daddy believed.

" 'Scuse me, lady. Got somethin' to eat?" A skinny woman stood inches from Jordan's shoulders, calling her attention back to this subway car on this Wednesday afternoon as she hurried to work at the Dream Time Tavern. The woman was eye level with Jordan and wore an old army jacket, black sweat pants, and shoes with holes so big in the front that her toes stuck out. No socks. That bothered Jordan, considering it was an unusually chilly October day. The woman's face was leathery, so Jordan couldn't quite guess her age, though she figured the woman was probably a decade or so older than she was.

"Nothin' to eat? That's okay. Okay. I'm okay," the woman muttered quickly as her face turned from Jordan's. It was the first time in months someone in the subway had asked her for food instead of money, and Jordan felt her heart rate speed up. She tapped her foot to a quick but silent beat and took off her red-framed glasses, pretending to clean them. Usually, she'd put a quarter or a dollar in someone's hand, look him right in the eye, and tell him to take care.

"Always take care," she'd say, "you never know what might happen."

Jordan knew from personal experience it wasn't easy living in this city—or anywhere else for that matter. She knew how tough it was to earn a dollar one day and how easy it was to spend it the next. So she gave when she could.

Barry told her she was too soft, that she'd go broke giving to everyone who begged her for a buck. These guys knew how to prey on the soft ones, he'd lecture her, when they would really just go and buy a beer with her money. But Jordan said it was how she'd been raised: you gave to anyone who asked.

Unless you were family, that is.

Besides, she was already broke, so what did a dollar every now and then matter? Barry would laugh at his friend, shake his head, and pat her on the back, telling her someday she'd grow up.

When Jordan put her glasses back on and looked at this woman's face, though, something inside her told her this was for real. This woman's stomach was empty.

The Chinese woman glanced at Jordan to see how she'd respond. A large man sitting across from her took a small orange from his bag and handed it to the woman, who received it as if the kindness was more nourishing than the fruit. She thanked him by nodding her head and chanting "thank you" over and over in a monotone voice. Then she began peeling the orange and putting each peel neatly into her jacket pocket while she dropped the fruit into her mouth. She smiled at its sweetness, closing her eyes while the flavors slid down her throat.

Jordan stared. She couldn't help it and she wasn't sorry she did. As the train slowed to a stop at Seventy-second Street, Jordan instinctively tapped the woman on the shoulder and motioned for her to follow. When the doors opened, the two stepped out. They walked up the steps—Jordan taking small quick steps, and the woman taking large uneven ones—out of the subway and onto Broadway and Seventy-second Street.

"I know where you can get a sandwich if you want," Jordan said. The woman lowered her eyebrows like a drawbridge and shifted her weight from one leg to the other. "Okay, okay. Okay," she said in the same monotone voice, still rocking on the sidewalk. Then Jordan extended her hand.

"I'm Jordan."

"Like the river?" The woman stopped still at the sound of the name she'd just heard, her tired eyes searching the face of the woman standing before her. She took Jordan's hand, and Jordan felt skin as callused as an old farmer. The woman held tight.

"Yes, um, sort of, like the river." Now Jordan shifted a bit.

"I 'member that story from church. Nice story. Nice. Lucy, I'm Lucy. That's who I am. Lucy," the woman's taut face loosened slightly as she introduced herself, still keeping Jordan's hand in hers.

Suddenly, she was as familiar to Jordan as the women she'd known growing up—before her father moved them back to Jack-

The Sound of My Voice

son. The image of such women lingered often in Jordan's head: once proud women hanging to a last thread of dignity, coming to her family's front door, standing on the steps with their shoulders held high, and wondering if Jordan's parents would buy a piece of bread from them. They always did. The women would leave a little taller. And for the second time that week, Jordan felt an unexpected nostalgia fill her eyes and roll down her cheeks. She squinted down the street and brushed her face with her hand.

"Pleasure to meet you, Lucy," Jordan finally responded with southern courtesy. Jordan looked up into the woman's face, a touch of sunlight throwing shadows across her brown skin. "Now let's get you something to eat, okay?"

"Okay, okay. Okay," Lucy said, letting her fingers drop to her side and her eyes drop to the sidewalk.

Jordan led Lucy up Broadway, past the organic grocery store and Lowe's Cinema and around the corner toward Central Park. What was this woman's story, she wondered. Had she worked a good job in midtown, gotten laid off when the economy took a turn, and then ended up on the streets? Had she been holed up in some rehab center or shelter trying to get her life together? Or had she come from a small town in the South to New York City in search of a dream, hoping to break into show business but instead wound up asking strangers for food?

Anything was possible. Anything could happen. That much Jordan was painfully sure of. Especially fighting each day to keep life in your goal. Jordan knew. She looked at Lucy again and was surprised to feel a surge of thankfulness rise in her bones for the little things in life, for beds and bathtubs and ceilings in studio apartments.

After a silent walk, Jordan opened the door to the Dream Time Tavern, held it for Lucy, and the two entered just as quietly. The room was darker and louder than outside, and a few clouds of cigarette smoke greeted them. A rugby match was playing on the television that sat on a shelf above an old wood bar. Half a dozen men gathered around it, each cheering the teams on the TV with one fist in the air and the other gripping frosted mugs of dark beer. No one noticed the women entering.

On the wall behind the men was a huge mural brightly painted with earth colors. A life-sized kangaroo and emu stood in the middle of the painting, and a half-naked black man sat on the ground beside the animals. He held a long hollow log no wider than his palm to his lips while the fingers of his other hand formed an *M* above his head. Below him, the words *Didgeridoo in the Bush* were painted in the same red color as the clay road he sat on in the mural.

"Welcome to the Dream Time," Jordan announced to Lucy, placing her hand on the woman's shoulder. Jordan felt the bone beneath Lucy's jacket. Then she pointed to a table for Lucy to sit down as she walked toward the kitchen not far from the bar.

"G'day, mate," Jack bellowed his Australian accent as he almost ran into Jordan in the kitchen. "Always nice to see that gorgeous face. Got some good specials tonight, mate." Jack's wavy brown hair was pushed down beneath the white skipper's cap he wore. A few whiskers speckled his chin. The tight yellow apron that hung around his neck and covered his chest seemed a strange contrast to the husky man beneath it. Ever since Jordan began working for him, Jack Ross wore his apron, especially when he was cooking. He didn't care what it looked like. This was his restaurant.

"I'll wear what I bloody well want to," he'd chuckle at his employees.

They, however, were obliged to stay in uniform: flower-print shirts, black jeans, and red bandanas hanging from their back pockets. Jack also didn't care what color of floral shirts they wore as long as they "looked like Aussies," he'd say. And as long as they earned their wages. He wanted his customers to enjoy their food and drink, and that meant everyone from the bartender to the busboy better make sure they did. No exceptions. If you worked hard for your customers, you scored points with the owner of the Tavern, points that lasted a long time.

Since her first day on the job three and a half years ago, Jordan sincerely enjoyed waiting on her customers, so much so that many came back regularly to the Tavern and requested one of her tables. Jack Ross noticed her natural hospitality and scheduled her for more shifts. Before long Jordan was deluged with teases from other waiters that she was the boss's favorite. Every time she heard this, she felt her cheeks turn colors. She just needed the work.

Still, she had to confess, a little favoritism from the man in charge wasn't such a bad thing, since her father would surely disapprove if ever he knew where she was working. Which he didn't. So Jordan clung to her vision as a playwright in this city to help her realize she wouldn't always have to wait tables. It woke her up mornings. And she would do what she had to even if that meant taking extra shifts at the Tavern or a temp job in some stuffy office and saving paychecks from both to pay for Vinnie's workshops. A little preferential treatment certainly couldn't hurt.

Especially at times like these.

"Jack, um, I brought a friend in for a sandwich," Jordan said. She was studying his face, hoping that today was a good day for him, that it might be one where he could tolerate another of her "charity cases," as he called them. Jack stopped chopping tomatoes, looked up at his waitress, and exhaled as if he'd just taken a long drag from a cigarette. He set down his knife and walked to the kitchen door, peering out the window at Lucy, who by now was testing each chair at the table to see which was most comfortable. Around she went as if she were participating in a game of musical chairs. The men at the bar cheered louder at the television, oblivious to Lucy's antics, jumping off and on their barstools whenever their team made a good play. Jack glanced at Lucy, then back at Jordan, who had followed him to the window.

"Again? Listen, mate, today's not..." He stopped, gave her a gentle push aside—like a big brother would his sister—and returned to his cutting board. Jack liked to call everyone "mate," the Aussie term men used for friends. Though to Jack, everyone, male and female, were mates, which baffled Jordan, because she was never quite sure if her boss had any real friends at all. She'd never known him to have a life outside of the restaurant, at least that he talked about at the Tavern like all the other employees and managers did. He lived in the apartment upstairs and only left New York one Christmas that Jordan knew of, when his father got sick suddenly in Melbourne.

"I'll pay for it, Jack. She'll take a hamburger, please, medium rare, and chips," Jordan said as she tied her long auburn hair back in a ponytail, put a short black apron around her waist, and began stacking salad plates for the evening's business. Jack shook his head slowly at the southern woman working beside him and glanced at her elbow.

"Since when did you start getting tattoos?" He pointed at the bell with his knife.

"Since this morning," Jordan said, shrugging her shoulders and admiring the art on her flesh. "You like it? I do. And would you believe the artist who did it was from Mississippi?"

"Small world. Reckon he's going to do a catfish next, on the other elbow?" Jack joked, walked to the refrigerator, and grabbed a small round burger. He paused for a second and stared at the size of it. He tossed the small one back in the cooler and picked up a thick piece of ground beef, the same kind he'd use for the famous Bush Burger his restaurant was known for, a half-pound piece of meat with a thick slice of "Australian" cheese across the top. He threw it on the grill, picked up his knife, and sliced another tomato.

"I think a bell is plenty. For now," Jordan said while she watched Jack prepare Lucy's burger. She patted his shoulder and smiled.

"Uh-huh," Jack shook his head, smiled, and went back to chopping.

"Specials look fantastic, Jack. They're going to love that Kangaroo Pie. 'Course there's not real kangaroo meat in it, is there?" Jordan asked. She pointed to the chalkboard that hung next to the kitchen doors where each special was neatly printed every night. Jack grunted. He turned toward the grill and flipped the burger. He pulled a plate from the shelf, placed two pieces of thick sourdough bread and a dill pickle on it, and dished some fries from the fryer on the plate.

"Order's up," Jack said as he put the Bush Burger platter on the counter and walked into the prep room. Jordan watched him before taking the meal to Lucy. Even when Jack tried to be tough, Jordan had seen him offer a burger or a beer to someone who couldn't always pay the bill.

"Thanks, boss," she hollered after him. "I owe you!"

"Yes, you do," he yelled back.

When she set down the plate, Lucy's eyes filled her face. She shifted again but kept staring at the burger, picked up her napkin, set it down, and picked it up again. She swallowed some water.

"Okay, okay. Okay," she said finally. Jordan put her hand on Lucy's shoulder.

"Let me know if you'd like anything else, okay?" she said. The men at the bar jumped again and cheered. At the same time, two young men in flower-print shirts and black jeans walked through the door, waved to Jordan, and immediately headed toward the bar to catch the final minutes of the match. Lucy was alternating between bites of the burger and a fry, and Jordan got busy.

She prepped the salad bar, laid green tablecloths across each four-top, and gathered enough forks and knives for the place settings. Soon the Tavern began to fill up with its usual dinner crowd, growing increasingly rowdy from a few too many pints of beer. Cigar and cigarette smoke hung over the bar. When the rugby match finished, the bartender switched the channel to a surfing contest.

Jordan had three orders in to Jack before she remembered

Lucy. She glanced toward the table where she'd delivered her burger. Lucy was gone. When she approached the table, she found Lucy's plate shiny and clean. She also saw that the sugar packets were gone and the green cloth napkin was neatly folded on the chair Lucy had finally decided on. As Jordan cleaned up the table, she noticed a brown piece of paper torn from a grocery bag and folded as neatly as the napkin. A note was scribbled inside: *RiVEr LadY thank U 4 a reely nice DinnEr. LUCY.*

Jordan smiled as she tucked the note into her pocket and cleared the table. She spent the next few hours serving a dozen more Bush Burgers along with shrimp cocktails, Kangaroo Pie, and bowls of cream pudding. She wasn't sure if it was the specials, the cold fall weather, or mere favoritism, but tonight's customers seemed unusually generous for a New York crowd, leaving her twenty and thirty percent tips. Jordan could certainly use the extra money; tuition for Vinnie's class was due in full next week. So far she'd managed to make the first two payments. But after paying her rent, she wasn't sure how she was going to pay the final bill. And there was the next term.

Jordan felt the wad of tip money in her apron and laughed at the unnecessary worry.

"Order's up, mate!" Jack was hollering again to Jordan to get three platters of sandwiches to one of her corner tables. She balanced the plates on her wrist and elbow and walked toward the table, shouting back to her boss as she went, "Thanks, mate!"

The order never made it. Barely out of the kitchen, Jordan came to a sudden halt, as if she'd just witnessed a horrible collision. She froze at the sight of three people coming in the door, a boy with two tall adults who were probably his parents. He stood about five feet and his auburn hair curled off his head and onto his shoulders. The boy wore a white T-shirt, blue jeans, and a purple unzipped sweatshirt that hung off his skinny but wide shoulders. As the boy looked up at Jordan and their eyes locked, the three plates slipped from Jordan's hands, crashing onto the floor and creating a mess of shattered ceramic, upside-down burgers, and splattered salads.

Jordan did not move. The boy and his parents hardly noticed as they were seated at a table across from the bar. Two flower-print shirts appeared instantly with brooms and dust pans. Customers glanced at Jordan, then at her mess, and back at her again, wondering why she was still standing over it, paralyzed. Her shoulders started to shake, and she was gasping for any air she could find, her eyes still locked on the boy who was now reading a menu.

"Mate, what's the matter? What's goin' on?" Jack was beside her now. Jordan couldn't breathe. Her entire body was shivering, and her flesh was stone cold. Jack put his hand on her back and started to rub it gently, leading his top waitress into the kitchen. He demanded one of the flower shirts bring him a paper bag. One instantly appeared. Jack slipped off Jordan's glasses, placed the bag over her mouth and nose, and simply whispered, "Breathe, woman. Breathe."

The air came back into her lungs. But Jordan's eyes now flooded, and she started sobbing and shaking again like someone whose whole world just turned black. Jack led her into his office off the side of the kitchen, sat her in his big leather chair, and closed the door. He found a box of tissues from under a pile of papers on his desk, handed her one, and kept his hand on her back until the tears slowed down. A small rotating fan buzzed behind them, the only noise between Jordan's sobs.

They waited in the near quiet. Neither had seen this coming.

"You're done for tonight. I'll call you a cab and get you home, okay?" Jack was picking up the phone before she could answer. Not that she had the energy to anyway. What had just happened? Where did she just go? How was it possible to have seen *his* face? Every part of her body was sapped, weary even in her fingertips. She wasn't sure she could walk out the door.

Jordan breathed in a big puff of air, exhaled, and tried to relax. Her foot beat hard against the cement floor. She breathed again and stared at the man who was now on the phone with a car service company, rattling off the address of the Tavern. She stared at Jack not for any reason in particular but because he was simply in her line of vision, blurry without her glasses. She took them from his shirt pocket and pushed them over her nose. They didn't seem to make much difference. He might as well have been moving in slow-motion for all Jordan was seeing. The room, his face, the Tavern, the boy, all were a dark blur in her head that kept her feet pounding and her shoulders shaking.

"What...was...that?" she mumbled. Jack looked up at her and finished his call.

"I'd reckon that was the nearest bloody thing I've ever seen to a panic attack," Jack said calmly. "You'll be okay, mate. You'll be okay."

Jordan stared into his green eyes and hoped with all her being he was right.

She didn't remember the cab ride. It seemed to fade into the faces and blackness of the Tavern. Somehow she climbed the five floors to her apartment, found her keys in her bag, and turned the two locks on the door. A sandwich bag of chocolate-chip cookies was taped to the door with a note from Barry. She left it hanging. Jordan sighed in relief at the familiarity of the apartment inside. She dropped her bag on the floor and fell on the sofa bed, still wearing her apron from work.

For a long time Jordan stared at the ceiling. Her shoulders had finally stopped shaking and now she felt chilled. She pulled a blanket over her. Each bone, each muscle in each part of her body was exhausted, void of any ounce of strength. But she could not close her eyes. Every time she tried, the black whirl of faces—*his* face—dizzied her, and she'd open them quickly to see the ceiling above her.

She stood up to put the teakettle on the burner and noticed the light on her answering machine blinking. Messages. Another chill went through her spine from the cold of the room. She put a blanket around her shoulders and by instinct pushed the button on the answering machine while she waited for her tea.

"Hello, love. Vinnie here. Listen, I'm thinking we should talk more about that scene. How about coffee tomorrow at the Blue Swan, say 11? I'll be there. Hope you will be too."

The teakettle whistled as Vinnie's message ended, and Jordan had to concentrate on the mug while she poured the boiling water. She was so tired. It occurred to her that Vinnie had never called her before. Strange. Hearing the smoothness of his voice, though, relaxed Jordan a bit, reminding her of better things. Theater. Words. Stories. Her mind wandered to his face and his neat black hair. Until another voice suddenly spoke out of the machine.

"Hi, hon. It's Mom. Wanted to see how you were doing. I'm thinking of coming up for a weekend next month to see you. Let me know when's good for you. How about Thanksgiving? Love you."

The click at the end of her message was too sudden for Jordan, and she almost spilled her tea. How did her mother seem to know when to call?

Jordan hit the replay button to listen again to her voice. When the intimate sound sang into her tiny apartment, Jordan set down her cup, got into her bed, and began to cry and rock like a little girl who just lost a friend.

Finally Jordan fell asleep, her face wet, her shoulders aching.

FOUR

eter Riddle was having a little trouble breathing. His lungs
weren't the problem—he had always been able to drink in
air like it was cool water on a July afternoon. He thought
of himself as a sturdy man, jogging each morning to the river and
back, a three-mile routine that kept his energy up, his blood pressure down, and his lungs working as they were made to. The runs
helped him focus. But on this Wednesday afternoon, Peter's path
to oxygen was being cut off by the thick brown arms, shoulders,
and chest of love.

Miss Mary was known for smothering anyone who brought
her lilies or daisies. The sixty-two-year-old woman stood four
inches higher than Peter, and her large, full frame jiggled whenever
she saw fresh flowers. She wore a flower-print sleeveless dress every
day, even Sundays. Today it was sunflowers. When she saw Peter
walk into the Cherry Blossom Center, his hands full of fresh lilies,

the sunflowers all but jumped off the cotton. Her gratitude was as big as her body, and Peter was suffocating now from both.

"I knew you wouldn't forget 'bout us today, Pastor!" Miss Mary's voice was a foghorn above Peter's head, and he began to jiggle in sync now with the woman who was hugging him. Her laughter became his, which made breathing for him more difficult, and the muscles in his neck tensed as he lifted his head from the cushion of her sunflowers. A strong scent of lilac perfume burst into his nose and landed in his throat. When she heard Peter's quick cough, Miss Mary moved her pastor an arm's length away and patted his back with a force almost as great as her enthusiasm for flowers.

"Glad to see you too, Miss Mary," Peter was clearing his throat as he recovered his footing. He took the woman's hand and asked how her day was going. She laughed again.

"Better now!" she boomed. Then she walked into an office, emerged with a clear glass vase, and one by one arranged the lilies in upright position while Peter watched. They looked beautiful, as always. When she was finished, she marched around the corner and down a white corridor lined with wood railings. Peter followed.

Miss Mary was the volunteer coordinator at the center, and almost more than her job, she loved placing fresh flowers in all the rooms so her seniors could enjoy them. She had been a faithful member at Second Baptist since Peter came on staff, and she was one of the few black women in the largely white congregation who came each week to hear Dr. Stately's sermons. One Sunday morning she stood up during the announcements and asked if anyone could volunteer to help her at the senior center. Peter admired her boldness and had been coming ever since, leading a Bible study when she asked him to or visiting with a particular man or woman. And always bringing flowers.

Peter was glad for Mary's towering presence at the church. Second Baptist had come a long way in terms of race relations, though no one would argue it still had a long way to go. At least in public. Privately, some folks thought things were getting a bit uncomfortable, but Dr. Stately had always preached—as Peter would as well—that everyone was welcome in God's house, no matter what color they were. That in itself was no small thing in a state where lynchings were real memories, not paragraphs in history books, and segregation was a way of life that still kept families worlds apart. Racial scars had not been healed with the civil rights movement, and progress in this area was as slow and difficult as a day in August. Folks did not deal easily with its uncomfortable heat.

That was a tragedy of the church, the senior reverend often said. Peter respected him for it. Of course, Dr. Stately's verbal disdain for racism translated—like everything else seemed to in his life—into deeds as well. He organized "encouragement" breakfasts with pastors from West Jackson, initiated multichurch, interracial picnics in Civic Park downtown, and invited choir swaps on Sunday mornings. He was willing to try anything to break down racial barriers.

"Christian love requires us to be together," he'd proclaim. Peter—and Miss Mary—agreed.

They were small steps, Peter knew, but steps nonetheless he was proud to be a part of. He had always been bothered by the deep-rooted biases he'd watched growing up in Jackson: the black men who were called "boy" by white teenagers; the black cleaning women who came in the back door of a neighbor's house, not the front; the farmhands who worked his uncle's land outside of town but weren't allowed inside his house. It confused him as a child how someone's skin color could make him or her better than anyone else. And he certainly didn't understand why black people did not live in his neighborhood.

"That's just how it is, hon," his mama would tell him when he asked. "But that don't mean we're any better."

Now, as an adult, he had to credit his parents: for all their non-chalance toward matters of Christian faith, they never failed to teach him that all people were basically the same. No one was better than anyone else, they'd lecture him and Cynthia Sue, although some people mistakenly thought they were. Riddles were not like that, they insisted. We would respect all people, was that clear?

It was. So Peter grew up watching the tension outside his home but feeling helpless to fix it. That is, until the night Jesus saved his young soul and Peter discovered a better way. The message of his Savior, it seemed to him, was one for any person anywhere, regardless of what he looked like or where she lived—Jackson, Mississippi, or Suva, Fiji.

Or New York City for that matter. Jesus was the only solution to any life of sin. Peter's job was to help them see that.

"Hey y'all! Look who stopped by to visit us," Miss Mary announced. Seniors filled the community room and looked toward the white man and black woman as if their interracial presence was a normal fixture in this place. Two men with thick white hair looked up from their card game and waved at Peter. A thin woman whose gray hair was braided neatly into a crown on her head turned from her canvas and gave Peter a smile and a wave with her paintbrush. A chorus of "Hey Pastor!" came from a couch where men were working crossword puzzles and women were reading various sections of the *Jackson Tribune*.

Miss Mary set the bouquet in the middle of a large oak coffee table and told her seniors that "the pastor had done it again!" She stood for a second admiring the flowers, hands on hips and face filled with a broad gentle smile. The sunflowers on her dress moved back and forth as she delighted over the sight of the lilies. Then she floated from senior to senior like a senator campaigning, pointing to the flowers and gazing into the older faces to see how each was doing. No one under Mary's care could be cranky or curt. It was not allowed, nor consistent, with her disposition.

"These flowers remind us how beautiful life is," she'd say, not waiting for a response, and then continue: "How do I know? Because God is good. Period." End of discussion. Peter was never quite sure if people conceded to Mary because of her contagious enthusiasm or because of her jiggling size. Or both.

"Did we tell you, Pastor, that our folks here are putting on a little performance?" Miss Mary turned her full body toward Peter and looked down into his eyes. Like any good story it could not stay long in her soul, and within seconds Peter heard every detail. How Hattie Mae and Henry wanted to raise some money so the kids at the school down the street could take more field trips. How Slim, Will, and Betty suggested they put on a variety show and sell tickets and within a few days the whole thing was planned. They'd even set a date: October 27. Now they just needed a few more rehearsals, Mary explained, and the show would "raise the money and the roof!" Her deep rich laugh shook the room and her sunflowers, convincing everyone that this event might as well be recorded in the history books.

"Hey Rev, doesn't your daughter do shows or something like that up there in New York? Maybe she could help us out," one of the card-playing men—Henry—was calling out to Peter.

"New York City! Theater? Like Broadway?" Hattie Mae's hand covered her mouth after she spoke.

"That's kind of a wild place, ain't it, Pastor?" Slim threw out the question as he tossed down a card in front of Henry.

"I've always wanted to go to Broadway," Hattie Mae said, dreamy. Mary's laugh slipped suddenly into a polite whistle, and she noticed Peter's foot begin to tap. He glanced at his watch, coughed, took off his glasses, and began to clean them with his shirt.

"She's not exactly in the business of helping, Henry," Peter said, his eyebrows pressed forward, his cheeks forcing a grin. "You know how young people can be these days. Only interested in themselves. Good thing they have all the answers!" He chuckled at his own comment, shrugged his shoulders, and raised his hands like he didn't know what else to do.

Miss Mary rescued him. "That's right, Pastor. Lord have mercy on these young folks today. What a world they have to live in. We thought it was tough when we were young, but 1995? Heaven help 'em!" she said, looking at the faces around her and inviting them into the discussion. Henry piped up and agreed that it was much tougher these days for kids than when he was growing up, and that pushed almost everyone in the room into lively conversations about their pasts. The verbal nostalgia created a noisy buzz in the community room, and Peter drank in a long breath of air before he let it out again.

He saw in his mind the small U-Haul truck as it pulled out of his driveway almost four years ago, his daughter's long auburn hair flipping back and forth from behind the steering wheel as she looked to check for cars in the street. His wife, Jeanie, standing on the lawn, waving to their daughter while he watched from the bedroom window through the blinds. The girl was making a big mistake as far as he was concerned, and he was not about to endorse it by sending her off. So Peter stared from the window and asked God to forgive his child.

He had not seen her since.

As a parent he had to let her go, had to let her fail on her own if that's what it took, like the father did with his prodigal son in Christ's parable. It was not what Peter would have chosen for his little girl, but he hadn't been able to change her mind. As much as he'd tried to convince her that she could be of much more use in Jackson, that he wanted her closer to him where he and Jeanie could be near by, she claimed she could not ignore the dream in her heart.

"It's my life, Daddy," she'd said to him. "It's like a fire in me I just can't put out. Please understand."

But he did not understand. New York and theater and art did not fit any church plans or ministry strategies for him. They never had, and as far as he could tell, they never would. What, after all, did those things have to do with God's kingdom?

The muscles in his neck tightened at the memory of their last exchange. He pushed his thumb into the flesh above his shoulders and rotated it deeply, forcefully.

"How 'bout some lunch?" Mary's hand was gentle on Peter's

shoulder. Cooks and busboys were setting up a buffet in the corner, and the elder woman was guiding her pastor toward it. He glanced at his watch and remembered his to-do list.

"Thanks, Miss Mary, but I've got a pretty full day ahead of me," Peter said as he glanced at the flowers.

"You always do." Mary's smile never left her face. "Now don't work too hard, Pastor, we need you back here next week for rehearsals." And with that Miss Mary's tall sunflowered body smothered her friend for a second time until she marched back toward her seniors. Peter walked out of the Cherry Blossom Center with nothing in his hands and nothing, surprisingly, in his soul.

Peter put the key in the ignition and backed out of the parking lot. He glanced in his rearview mirror, expecting to see Miss Mary or Henry waving him off, but no one stood at the center's entrance. His lungs reached for air, any air, but the struggle was great. What was this? He'd gone for his morning jog, so his breathing should be strong. He waved his hand in front of his face, back and forth like he would with flies, thinking that might allow the oxygen to flow. His chest ached. His shoulders rose and fell until he had to pull the car over, turn off the ignition, and try to relax. Try to catch his breath.

"Move...past...it," he said between breaths. He raised his arms above his head to open his lungs. His chest felt like it was being squeezed. He breathed slowly, deliberately. *Focus,* he told himself.

There were other needs he had to meet, other responsibilities to fulfill. After all, a busy life was a productive one. It was the least he could do.

As he turned onto Applewood Lane, his nerves calmed, but his stomach growled louder than the engine of his car. Food to him was often an inconvenience, a necessary burden that interfered with his list of responsibilities. He never minded church suppers or breakfast meetings, because at least he could get some work done by interacting with the people who attended them. During business hours, though, lunch was a problem he did not have time for. His schedule was already tight.

So Peter did today what he usually did; he pulled his car into the drive-through of Captain Billy's Chicken Pickup and ordered a deluxe sandwich, enough of a meal to get him to dinner. Billy's supplied him with all he needed: a fast, fresh sandwich prepared by an old friend who wouldn't steal his time. Peter and Billy had known each other for years—they'd played on the same baseball team growing up—so he never minded grabbing a few dollars from his wallet to support the small businessman. Billy, in turn, gave Peter only what he came for: a sandwich. No demands. No requests for pastoral advice. Just chicken.

"Hey Pete. Busy day again, huh?" Billy was leaning out the drive-through window to hand the pastor his lunch. He looked more like a country music singer with his thick mustache and cowboy hat than he did a captain or a chicken connoisseur. But he was a happy man who was rarely bothered by anything. Serving friends chicken sandwiches was contentment enough.

"You know how it is," Peter answered as he took his lunch and handed Billy a five-dollar bill.

"Nope. Sure don't. But I know you gotta eat," Billy smiled, dropping extra napkins and $1.74 in change in the pastor's palm. "Thank God for chicken."

Peter laughed at Billy's comment, knowing it was more of an economic response to his purchase than a spiritual adulation. Billy didn't see the point of religion, he'd tell his old baseball buddy whenever Peter invited him to church. But he'd be glad to have all the religious folks in the world come into his chicken stand. After church, during the week, any day. Those were the times Billy's interest in religion soared.

Peter waved to Billy, pulled out of the drive-through, and opened the bag simultaneously. He had long mastered the art of driving a '91 standard Toyota while eating a chicken sandwich at the same time. He'd pile his lap and shirt with napkins, shift from second to third, then third to fourth gears between bites, and set the sandwich on the passenger's seat beside him as he chewed and swallowed. Even if he had to slow down and downshift for a traffic light, he'd manage to keep the chicken with all its fixings from spilling out of its bun. By the time he arrived at the church office, he'd have lunch over with minimal mess, and he could get on to the next item on his list.

Time management at its best, he congratulated himself.

Three messages written on pink memo paper were waiting for him when he slipped into his office across from Loretta's. Since he hated having things hang over his head, he picked up the phone and made his first call. Cynthia Sue answered.

"Hey little brother. Thanks for calling back," she said. They talked for a few minutes about the weather in Mobile and Jackson as well as the latest stories in city hall. His sister had been a reporter ever since he could remember, and if he needed to know what was going on in the world, Cynthia Sue was his source. A few years ago, though, the *Mobile Beacon* asked her to be editor for the arts and leisure section, and she left Jackson. It was a great step for her, and though she was four hours away, the sister and brother still managed to talk at least once a week.

"When are you and Jeanie coming for a visit?" Cynthia Sue asked as she always did, knowing the answer she would get. She was persistent.

"Soon," he answered. "Soon. It's just been so busy." He just didn't know when he could afford to take time off to get down to see her. He wanted to, though, he'd tell her.

"Well, the beach is nice this time of year, and some good shows are coming to town. Don't be a stranger now, ya hear?" He heard.

Peter hung up the phone, tossed the memo in the trash, and made the next two phone calls. No answer. He dropped the pink memos into a yellow folder marked, *Follow-up*.

He looked at the next task on his list: *2. Study 1 Timothy; prepare notes for prison worship service* and reached for his Bible and commentary. This was Peter's second year of helping the prison chaplain in leading Bible discussions at the Mississippi State Correctional Facility. This particular group was just beginning their study of the apostle Paul's letter to Timothy, one of Peter's favorites for helping others understand their sin. He scribbled some notes about why Christ came into the world, wrote down some questions for the inmates, and glanced over the commentary on the text.

Peter spent the next few hours making more phone calls for Senior Sunday, finishing a letter that he asked Loretta to edit, and writing checks for bills that needed to be paid by the end of the week. He and Jeanie didn't have a huge income from the church and the school where she taught, but they were able to get a decent mortgage for their house and put away a bit each month for savings. Just in case.

He glanced at her picture on his desk. Jeanie was wearing a light blue, sleeveless dress, and he remembered how long it had been since he'd seen her face so tanned. Lately he noticed her cheeks growing pale and the lines around her eyes getting darker. She seemed thinner than she had in years, and whenever he asked her about it, she told him she felt fine. Great even. No need to worry about her, she'd say. He had enough to do at the church.

He adjusted the glasses on his nose, picked up the phone, and dialed the number he'd dialed for years: Dr. Hollander's office. He'd been their physician since they returned from the mission field, and anytime his daughter or wife had caught a cold, broke a bone, or just needed a checkup, Dr. Hollander rearranged his schedule to see them. Peter rarely visited him because his own schedule was always full and he found his colds or pains would go away eventually. When he was honest with himself, he admitted it was because he didn't much like doctors in the first place.

They never seemed to get it right.

"Doctor's office. How can I help you?" The woman's voice sounded at first like a recording, but Peter realized he'd gotten the receptionist. He ran his fingers nervously through his hair as he scheduled his wife's annual checkup for her as he promised. Jeanie was in class during the day and wasn't able to make personal phone calls. So Peter organized most of her life, something he was familiar with and more than willing to do. Jeanie had been his steady hand for almost thirty years now. It was his job to take care of her, and he considered this a small task considering all he'd put her through.

He tried to forget. He closed his eyes tight hoping it would wash out the memory.

The phone rang and startled Peter back into the present, grateful for the diversion. It was the prison chaplain explaining that tonight's Bible class had to be postponed. The warden had scheduled extra time for the inmates in the gym, and most of the men who regularly attended had decided to build their physical muscles rather than their spiritual ones. Could Peter come next Saturday instead?

Of course he could. He turned his calendar to a week ahead and wrote down *Prison Worship Service* for that Saturday morning. The cancellation gave him more time to prepare and an unusually free night. Maybe he would take Jeanie out to dinner for a change. Surprise her with something he knew she loved but that they rarely had time for: an evening out together.

At four o'clock the church bells signaled the time school let out, the time Peter was due to pick up his wife. He straightened his desk, crossed the last item off his list, and was almost out of his office when he heard the phone ring again. He hesitated, debating on whether to let his message service pick it up. It rang again and Peter hurried back to the phone.

The voice was calm, cold even. Jeanie was en route to Jackson State Hospital. She'd collapsed at the end of the day and an ambulance had come for her.

"Could you come right away?"

The world went dark.

A dial tone came over the phone, but Peter held the receiver anyway, staring at her picture, shaking.

Not Jeanie. No, God, please. Not Jeanie, too.

He grabbed his car keys and ran to the parking lot. The drive through downtown Jackson was a streak of black and gray. Buildings were tiny cinder blocks Peter saw out of the corner of his eye as his foot pushed harder on the gas petal. He spun into the hospital parking lot within minutes, his heart pounding and his lungs working harder than ever that day. Peter wiped his palms against his pants and glanced at his watch out of habit. He pushed his glasses up closer to his eyes as he followed the signs to the emergency room and approached the patient's desk.

Jeanie was undergoing tests now, the receptionist told him. She'd let the doctor on duty know he was there. In the meantime Peter could take a seat in the waiting room. She would let him know when his wife was being moved to a recovery room as soon as she was given that information.

Peter instead went to the pay phone in the corner, dropped a quarter in it, and called Dr. Hollander's number for the second time that day. This time he did get a recording, and he left an emergency message for the doctor to call the hospital as soon as possible regarding Jeanie Riddle. Peter hung up the receiver and clinched his jaw. He stared at the silver slot that had taken his quarter and wondered why someone as fragile as his wife had to endure so much. He imagined her face in the photo and begged God for mercy. Then he turned around to look for a seat.

His foot knocked the back of a chair in a quick rhythmical beat. Peter shifted uncomfortably and squinted at the receptionist like she was a bull's-eye he'd narrowed in on. She moved graciously between phone, computer, and traumatized family members waiting for news. Peter stared hard at her, hoping that might bring him the only news he wanted to hear.

A big man in surgical scrubs appeared and started talking to the receptionist. Peter thought he looked more like a linebacker than a doctor until he turned his face toward Peter, peered through his glasses, and waved him over to talk.

Apparently, when she was turning in her attendance sheet to the principal at the end of the day, Jeanie's face went pale and she fainted. The principal's secretary immediately called 911, and the ambulance was at the school within minutes. Jeanie was given oxygen and brought to the hospital.

"We'd like to keep her overnight for observation," the doctor said. "We'll let you know when we move her into a room." He smiled an obligatory smile, as if the news was good enough and Peter ought not to worry. It did not help.

Peter's shoulders were thick and heavy, his palms moist.

He walked to the phone again, dropped another coin in the slot, and dialed Cynthia Sue's number. He took off his glasses and waited for her to answer. When he heard the familiar balm of her "Hello," Peter leaned against the wall to hold himself up.

"It's Jeanie, Cyn. She's in Jackson State Hospital," Peter's voice faded.

"I'll be there as fast as I can. Don't you worry," Cynthia said. And the line was dead. Peter placed the receiver back in its cradle and hurried to his chair again. His foot knocked quicker against the metal leg. He glanced away from the carpet beneath him—which he'd been staring at without realizing it—and saw a small girl watching him, her straight blonde hair touching the tips of her shoulders.

He hadn't noticed her or anything else before. Now he saw that her legs barely reached over the seat of the chair and her hands lay still on her lap. Her blue eyes, though, were old and knowing, and they did not leave Peter's. Slowly, the corners of her lips turned upward at him and it was clear she wanted to give him something. Anything to make him feel better.

He stared back at her face, and it became the face of another little girl at another time in his life. His eight-year-old daughter was watching the birthday candles on his cake, aching to help her daddy blow them out. She giggled and squirmed in her chair, an ocean of life bouncing out of her tiny body. She was singing as loud as she could with every ounce of her being, thrilled just to be with him to celebrate his birthday. When the flames were gone and smoke rose from the candles, his little daughter jumped from her chair and clung so hard to his neck that he almost lost his breath, smothered by eight-year-old love. Her laughter became his.

Peter's cheek was wet. The little girl in the waiting room was not smiling anymore. She got up from her chair and simply stood in front of him, her little hand on his knee. The air around his face felt fresh and his shoulders loosened as he sighed.

He looked beyond the child toward the receptionist and heard the noise of the waiting room for the first time since he'd sat down: television blaring, babies crying, people chattering. He wiped his palms on his pants and his eyelashes flickered like the florescent lights above him. The little girl sat back down in her seat.

"Mr. Riddle," he heard from the desk, "your wife is in room 854. You can see her now."

Peter stood to his feet, coughed, and walked toward the elevator. The girl watched him move slowly through the room. Then she lifted her tiny hand in the air and waved after him, but Peter was concentrating on the elevator numbers above him.

FIVE

The sand was hot between Jordan's tiny toes. She reached down to brush it off, but no matter how fast she raced her hand across her skin, the sand seemed glued to her feet. In fact, the more she brushed, the coarser and thicker it became until finally her feet and shins were buried in a white dune up to her knees. She looked up at the pale blue sky, then out at the water in front of her. The more she stared, the blacker the sea turned. She glanced toward the sun and felt its power turn her white skin pink, then flame red within seconds, until the little girl's eyes filled with huge drops of pain.

Jordan twisted her feet from the sand back and forth, trying to get them out, but they would not budge. The burn went deeper into her arms, rubbing them raw, and quite suddenly as if God snapped his fingers, the sky lost its blueness and turned into a dark swirling funnel. Black rain spit stones against her back, and mud began rising all around the little girl, smashing against her legs, then her hips, and onto her stomach. She opened her mouth to scream for help, but no sound came out, and no one was nearby to hear her if it had.

An angry wind slapped strands of hair against her face. Jordan was stuck, trapped now in a river of mud and storm, her body aching. Panic filled her bones, and she shook with all her might to get free. But she could not. She watched in terror as the sky fell. Dark whirl. Smoke everywhere. Trees uprooted. Waves crashing. Screams. Trembling, aching, water cutting her flesh like a whip.

And then the wind became a breeze, gentle and cool on her cheeks, calming her and stroking her forehead. Jordan's shoulders began to relax. She opened her eyes and saw two bright brown eyes staring down at her. He held an oriental fan in his hand, moving it slowly up and down above her, and small words landed tenderly in her ears, "Baby, hey, it's all right, it's all right. Really bad dream. You're okay."

Barry's whisper was a gift to Jordan, a peace offering nudging her back into the real life of New York City and far from the horrifying island of her subconscious mind. She was relieved to see the clean-shaven chin of her neighbor, and as she stared at Barry, the storm of her nightmare moved further away. She reached her fingers up to touch his face, and when she was sure he was more real than *that* place where she'd just been, she turned her head to see the bathtub still in the middle of her apartment, the piles of books climbing to the ceiling, and the teapot on the counter by the sink. Then her eyes hurried to her old black laptop, and Jordan smiled when she saw it where it always was: on the fat pink chair she'd bought from the Salvation Army thrift shop on Ninety-sixth Street.

"You okay? Must have been some night," Barry was still fanning his neighbor as he studied her face. His question triggered Jordan's memory, calling up the previous night like a computer file: the kitchen, the boy's familiar face, Jack's office, the cab ride. Yes, the fog in her brain was lifting. But her head ached and throbbed across each part of her skull, and her eyes stung from dryness.

"How'd you get in here?" Jordan sat up quickly as the question occurred to her. She shot quick glances around the apartment to make sure everything was where it belonged. Barry dangled a set of keys attached to a bright red ILUVNY key chain in front of her face.

"You left them *in* the door last night. Along with my very beautiful chocolate-chip cookies, I might add, and I am deeply offended," Barry said, glancing toward the window for dramatic effect. "Good thing for you I know how to be a neighbor, in the biblical sense of the word, which would no doubt relieve your righteous daddy. I mean, who knows what evil urban minions were lurking around the corner, just waiting to devour the good little southern girl who left her keys *in* the door!"

"It was a rough night," Jordan mumbled, crawling off her

couch, still wearing her uniform, her hair a mess of stretched pony-tail. The thought of her "righteous daddy" right now put a sour taste in the back of her throat, and she swallowed hard to wash it out. Then she planted both feet on the hardwood floor, firm and still to get her balance, shut her eyes for a second, and groaned as she rubbed her neck. Barry stood beside her, his long thin arms cupped behind her in case she fell. But Jordan walked toward the stove and put the teapot on the burner, grabbed two mugs from the cupboard and a box of herbal tea—variety pack—which she held up as a nonverbal question for Barry.

"Something fruity, of course," he laughed at his own joke and just as quickly turned serious. "Nothing personal, Jordan, but you look like either someone slugged you or you slugged down a few too many. Cucumbers are great for that kind of thing."

Jordan strolled toward the mirror in her bathroom. Barry was right: she looked as terrible as she felt. Her eyelids were puffy pock-ets of skin, and the dark shadows beneath them were swollen too from the crying. Her face drooped in a pale weariness. She reached down into the sink and slapped a handful of cold water onto her face, hoping it would bring some life back into her. Strange, she thought, how something so soothing as water could just as easily pound the breath out of a soul with its power. A long, slow whistle of air moved up through her lungs and out of her mouth and nose. Jordan noticed a small crack in the paint on the bathroom ceiling and sighed again. Then she prayed for strength.

She walked back to the stove and waited beside the teapot. She wanted to tell Barry what had happened the night before, knowing that he would be expecting to hear every detail, but words seemed like too much work this morning. Usually she loved recounting her Gotham tales to him, building on each experience like it was a new chapter in an adventure novel. She was a natural storyteller, and every day the city gave her plenty of material to work with. This morning, though, reliving the story of that boy's face—her brother's face—inside her restaurant, the jolting collision of past and present, and the ensuing panic that rose up through every muscle in her body, well, it was too exhausting right now.

"Breakfast?" Barry was putting his cookies on a plastic plate he'd found on a shelf above the sink. He arranged them in a circle with one in the center to punctuate his efforts. He set the plate in the middle of Jordan's couch and pointed to a spot for her to come and sit. She obeyed. When the teapot steamed, he poured two cups of Lemon Zinger and sat beside Jordan. Carefully, he placed the mug in her right hand and a cookie in her left. Jordan let him, though she wasn't much interested in either.

Barry, however, slurped his tea and munched on one cookie, then another, thrilled to be a friend right now to the woman who had first befriended him three years ago when she moved in across the hall. No one else in the building had bothered to knock on his door to introduce themselves—except Mrs. Gonzales when the rent was due—and the few times he had tried with the others who lived in the building, he was met with disapproving, or disinterested, stares. But this young woman from Mississippi, the playwright in waiting, was eager to meet her neighbors. She even invited Barry over for home-cooked dinners on a regular basis—a novelty in the City of Perpetual Restaurants—and made a habit of offering him comfort food whenever he needed it, like the times he'd fought with his boyfriend or flubbed an audition. Jordan was one of the few women besides his mother Barry really loved. So he didn't mind sitting with her this morning, especially since, in his mind, she looked so awful.

Obviously, he would have to take matters into his own hands if his neighbor was going to snap out of it. He chomped a third cookie and washed it down with a final swig of Lemon Zinger. Jordan had been staring at the dust fluffs on her floor and hadn't eaten any of her breakfast, so Barry took the cookie from her hand and put it back on the plate for later. Then he gently pushed her mug toward her mouth, pulled her lips apart with his fingers, and began to pour the tea—which was now lukewarm—into her mouth like he was watering a plant. He couldn't help but laugh at the sight of Jordan's teeth—something he was not exactly accustomed to observing—and broke into his best dentist impersonation.

Within seconds Barry had Jordan giggling and snorting with affectionate abandon. Away she went laughing and howling from sheer emotional release. Just as she would wind down from one round, Barry would squeeze his lips together like a fish or twist his tongue sideways, and they'd be off again—two friends howling at the zaniness of the morning until their eyes filled and their stomachs hurt.

When the humor finally subsided, Jordan reached instinctively across the couch and hugged her neighbor. Tight. He patted her back and whispered something about being the "Best Florence Nightingale you could ever want!" Jordan's throat filled with chuckles again, and she jumped up on top of the couch with her arms in a victory sign.

"I don't know whether to sing 'I Am Woman' or the theme from *Rocky*," she announced from her throne.

"He-len! He-len! He-len!" Barry chanted. Then he sprang up, and together they belted out the strangest rendition of "I Am Woman" the rest of their fifth-floor apartment building had likely ever heard. They dissolved into laughter again until Jordan happened to read the clock on the counter: 10:35. She ran into the bathroom, grabbed a towel, came back out to the bathtub in the middle of the apartment, and turned on the nozzle.

"Sorry, Bare, I almost forgot. Vinnie called last night and wants me to meet him at the Blue Swan. At eleven! Gotta jump in the shower."

"Go! Go! That's a date you don't want to miss," Barry called out as he darted out of her apartment and into the hall. "Glad you're better! See you at the theater tonight!"

She hollered through the shower that she'd be there. Barry unlocked the door to his apartment and went home.

The Blue Swan Diner was two subway stops from Jordan's apartment. She ran down the steps toward the platform. At the same time she arrived, a train was just pulling into the station, so she jumped on and found a seat near the door. She pulled a brush from her black shoulder bag and began to smooth out her hair into one thick piece, twirling it around her finger and gathering it into a brown plastic clip she squeezed onto the back of her head to get the hair off her neck. That would have to do today, she thought. This was a meeting she couldn't miss.

She rummaged through her bag to make sure she'd brought her script. When she found it, she pulled it out and read a few lines but was interrupted by the announcement of the subway conductor: "Next stop, Fourteenth Street. Transfers are available for the N, R, 2, 3, and 9 trains."

Jordan stuffed her manuscript back into her bag, smoothed her hair with her hand, and stepped off the train at Fourteenth Street. She found the exit toward the southeast corner and hurried up the steps, still humming "I Am Woman." Even though she'd graduated from high school in 1984, she'd always loved the music of the early seventies, everything from James Taylor and Carole King to Bread and Helen Reddy. Maybe the seventies radio station had been the only one she could ever get on the transistor radio she had as a kid, but she still knew each song by heart. Their sounds were never far from her mind. Like old friends who'd greet her anytime she entered a department store or café, they'd be singing over the intercom, inviting her to sing along. Which she did, of course.

As a kid Jordan snuck her radio underneath her covers at night so her father wouldn't know she was listening. She turned down the volume as low as she could to hear it, hide under her sheets like she was in a tent, and whisper along to the words of each song. Sometimes, if she was sure her father was deep in conversation with church elders in the living room, she'd poke her head out from her covers and pretend she was singing backup for Barry Manilow or Karen Carpenter, holding the radio to her ear.

One night her brother crept into her room, and together they mouthed the words to the Carpenters' hit "Top of the World" as if they were on a television variety show. When it finished, the two children dissolved into giggles, putting pillows over their faces so their father would not hear them singing such songs. Hymns like "Great Is Thy Faithfulness" and "Nearer, My God, to Thee" were about the only music their pastor-father would allow them to sing, in public anyway. *What he doesn't know won't hurt him,* her brother whispered as he tiptoed back to his room.

Her sweet brother.

꙳

Jordan nearly ran into a hot dog vendor when she realized how lost in her musical memory she'd been. Just before she was about to knock off the ketchup bottle and napkin container in the middle of the crowded Fourteenth Street, she caught herself and apologized to the gray-bearded man with the turban on his head who stood behind the cart. Order was kept and the two transplanted New Yorkers smiled at each other for maintaining the peace.

But Jordan's head suddenly throbbed again, so she hummed the Reddy tune a little longer in hopes that it would defeat the pain.

Vinnie was already halfway through a stack of pancakes soaked in syrup when Jordan found him at a booth in the back of the Blue Swan Diner. She first spotted his thick black hair, noting it was—as usual—perfectly combed. When she neared the table, she noticed the sleeves of his starched denim shirt neatly rolled back to the middle of his forearms. Vinnie's eyebrows rose as he spotted his student and pointed with his fork and knife to the seat across from him. Jordan tossed her bag in and sat down. When he saw Jordan's puffy face, Vinnie stopped midbite but didn't ask her about it and stared back at his plate. A pile of manuscripts sat on the table next to the salt and pepper shakers, along with a folded copy of the arts section from the *New York Times* on top.

When he finished chewing, Vinnie smiled at Jordan and cleared the papers off of the table. He waved to a waitress across the room who dodged tables and busboys to accommodate Vinnie.

"What'll you have, love?" he asked Jordan, that smooth voice gliding over the din of the restaurant noise and straight into Jordan's being. She shivered and suddenly pretended to be very interested in the menu.

"Oh, uh, just coffee. No, make that mocha," she told the wiry woman standing above her, who was clearly puzzled by Jordan's youthful presence across the table from this gorgeous older man. He was closer to her age than Jordan's.

The waitress shook her head and tried to be patient. "How about hot chocolate, hon? Or coffee?"

"Sure," Jordan responded without thinking. Why did she suddenly feel so nervous sitting across from Vinnie? She'd been in this diner a dozen times before, alone and with friends, and had never felt uncomfortable. Then again, she had never come here—or anywhere for that matter—with her playwriting mentor either.

"What? You want me to surprise you?" The waitress was tapping her pencil against the pad of paper in her hand and looking everywhere but at the customer in front of her. Jordan cleared her throat.

"Sorry, no. Coffee. Black. And a toasted onion bagel with butter," Jordan asserted, remembering her song. The waitress shuffled away, but before Jordan had even blinked, the woman was back in record time with her order, setting down her plate and cup in front of her.

"How do they do that?" Jordan looked up at Vinnie, shaking her head in awe as she pointed with her thumb toward the super-human speed with which her order appeared on the table. The once-impatient waitress was now merely a Dickens-like specter across the room. Vinnie chuckled and rubbed his chin.

"This is New York, love. They do everything fast here." Vinnie was lifting his shoulders and hands at the same time he answered her, a half-grin on his face. While Jordan buttered her bagel, Vinnie sipped his coffee, wiped his mouth, and spoke.

"Your work has been improving over the past three workshops, love, and I certainly see where you're going with this play," he said, looking directly into her eyes. Jordan focused on her bagel. "Yes, it needs some work, we both know it. But I felt you could use sort of a personal strategy session to think about the best ways to nurture your talent in general and this play in particular."

The lump in Jordan's throat was heavy. She swallowed some water to wash it down as she listened to Vinnie talk about a small theater company in the Village. He knew the director there and a few of the actors, and that they were looking for promising pieces to develop for their upcoming season.

"I think your play would be a good fit with them," Vinnie said, tilting his head and punctuating his comment with a smile.

It didn't *really* matter that this was her *fifth* workshop with

Vinnie, Jordan thought. He had a lot of students, so it was possible he'd never noticed her work during those first two sessions. She did agree, though, that she was growing as a playwright, and she needed to think more about how to move her plays from manu-script to the stage where they belonged. The half-dozen times she'd invited Barry and other actors to her apartment for readings had been helpful to her, if nothing else, just to hear the sound of human voices infuse her words with emotion. And the few responses she'd gotten from artistic directors at regional theaters had been generally positive, with talk of future summer programs.

Still, Vinnie was right—again—it *was* time to take advantage of being a playwright in the city whose fame came largely from the Great White Way, nicknamed after the lights of Broadway, the world built by Ziegfeld's *Follies,* George M. Cohan's musicals, and Arthur Miller's dramas. She set down her bagel and picked up her courage.

"So, what do you think the next step should be?" As soon as the question popped out of Jordan's mouth, Vinnie's mobile phone rang. He held up his hand for her to hold that thought and pushed the button on the small black phone. He smiled when he heard who was on the other end, and Jordan sipped her coffee trying to appear inconspicuous. She glanced at the smudged wide window in the front of the diner and saw the sun had stopped shining. A northeastern rain was starting to come down on this October morning, a slow drizzle at first, then a furious downpour. She noticed Vinnie's bag included an umbrella, of course, and she rolled her eyes at her own forgetfulness.

Vinnie hung up the phone, quickly packed his scripts into his bag, and took out his umbrella and his wallet. He paused to swallow the last of his sparkling water. He found a twenty-dollar bill in his wallet and put it under his plate. Then he rose from the booth.

"Sorry, love, that was a producer uptown. Needs a little doctoring of a script before they open next week." Vinnie put his bag over his shoulder. Jordan nodded her head in support and was about to tell him not to worry about it when Vinnie suddenly leaned down and kissed her cheek. Then he said to her, "Let's continue this later. My treat."

And for the second time that day, Jordan shivered at the smoothness in Vinnie's voice. He was out the door before she realized how stunned she was by what just transpired. She reasoned with herself that people in New York often greeted one another with a kiss on the cheek, coming or going, that they lean into each other's faces with a little peck. Pure affection. Social etiquette. Of course, it had taken her a while to get used to it when she first arrived in the Big Apple, since the only people you kissed in Mississippi were your great aunts, uncles, or grandparents. Still, she'd accepted it now as a normal part of New York social life, though she had to admit this morning it had not been a normal part of her life with Vinnie. This was a first.

By the time she finished her coffee, she had convinced herself that Vinnie was merely interested in her career—showing concern for an ambitious student. His behavior was perfectly consistent with the professional culture of the theater, so she needed to stop blowing this out of proportion, Jordan lectured herself as she grabbed her bag and headed toward the door. And the rain.

She stood in the downpour, thinking the moisture might wash out some of the strange cobwebs that had formed in her head during the past twenty-four hours. Instead, when she was completely drenched, and still unsure what she should do that day, she instinctively started walking toward the uptown subway. Jack had given her the night off, and she didn't much feel like working on the next scene in her play back at the apartment. Besides, she had until next week to finish it for the class with Vinnie. It seemed as if there was something else she was supposed to do tonight, but for the life of her, she could not remember. So she did what she usually did when she came to these moments of indecision, confused by the swirling city around her: she traveled north to her sacred place, her corner of peace.

Jordan ducked into the subway station and tried to comb the rain out of her hair with her fingers. Her glasses had fogged up from the moisture in the air, so she had trouble seeing as she dropped in her token and waited for a train to take her uptown. She felt soggy all over, from head to heart, and suddenly felt too tired to process the past couple of days. Jordan let the flow of the passengers carry her onto the train and into a narrow seat between an African woman in a turquoise wraparound dress and a wide white man in a navy blue doorman's uniform. She squeezed into the spot and waited until the conductor announced the stop she was waiting for: 110th Street. One block from the Cathedral of Saint John the Divine.

Slowly, Jordan rose from her seat and stepped onto the subway platform. Routine took her immediately to the stairwell, which led onto Broadway and 110th Street, what New Yorkers know as the Upper West Side of Manhattan. Soaked anew from the storm, she walked one block up and one block over until she reached the stairs of the cathedral. But by the time she came to the steps and began to climb, the rain lightened until she got to the top, and then the rain clouds passed over completely. Just stopped. Her skin, jeans, and bag still felt wet, but the freshness of the air around her blew softly across her eyes, restoring to Jordan a vigor she'd forgotten about these past few days. She saw a thin woman walking out of the cathedral, her face reminding Jordan of the homeless woman she'd taken to the Tavern the night before for a sandwich.

Lucy was her name.

But this was not Lucy now. Jordan exhaled the memory of the day before and walked to her hallowed space in the cathedral. The American poet's corner in the northwest section of the church was one of Jordan's favorite places in the city. Yes, she was moved by the glorious gothic ceiling and the astonishing stained-glass windows that lined the walls. But it was the poet's corner, the stone slabs recognizing the life and wisdom of writers and poets that most renewed her perspective. Here she could pay homage to Walt Whitman, Emily Dickinson, Anne Bradstreet, Langston Hughes. Others like Hawthorne, Eliot, Twain, even Fitzgerald, were all given their own unique stones to honor their creative contributions to society. There was something amazingly right about this in Jordan's mind, about a church appreciating the process and impact of creative efforts like those honored here. To Jordan this seemed as consistent with the idea of religion as prayer or worship.

Of course, though, this had not been anywhere near her experience growing up, which was probably why the sheer novelty of Saint John's attribution encouraged Jordan. In Mississippi she'd never heard of a church mentioning the word *poetry,* let alone honoring its poets or writers, though Mississippi certainly could claim many. After all, it could boast of William Faulkner, Tennessee Williams, Eudora Welty, Shelby Foote, Willie Morris, and her favorite, the Jackson playwright, Beth Henley, who'd won a Pulitzer Prize for her drama, *Crimes of the Heart.*

Once when she was studying at Bellreed College, Jordan had asked the librarian in the Eudora Welty Public Library why their state had produced so many great writers. Jordan waited as the tall elderly man scratched his head, furrowed his eyebrows, and looked at the linoleum library floor before he answered.

"Well, I reckon it's 'cuz they ain't got nothin' else to do here," he said with genuine southern seriousness. Jordan could not have agreed more.

So on busy or confusing days, when the crowds got too pushy or the subways stalled or the sheer number of shows, concerts, and exhibits to choose from seemed overwhelming, Jordan found herself longing for a bit of home where there was "nothin' else to do." At those times she'd find her way here, to the poet's corner of Saint John's, where she knew the doors would always be open and she could just sit in the silence of the church, soaking in the creative power of faith and words and peace. This was her secret refuge. It was her place to reconnect.

Maybe it would make yesterday go away.

"Rough day?" Sister Leslie had slipped into the pew beside Jordan and looked straight ahead to the cross in the nave. Last year Jordan met the Episcopalian nun on one of her miniretreats to the corner. They shared an equal admiration for the writers and artists honored here and had been friends ever since.

"Sister!" Jordan looked up, surprised and relieved to see her friend, if one can be both at the same time. Without thinking of anything else, Jordan released her tension in a river of stories about the last few days. The homeless woman at the restaurant, the boy's face reminding her of her brother's, the ensuing panic that overwhelmed her, even hearing her mother's voice at the end of the day. And this morning, well, it was just plain weird meeting her playwriting teacher for breakfast. Now she needed some time to regroup, to remember why she was in New York in the first place, regardless of the circumstances or the tapes that played in her mind of her father's disapproval.

Sister Leslie listened and nodded to Jordan as she continued looking toward the nave of the cathedral. Then she placed her arm around Jordan's shoulder and sat quietly beside the young playwright. A soft tear rolled down Jordan's face and her heart offered a silent prayer, a plea for direction and help as she tried to make sense of the dark ache within her. Comfort sat on both sides of her now, gently, wordlessly, like the fresh air that met her at the door.

Jordan reached into her bag and found a tissue. Sister Leslie pulled her arm back and leaned forward on the pew. She was only a few years older than Jordan, but her eyes were lined with the type of joy and contentment usually found on women twice her age. Hers was a happy life, a sacred, purposeful one that moved her easily around the community of St. John the Divine and the Upper West Side. Her gentle wide gaze held Jordan's as she stood to return to her office in the back.

"If you don't have dinner plans tonight, Jordan, we're having a community buffet in the hall." The nun shrugged her shoulders, grinned, and pushed her eyebrows upward, like a child might do before deciding whether to go outside to play. She was a few inches taller than Jordan, though her frame seemed tiny and buried beneath her black-and-white habit. Jordan thanked her for the invitation and thought she might just be there since she couldn't remember what else she was supposed to do.

But as Jordan stood up to leave her corner, she was caught by the colorful stained-glass window above them: people crowded in the picture around the Christ child, a light shining on his face, wood floor beneath them as if they were on a stage.

Jordan turned quickly to her friend. "I'm sorry, Sister, I'm supposed to usher tonight at the theater with my neighbor. I just remembered. Thanks, though." She reached across to the woman, put her arms around her shoulders, and hugged her. Tight. The nun smiled again and waved at Jordan as she strolled out of the cathedral.

The rest of the afternoon was clear as glass—a cloudless sky— and Jordan decided to revel in it. She wandered down Broadway on the Upper West Side, sometimes exploring bookstores or thrift shops, sometimes just sitting in cafés and watching the families of people walking by. Her shoulders were light and the puffiness on her eyes gone.

Barry was waiting for her at the theater and whistled when he saw her.

"Girl, you look like a million bucks! I should sing to you every morning." He laughed at the thought and then looked into the relaxed green eyes of his friend. "Don't tell me. You've been to church?"

"Well, sort of." Jordan grinned as she grabbed her friend's hand and they hurried into the theater. The show tonight was only average, she and Barry decided on the way home, a revival of an O'Neill play about a daughter who tried to survive on the farm with a difficult father and a materialistic brother. Not much redemption, the two friends concluded as they climbed the five floors to their apartments and said good night.

The phone was ringing as Jordan unlocked her door. It was Aunt Cynthia.

"Hey Jordan. I figured I'd catch you about now. Just coming back from a show, I'll bet?"

Jordan laughed and sat on her couch. She held the phone close to her ear, happy to end the day by talking with someone from home. Someone like her aunt.

"It's your mama, hon. I don't want you to worry, but she went into the hospital late this afternoon. I'm there now. But like I said, don't worry. She's fine. Just tired." Jordan's eyes suddenly stung again as she listened to the story. She knew her mother had been pushing herself too hard, as usual, what with the fall programs and parent-teacher conferences and church events. She'd fainted at work. Again.

"I could fly home."

"No, sugar, your mama's probably being released in the morning, and doctor's orders are to take it easy. Call her tomorrow sometime, she'd like that."

Jordan thanked her aunt for calling, promised she wouldn't worry, and hung up the phone. She turned back the covers and slid into bed. Her body craved sleep, but her mind now was full, troubled for her mother and for what it might have meant if Jordan had had to fly home. It'd been four years since she'd seen her father, probably not long enough in his book, and Jordan did not want to rush it if she didn't have to.

The image of the poet's corner suddenly dropped into her mind, covering her like a blanket with the peace she always found there. She let out a bit of air, closed her eyes, and started to hum. Not a song from the seventies as she'd been singing earlier, but surprisingly one that took her back to her mama. It was a song Jordan had heard her mother humming in the kitchen as she prepared dinner or when she worked in the garden. Funny, she couldn't ever remember singing the song at Second Baptist. No, this was her mother's song. The words echoed from the memory into Jordan's tired mind now:

When peace, like a river, attendeth my way,
When sorrows like sea billows roll,
Whatever my lot, Thou has taught me to say,
It is well, it is well, with my soul.

It is well, with my soul,
It is well, with my soul,
It is well, it is well, with my soul.

That night Jordan fell into a deep hole of sleep, one where childhood wounds and adult fears were buried and covered in monster masks and familiar faces, the kind that, thankfully, created only a fuzzy image the next morning when she woke up. When she heard her alarm clock, she felt rested and glad to be awake. Grateful to be in New York, not Jackson.

SIX

Jeanie's face was as pale and tight as the hospital sheets beneath her. She tried to smile when Peter walked into the room, but it was an effort even to move the muscles in her cheeks. She was so tired. Instead, her small brown eyes simply followed the steady frame of her husband as he hurried toward a chair in the corner, picked it up with one hand, and plopped it down beside her. Close.

"I'm sorry, Peter," Jeanie's words were notes that hung quietly in a dark, familiar song. Peter had heard it for years now. His wife often felt responsible for each blemish on their life together; whether it was a dying azalea bush in the backyard or a lost friendship over the years, Jeanie blamed herself for the rain in their lives. And if there was any reason behind what sunshine did stream into their days, Jeanie said it was because of Peter. God heard the prayers of her husband.

Peter pressed his lips to his wife's forehead, being careful not to press too hard, and then leaned his mouth toward her ear. "Hey hon," he whispered, ignoring her apology and trying not to react to the cold of her skin. He sat down slowly, smiling at the woman he'd been married to for more than thirty years, placing her small pale fingers in his hand. Her eyes watered.

He stared at her, pained by the fragile figure on the bed, long thin tubes running from her arm to the IV stand above her and pillows propped under her knees. He brushed the brown curly hair back from her face with his other hand, stroking his wife's head. As he did, Peter noticed gray streaks in her hair and wondered how long they had been there. Maybe the hospital light was playing tricks on him. Certainly, *his* Jeanie could not be getting older.

"How you feeling?"

"Fine. I don't know why they brought me in here, why all the trouble," she answered, pulling her hand from his and looking toward the wall. She clasped her hands together and rested them on her stomach. Peter cleared his throat.

"Well, you look as good as you did the first day I saw you," he said.

The corners of her lips turned slightly, but she did not look back at her husband.

That picture dropped into Peter's mind as he stared at her. It was 1964 and they were both barely twenty years old, second-year students at Jackson Baptist Bible College. She was walking into the dorm cafeteria, surrounded by her friends and balancing a pile of books in her arms. Peter was eating with his roommate when he looked up from his plate and saw Jeanie's wavy hair bouncing with each step she took. He watched her cradling her books, laughing with the young women around her, and finally sitting down at a table a few feet from his. The light blue sweater she wore still lingered in his memory, highlighting the soft features on her body and face, and the tender grace with which she moved.

But it was her eyes that most drew Peter. Rich brown eyes with a hint of topaz glistening from her soul in a way Peter had not seen before in anyone else. This woman had depth, he thought, and he wanted to know her. He pushed out his chair, left his half-eaten dinner on the table, and walked over to where she was sitting. When she looked up at him, though, Peter's courage suddenly dissolved, and he stood staring like a child on his first trip away from home. He gawked.

"Your dinner's getting cold," Jeanie smiled and pointed to the table he'd just come from. The sound of her voice brought Peter back to himself. He laughed, glancing over his shoulder to the plate across the room and then back to the eyes that caught his heart.

"You're right. Mind if I bring it over to this table?" Peter had regained his confidence. Jeanie's nod was all the encouragement he needed to dash back to his dinner, scoop up his tray, and all but throw it on the table across from the young woman in the blue sweater. His roommate sat alone, grinning.

"Mind if I bring my dinner over to your table?" he whispered to his wife now as she lay still in the hospital. Jeanie's head turned slowly off the pillow and toward her husband, the color in her eyes clouded by weariness.

"What are you talking about?"

"Remember the dining hall in college?"

"What about it?"

Peter looked away, thinking of the thousands of meals they'd shared there, the dinners and picnics and breakfasts where he and Jeanie had talked about everything from children and trips to books and dreams. Their companionship was easy from the start, both certain that the only way they wanted to spend their lives was in service to God. She would be an elementary teacher; he a pastor of his own church. And together they would be a powerful combination in helping others find their purpose.

Youthful zeal, though, never plans for tragedy, one that strains even the most devoted relationships.

Jeanie lay motionless on the hospital bed, still waiting for her husband's answer.

"Never mind," he said. He clenched his jaw so it moved back and forth on his chin.

Jeanie closed her eyes, her hands still resting away from Peter's. He looked at them. The lights from the parking lot outside her window cast strange shadows on her bed. He stared at her face, then down at the green hospital gown that covered her shoulders, her breasts, and her hips. He looked at her strong short legs and even her toes. He pulled the blanket up to her neck to make sure she was warm.

Peter brushed his eyes from under his glasses, certain his wife would need to see only strength from her husband. His foot began to knock the metal leg of the chair. He propped his hand under his chin and fought off a war of words that flew through his mind. Conversations they had had last week about credit-card bills and checkups bounced around his head. They weren't arguments exactly. Just sentences and concerns that came mostly from him while Jeanie glared at him, offered a small defense, and went quiet. It was a pattern in the past five years or so, one far different from their early dining room discussions.

Refocus, he thought to himself. Work at it. He shut his eyes tight for a second, hoping that would help him concentrate on how to help his wife now. Maybe he should try to distract her from her pain. He decided to whisper a hymn Jeanie had loved for years, one they rarely sang on Sunday mornings at Second Baptist, but one he'd heard her hum often around the house, hoping its familiarity would bring some comfort to her. *"When peace, like a river, attendeth my way / When sorrows like sea billows roll…"*

Tiny lines formed at the corners of her eyes like she was squinting to see, though her eyes remained shut. Then Jeanie's breathing

Jo Kadlecek

eased and her eyelids loosened slightly as Peter continued to hum so that he could see a sliver of white behind her lashes. Her lips dropped effortlessly on her chin forming a tiny *O*, and before he got to the refrain, Jeanie was asleep.

Peter turned his wrist to see what time it was: 9:10 p.m. He drew his head back, surprised that so much time had passed between the present and when he first got the call earlier that afternoon. How long had he been in the waiting room where the little girl watched him? Time to him was a map, one with destination points he carefully plotted each day. Every hour was planned, filled, and accounted for. He controlled it. He wrote each meeting down in his daily calendar, slotted out study and sermon preparation time, and penciled in appointments with people, in case they needed to reschedule. Church work was demanding, and he had to be organized.

It was easier this way.

Tonight, though, he had lost track. He'd even left his Day-Timer in the car as he ran into the emergency room. Usually, he carried it with him everywhere he went—an addendum to his Bible, guiding his daily interactions. But tonight the lost hours, the unplanned event, the empty ache that always came with waiting—especially in hospitals—made him forget about his schedule. Whenever he'd lost track before, his stomach turned into knots and he became queasy, as if he were seasick. Tonight, his stomach just felt empty.

He loosened his tie, set his glasses on the table beside Jeanie, and turned off the lamp. Peter settled back into the chair and stretched out his legs. He felt the muscles and bones in his body go limp; he hadn't realized how tired he was. Then he leaned back his head on the top of the chair, closed his eyes, and fell into one of those gray places in sleep somewhere between worry and rest.

About four hours later a gentle hand tapped his shoulder. Peter looked up and saw two round eyes lined with black mascara and eyeliner staring at him. His sister's face was shaded with a lifetime of adventures and experiences; her nose was long and narrow, and light foundation hid well the lines of age that had formed on her forehead and chin. She motioned her brother to follow her. They walked in silence out of the dark room and into the corridor.

"The doctor says it could be anything, but probably mostly she's not getting enough rest," Cynthia Sue was speaking with her usual authority. She'd cut her hair short, just above her neck in a kind of bob, since Peter had last seen her. Almost every time Peter saw his older sister, she had a new hairstyle. Granted, it was always one that reflected the inherent dignity she seemed born with, a quality Peter admired but one he thought had missed him in the birthing process. Even in the middle of this night, he couldn't help but notice how her hair, makeup, and dress seemed as assured and poised as she always did.

"How do you know? I haven't even seen the doctor," Peter was groggy and short. He was, however, relieved to see his sister.

"I'm a reporter, remember?" She announced it as if she were suddenly breaking a story. Cynthia Sue had left the newspaper office as soon as she met her deadline and made the four-hour drive from Mobile to Jackson in three. She'd called their parents from the road and found the doctor as soon as she got to the hospital. Once he gave her his diagnosis for Jeanie and she'd gathered as much information as she could from nurses, Cynthia Sue made one more call: to her niece. Peter's daughter. She had reached Jordan just as she came home from the theater and told her not to worry. Her mama was just tired.

Peter swallowed a big gulp of air when he heard this and released it through an odd but quick chuckle. He walked to a water fountain across the hall and leaned over for a drink. His throat was dry, his face sleepy. *She* was the last thing he expected to hear about tonight, and he was not completely ready for it. As he'd told his sister for the past four years, as far as he was concerned, his daughter was a distant ship in the ocean who'd set her own sail in a direction far from home. That was just how it was, he said, those were the choices she made when she decided to move to New York and away from all that he stood for. He splashed some water across his chin and returned to his sister.

"Well, she needed to know about her mama, Peter. You can't

argue with that," Cynthia Sue said, one hand on her hip and the other in the air like an exclamation mark. The nurses at the station glanced toward them, then back to their charts. A beep came over the intercom and a tall gray-haired nurse hurried down the hall.

"Thanks for coming, Cynthia," Peter's voice was gravelly, still tired. He rotated his neck to get out the kinks from having fallen asleep in the chair and ignored what he'd just heard about Jordan. His sister nodded and continued to relay her scoop.

"They looked at her blood pressure, heart, and lungs. They sent some of her blood to the lab to test it for anything from leukemia and cancer to STDs." Cynthia Sue laughed at this latter bit of information and then turned thoughtful again. "And, Peter, they scheduled an MRI for the morning to look at every possibility. They don't want to rule out anything."

"Why didn't they tell me any of that? I'm her husband." Now Peter's hands were on his hips, his shoulders perched. His eyebrows moved together. He was so serious.

"Why didn't you ask?" Cynthia Sue tossed it gently back to him. She knew of her brother's aversion to doctors, how he'd mistrusted them ever since they returned from Fiji.

"Besides, I'm the snoop in this family. You don't think you'd get more information than I would, did you?" Cynthia Sue said. She didn't mind talking with the doctors and nurses; she was used to it because of her work.

"I just wanted to help, little brother," she said.

Cynthia Sue reached across the sibling tension and put her arms around him. She drew him in close to her and squeezed his frame hard, rubbing the top of his shoulders on down to the middle of his back with her palms.

"She'll be okay, hon, she will," Cynthia Sue whispered into Peter's ear, still holding tightly to her only brother. Her confidence and her grip helped Peter relax. Still, he knew he was the one who was supposed to be the believer.

He let go of his sister, stepped back about arm's length from her, and looked into her face.

"I know. God is with her." Peter spoke firmly in a voice he often used when he was in the pulpit: low, deep, and full of conviction. Cynthia's face looked serious again, like it did when she was interviewing one of Mobile's politicians. Then she pushed her lips into a smile, patted her brother on the shoulder, and walked over to the water fountain. Her throat felt clogged suddenly, like she needed to wash down whatever was stuck. She took several swallows and saw out of the corner of her eye Peter walking back toward room 854.

In spite of their differences, she admired her brother's loyalty. She knew he would want to stay with his wife through the night. Cynthia Sue smiled again at Peter, but he was already inside his wife's room.

She walked into the Mississippi night, drove to her brother's house, let herself in, and slept in her niece's empty room. When Jordan had left for New York four years ago, she'd taken everything but her twin bed and the big travel agent poster of a Fijian sunset she'd bought when she was a kid. In bold letters across the bottom of the poster, the word *Bula!* was written in Jordan's handwriting, the native greeting on the island. Her aunt grinned as she read the word. And in spite of the sparseness in the room, Cynthia Sue still felt Jordan in here. This room had not lost her niece's fingerprint, and that made her glad.

By nine o'clock the next morning, Peter was helping Jeanie out of the car in their driveway and into the house they'd owned since moving back to Jackson. Coffee brewing and biscuits in the oven, Cynthia Sue met her brother and slow-moving sister-in-law at the door with hugs. She wasn't sure who looked more exhausted, Jeanie or Peter. Both came in and dropped on the couch like they hadn't sat down for days. Cynthia brought each a cup of black coffee with a bit of honey, the way they'd drunk their coffee for years. As soon as she set down the mugs, the phone rang. Peter pleaded with his eyes for his sister to answer.

Cynthia picked it up, listened, and then held her hand over the receiver.

"It's Miss Mary," she said. "Today's her day off at the senior center, and she wants to know if y'all could use an extra hand."

Peter shook his head in awe at how quickly word traveled in Jackson. He shrugged his shoulders toward his sister, and within seconds Cynthia was telling Mary, "Sure enough. Come on by. That's real kind of you, Miss Mary."

Jeanie smiled at the exchange, thankful for the help but awkward at the fuss over her. "I'm fine," she told her sister-in-law when she hung up the phone. "I just need some sleep."

The smell of freshly baked biscuits floated toward the living room as Cynthia brought the basket to her brother and sister-in-law. Jeanie took one bite out of her biscuit, put it on her napkin beside her, and tilted back her head to rest. Peter did the same. Cynthia Sue smeared some jam across her biscuit, took a bite, and slurped her coffee at the same time. She loved the way coffee flavored the jam and the flour. Or maybe it was the other way around. She did the same thing until her biscuit was gone and considered sneaking Peter's.

A knock on the door startled all three. At the same time Cynthia was getting up to answer the door, the phone rang again.

"Good Lord, Jeanie, you'd think you just got elected homecoming queen, all this attention!" She shared the laugh with Jeanie and pointed to Peter to go to the door so she could see who was on the phone. Peter forced himself from the couch and saw their neighbor Mrs. Mowery on the steps, an apple strudel in her hand.

She stood tall and awkward in a pink-striped housedress, her hair still in rollers, her feet in big flat slippers. She was from a long line of "pure" Mississippians and didn't mind saying so.

"Hey Pastor," she said as Peter opened the door. She caught her breath for a second when she saw how tired Peter looked. "I heard Jeanie had a little bit of a rough day yesterday, so I thought you might be needin' somethin' sweet to get you through." She paused as she stared at him. "I reckon I was right."

Only a few teeth showed when she smiled at her neighbor. Peter said he was much obliged, took the strudel from her, and apologized for looking such a mess. She chuckled, and as she did the rollers on her head moved up and down. She waved her "Don't you never mind" hand at him and marched back to her house next door. Peter watched her move along the sidewalk, her short deliberate steps, until she disappeared inside her small white house.

As he turned to show his wife their neighbor's gift, he saw Jeanie looking at Cynthia Sue, the phone close to her ear.

"No, hon, it's good timing," his sister was saying. "They just got home. I'll put your mama on." She shot a glance to her brother that dared him to behave and handed the phone to Jeanie so she could talk with her daughter. Then she slurped her coffee again loud enough to remind her brother that she was still the older of the two and he better not try anything he'd later regret.

His foot tapped anxiously against the floor. Peter coughed into his napkin and turned his wrist toward him again to see what time it was. Then he walked out the front door to the car to get his Day-Timer. When he opened the book, he saw three appointments listed for the morning. One he could postpone, but the other two were meetings he'd rearranged before, including a planning meeting with Dr. Stately. He could not miss that.

Peter walked back inside, saw Jeanie still on the phone with Jordan, and cleared his throat. His sister glared at him. So he hurried down the hall to take a shower. It bothered Peter that his wife was in touch regularly with his daughter. Sometimes he felt a hot burning sensation rise in his spine at the idea of the two talking about nothing in particular or everything important to them. Of the various conversations he'd had lately with Jeanie, only one had covered the topic of losing Jordan. And Peter cut that short. It was as if they both knew that talking about it would conjure up a pain—and a memory—neither wanted to confront.

The events of the day busied Peter's mind as he finished his shower, put on his blue suit, and reached for a tie. His muscles were weary and begged for sleep. He sighed. Then he combed back his auburn hair and walked back down the hall.

When he saw his wife was still on the phone, something snapped in Peter's gut.

"It's time to get off the phone, Jeanie, and get into bed." His voice was louder than usual, firm and forceful, with an angry whip behind it. Jeanie froze when she heard him. Her frail brown eyes pleaded with him. Peter took off his glasses and pretended to polish them. When he put them back on, she held up her index finger to him to signal one more minute, but before either could think about it, Peter yanked the phone out of Jeanie's hand and slammed it down on the receiver. Then he picked it up again and slammed it down one more time, harder and louder than the first, to make sure it was disconnected. He breathed quickly.

Jeanie slumped down in her chair, silent and shaken, her eyes wide and fixed on her husband. Cynthia Sue hurried across to her and stood beside her, her hand on Jeanie's shoulder. Neither woman said a word.

Peter put his hands on the counter as if to get his balance and stared at the floor. His eyelashes flickered behind his glasses as he breathed in, then out, trying to relax. After a few long seconds, he raised his head and looked at his wife.

"I'm sorry, Jeanie, but—"

"No, you're not," she said coldly. "You've never been sorry about what's happened with Jordan and—"

"But the doctor said, well, you just need to rest." He cleared his throat and combed his fingers through his hair.

"Maybe she's not the only one who needs to take it easy," Cynthia Sue's words were a gentle treaty. But Peter would not look at his sister.

"I've got to meet with Dr. Stately and some other folks at the church," he said, his voice gravelly again.

"Of course you do," Jeanie said, her voice barely audible. "You always do."

"But I'll be home early," he defended. He kissed his wife on the cheek, patted his sister on the shoulder, and thanked her for coming up. Then Peter put on his jacket and walked out the front door. His coffee cup still full and by now cold.

Halfway down the street, Peter punched the steering wheel with his fist, determined not to let his daughter get to him like this. She should not have taken so much time with Jeanie on the phone. She was selfish not to think about how her mother should be resting, rather than talking to her. But there were a million shoulds about Jordan that plagued Peter, and he knew if he kept thinking about them, he'd only get angrier and more distracted. He stared at the road ahead.

A few minutes later Peter shook his head and drove into the church parking lot. It was 10:15 and he was late for his meeting with his senior pastor. As Peter hurried in, trying to push the morning out of his mind, Dr. Stately was walking out. Peter stopped suddenly on the sidewalk into the church.

"Mornin', Peter. How's Jeanie?" Dr. Stately stood tall outside the sanctuary, his silver hair shining in the morning sun. His suit and face were smooth and sure, as always. Peter looked at his pastor for a second and then looked at the ground.

"Nothing to worry about. She's just been working too hard," he mumbled. "Teaching can do that. She'll be fine—as soon as she gets some rest."

"Well, that's good to hear. Listen, there was a cancellation at the club, and I hope you don't mind, but I've got to get a golf game in this morning. Could we meet later this afternoon instead?" The deep pastoral voice wrapped around Peter's raw soul like storm winds do trees. But Peter held on, nodded, and gave his pastor the same "Don't you never mind" wave Mrs. Mowery had offered him only an hour before.

Dr. Stately slapped Peter's shoulder and smiled. Even though the sun was bright, the October air felt chillier than usual as Peter watched his elder get into his Oldsmobile and drive away. Peter took out his Day-Timer and crossed off the morning meeting with Dr. Stately, penciling it in for three that afternoon. He looked at his watch again: 10:20. Tim Moody was coming at eleven for a counseling session, but Peter ached in emptiness. He had no idea what he could offer this parishioner. He looked up at the blue sky and watched the clouds moving in a line, almost hurrying to form a huge smoky ball plowing through the air. A storm was coming.

Peter's stomach growled. He thought about Mrs. Mowery's apple strudel, then Cynthia's biscuits, and realized he hadn't eaten much of either. It had been enough just to get Jeanie home. So rather than heading into the church office, he turned around, walked back to his car, and decided to drive to Captain Billy's for a sandwich before his 11:00 a.m. meeting. Maybe the drive and the food would clear his head and restore his purpose. Maybe the storm would pass.

Peter buttoned his jacket at the chill and yawned as he sat behind the steering wheel again. He put the car in gear and drove back onto the street. Tiny drops of rain began to hit the windshield. As he turned on the wipers, he felt the burning sensation climb up his spine again. His eyes stung from weariness, but he kept driving.

The rest of the day was a blur to Peter—another whirl of personalities and needs, meetings and conversations. He felt himself floating through each from a distance. He heard sounds and sentences come out of his mouth as if he, too, were listening and watching the day's interactions like he was somewhere else. His body felt far off. Whenever he saw a woman's face, it turned into either Jeanie's or Jordan's for a few seconds and then back into the woman's. The wind howled outside, and Peter's throat felt dry all day.

Dr. Stately never came back to the church that afternoon, though Peter hadn't noticed until Loretta was going home around 5:00 p.m. When he asked her about the senior pastor, she shrugged her shoulders, smiled, and waved as she walked to her car.

Peter had also forgotten about the missions meeting that night, so he didn't come home early as he had told his wife and sister. It wasn't until 10:30 that Peter finally pulled into the driveway. The lights were out in his house, and as he opened the front door, he could still smell the fried chicken Miss Mary must have cooked for Jeanie's dinner.

When he shut it behind him, his sister turned on a lamp in the living room. She had been sitting in the dark, waiting. He wanted to say something to her, but no words, no greeting, nothing formed in his mouth. Cynthia Sue stood up, walked over to her brother, and stared at him. He shifted his weight and tried to walk into the kitchen. She moved in front of him, not letting him pass, but still said nothing.

"What? What's the matter?" Peter's voice trailed off.

His sister's dark eyes shot through him.

"I've been at the church, sis. I can't expect for you to understand all that I'm doing in the ministry, but…"

Cynthia Sue did not wait to hear the rest of her brother's reason for coming home so late. She simply grabbed him, pulled him close, and hugged him.

When she finally let go, gathering her purse and bag, she turned to her brother once more.

"Peter, what you do at that church is your business. But I am here to tell you, you cannot wait forever." Her eyes held his. Then she walked out the front door and got into her car to drive back to Mobile.

Peter watched his sister from the window until her car was out of sight. He tossed his jacket and tie on the couch, turned off the light, and went quietly into his bedroom. Still dressed in his shirt and slacks, he lay down beside his wife. All he could hear was Jeanie breathing. He listened for a long time. The slow steady cadence reminded him of rain on the windowpane.

SEVEN

The October morning air felt good on Jordan's face and brushed her cheeks pink. She pulled her hair up into a ponytail on top of her head so that auburn strands flopped around in every direction. Then she bent over to tighten her shoelaces and stretch her hamstrings. She counted to ten and let her fingers dangle over her toes. As soon as Jordan pinched the start button on her stopwatch, she pushed her glasses back close to her eyes and took off.

Few things for Jordan compared with jogging around Central Park when the sun had just come up. In October no less—her favorite month in New York. Not too humid but not yet cold. And the autumn colors were always glorious. She'd gotten up when the sky was caught between dark and light, ridden the number 6 train to Fifty-ninth and Lexington, and walked the few blocks over to the park. The streets were quiet, void of the usual cab honks, bus engines, and tourist buzz. She could almost hear the wind.

Today Jordan felt groggy and kept hearing the sound of a phone slamming down in her ear. She hadn't gone for a jog since that morning last week when she had called home to check on her mother and had been dramatically reminded of how little she and her father had in common. She was worried about her mama's health but wasn't about to risk calling again; instead, she'd wait for a call from her aunt to keep her updated. Now she just wanted to clear her head and work her muscles. The six miles around the park would do both.

Jordan jogged north past the fountain in the middle, behind the Metropolitan Museum of Art, and around the reservoir. In each part of the park she saw yellow and orange fall colors splashed across trees. Bright red leaves burst off of branches and scattered on the ground beneath, crunching whenever Jordan stepped on them. Bushes glittered in the morning sun, shadowed every now and then by a few gray clouds that moved across the sky. The summer greenness of the Great Lawn had slipped into a pale canvas dotted with autumn leaves. There was no mistaking: New York's Central Park was a slow and beautiful refuge from the urban busyness of the streets. Sometimes when Jordan came for a jog, she forgot she was even *in* a city.

She wondered how New Yorkers would have coped through the years had city planners sold off this land in the mid-1850s to developers rather than build the park in what was then farm country. What foresight they had, she thought, considering all the skyscrapers and apartment buildings that had since been built around it. Sometimes a soul just needed green. Nature and leaves. Lakes and trees. And grass, not concrete, under her feet. As much as New York meant to her, Jordan understood how city life could sometimes wear down those who lived here.

Still, the Big Apple and everything it represented—the theater, the people, the distance from Mississippi—had become hers. The novelty had not worn off for the young southern playwright, and now, more than ever, she was determined to make it her home.

After all, there certainly was not much waiting for her back in Jackson. Jordan had taken far too many steps in the wrong direction for her righteous daddy to invite her back.

By the time she passed the Strawberry Fields John Lennon had made famous on the southwestern end of the park, Jordan glanced at her watch. She was ahead of her usual time by almost a minute; the autumn colors and internal conversations must have distracted her from the exercise and helped her keep up her pace without even realizing it. Once she had arrived at Columbus Circle at Fifty-ninth and Broadway, Jordan decided to catch the subway back to the Village. She stretched out and cooled off in front of the park entrance, greeted now by honks and tourist buses and street vendors setting up for the day. New York was waking up.

Jordan bought an orange juice and a *New York Times* at the

newsstand on the corner and skipped down the stairs to the subway. As she waited she flipped through the newspaper to the arts section, wondering what rising playwright she'd read about today. Several new shows were opening on and off Broadway, and she felt obliged to keep up with her colleagues. Maybe someday they would be reading about her. She smiled at the thought at the same time that she noticed a small rat crawling on the subway tracks below. Jordan went back to the newspaper.

Barry was walking out of the apartment building as Jordan came around the corner. She hollered after her neighbor. He stopped, turned around, and waited for his friend to catch up.

"Ah, my good-luck charm," he said to Jordan. His face was wide with a smile, but Jordan seemed to notice an emptiness in his eyes. They were darker than usual this morning, slightly puffy, and Jordan wondered if Barry had gotten much sleep.

"Ooh, is that sweat?" Barry was pointing to Jordan's forehead, trying to divert her attention. He looked at her running shoes. "Jogging, huh? Why do you do that again? Tell me what the point is now?" He was trying to make her laugh, as usual, but Jordan could tell Barry was feeling a familiar pain that often confronted him on cloudy mornings.

"I reckon it's supposed to be good for you," she said. "Bare, you should see the colors in the park. Absolutely brilliant." Jordan reached her hand across to Barry's arm, rubbed it, and smiled at him. Then she looked straight into his eyes and pressed her eyebrows together.

"You okay?" she asked.

Barry shifted his weight and shot a glance at a produce truck plowing by. He nodded his head, took off his Yankees cap, and ran his fingers through his thick brown hair. Then he put the cap back on and adjusted it. He forced a grin while playing with the zipper on his leather jacket.

"Me? Oh, couldn't be finer." His laugh got caught in the back of his throat and gurgled as if water were rippling through it. He stuffed his hands into the pockets of his jeans and let his shoulders sag a bit.

"Honestly, Jordan, I'm nervous as hell. I've got an audition in an hour for a part I'd love to have, haven't heard a thing from you know who and woke up wondering why on earth I was living in this messed-up city."

She knew what that meant. New York was easily the most competitive place there was for building an acting career; the best in the business came here, driven by the dream to see their name in lights. And you were in big trouble if the fire in your bones ever went out for the art. You'd never survive.

Barry stared into Jordan's eyes, and she saw the fear of a twelve-year-old boy. Neither said a word for a long moment. Another truck passed, obnoxiously loud.

"Other than that I'm dandy." Barry glared at the ridiculous truck trying to squeeze down a street between several cars that were double-parked and through a space that was barely wider than the truck. He rolled his eyes.

Jordan reached across the sidewalk and grabbed her friend. She hugged him for a minute, and when she let him go, she took off her glasses and held his gaze.

"You'll do great. God knows they'd be lucky to have you." Jordan was firm and confident in her encouragement as she held tight to Barry's hand. She was not about to let her friend go into the cruel world of theater auditions without an extra dose of affirmation.

"If you weren't so disgustingly sweaty, girl, I'd make you come with me." He laughed and Jordan was sure she saw a tinge of hope return to Barry's eyes. She let go of his hand and slapped his back.

"Break a leg!"

"I'm hoping to. The auditions are only a couple of blocks away," Barry rambled, "so I thought the morning air might do me good. If I bomb I'll head up to the park and drown my sorrows in the trees!" He hollered over his shoulder to Jordan and waved to her as he hurried down the street until he was out of sight.

A silent prayer for Barry formed on Jordan's lips. It astonished her. She'd thought of herself as a lapsed Baptist ever since moving here, though still a believer, and praying for friends as they ran off to auditions seemed more the stuff of Baptist inclination than of

New York pseudoreligious playwrights. But she lifted her shoulders as if it couldn't hurt, dug out her keys from her jacket, and began to climb the five floors to her apartment.

Maybe she should be praying more, she thought by the third floor. Maybe she shouldn't wait just for the tough moments in a friend's life or for the silence of the poet's corner at St. John's. Maybe she and God should pencil in a few more chats throughout the week than they did now. Granted, there probably weren't many other playwrights in this town who talked regularly with the God of the Bible, but by the time she unlocked her door, Jordan thought it might not be a bad idea.

Life was not exactly easy these days. She could use a little extra help.

When she dropped her keys on the couch, the old family photo she'd hung above it suddenly caught her attention. It was at least fifteen years old, but it was the last time her entire family had been together for a photograph—all four. Jordan swallowed the last of her orange juice as she stared at the photograph and leaned against the counter. It took her to the old Jackson house where she'd grown up. She remembered crawling out of bed and encountering her parents as they prayed each morning. They had to talk to the Lord first thing in the day, her mama on her knees in the living room, eyes closed, hands clasped, and her father hunched over his Bible at the kitchen table, cup of coffee next to him, glasses perched on the end of his nose. Neither would much notice the girl as she crept past them to the refrigerator for a glass of milk, trying not to bother either during such holy time.

Sometimes, as a child, Jordan was jealous of God. He seemed to get more of her parent's attention than she did. But the older she got, the more she understood why he should.

Even now she was still a little confused at their morning ritual since her father had deliberately taught her to say her prayers each night as he tucked her into bed. He'd help her talk to Jesus about anything she wanted. When she'd finish her last prayer, the two would sing amen as a chorus, and Jordan would pull her covers up to her chin. Then her daddy would lean over and surprise her with a kiss somewhere on her face. It was a game they'd play each night after prayers; she'd close her eyes—sort of—and wait, and he'd kiss her eyelid one night, her ear the next, her nose after that. Each time she'd giggle as she'd peek to see her father's familiar face dropping down toward hers. Each night she was thrilled to watch the delight her daddy showed in her.

But that was a long time ago.

Jordan tossed her empty bottle of orange juice in the trash and turned on the bathtub in the middle of her apartment. Her stomach hurt. She wanted to quit thinking about the family in that photo—about her brother, James—but she couldn't. Growing up, she hadn't minded the constant focus on being a "good Christian girl," nor did she object to the countless hours in Sunday school or summer Bible camp, learning stories from the Old and New Testaments. She still found a certain solace in reciting the Lord's Prayer or reading a psalm aloud. But these days she could no longer relate to the seemingly endless list of expectations she'd learned at Second Baptist. God, she thought now, was bigger and less predictable than a list—otherwise he wouldn't be God—and she figured the Christian life had to be about much more than merely trying to convince others to adhere to a bunch of rules.

At least Jordan wanted to believe it was that way. Whenever she had asked her father about this, especially the older she got, his face would go blank. She might as well have been asking him about Mars or the theater, because he'd take off his glasses, clear his throat, and stare right through her. He became wooden. Christianity was clear and simple and therefore easily believed, he'd tell her in his preacher's voice, his eyebrows creased across his forehead like lines in the sand. Why did she want to make it so complicated? There was no debating it, and there was certainly no other way to approach it.

As Jordan got out of the tub, she slipped a gray Ole Miss T-shirt under her overalls and poured herself a bowl of granola. She was still bothered by the photo. She wondered when her father had become so rigid.

What had turned him into a Bible fix-it man, as she referred to him now whenever Barry would ask her about her family? Scripture had become his only answer to everything. Whenever Jordan had a problem in high school or college, he'd quote her a verse from Romans or Ephesians. Jesus could fix everything, he'd tell her. Period. Everything was either black or it was white. She could not think of a time since they'd moved back to Jackson that he responded to her in any other way. He was so spiritual that sometimes she wondered if he was human.

Jordan combed out her hair, and as she looked in the mirror, she realized her daddy had not always been so stiff, so religious. She suddenly saw him singing at the beach in Fiji, laughing in the ocean, playing jokes on her mother. And her brother. What changed?

Had she made him so angry when she decided to be a playwright?

The phone rang and Jordan jumped at the sound, dropping her comb into the sink and knocking the cereal bowl to the floor when she turned toward the phone. *Forget about him. Let the questions go,* she told herself. What difference did it make now? It would be a long time before she'd ever see her father's face in more than this old photo.

"Move on," she said aloud. "Get it together... Hello?"

"Hi, love, I think I have just the director for you. They're looking for original new work, and naturally I told them about you." Vinnie gave Jordan the director's name and the address of the small theater not far from where they met for class. "They're interested in your play and want to talk with you—if you can get there before noon."

She scribbled down the name and address, thanked her mentor, and hung up. Then Jordan picked up her cereal bowl from the floor, grabbed the latest version of her play from her computer printer, along with her jean jacket, and walked out the door.

As soon as she shut it, though, she pushed it open again and marched back inside. She might as well grab her uniform for the Tavern since she had to work tonight. She sniffed the flower-print shirt, decided it was clean enough to wear one more time, and tossed it into her bag with her script. She threw off her overalls and pulled on her black jeans. Jordan shot a defiant glance at the man in the photograph on the wall and walked out of her studio apartment.

Mrs. Gonzales was mopping the floor. She stopped when she saw Jordan and leaned against the handle as if she needed a break. The tiny Mexican woman wore a long gold cross around her neck. She stared at Jordan with tired eyes.

Jordan tiptoed across the clean wet floor and waved at her landlord.

"*Muchas gracias,* Señora Gonzales," she exclaimed as she pointed to the freshly mopped tiles in the hallway. Her Spanish was terrible, but she at least tried with Mrs. Gonzales. The older woman shook her head slightly, smiled, and watched Jordan's tiptoeing before swishing the mop back and forth again along the floor.

The sky had turned grayer since Jordan had returned from her jog. Funny, she hadn't expected it might rain today—the weather reports called for blue sky. Black bags of garbage were piled in front of her building and along the street as she headed north to West Fourth Street. She passed a half-dozen abandoned buildings with graffiti sprayed across them, situated between busy apartment complexes, storefronts, and diners.

Jordan stayed with the flow of people, stepping around white tubs of fresh flowers for sale, mothers with baby strollers, and Chinese delivery men who were riding their bicycles on the sidewalk until someone yelled for them to get off. When she came to a red light, Jordan turned and kept walking toward the green light, changing sides of the street but still heading north toward the theater. The sky seemed to be fighting between blue and gray, she noticed, but her mind was firmly focused on her play. She was rehearsing the pitch she'd give the director, going over the strengths of the two acts and the few areas she still wanted to explore.

Jordan reached into her bag and pulled out her manuscript, flipping through the pages to make sure they were in order. Her glasses started to fog up from her breathing onto the paper, so Jordan looked up. The light on the corner was red and this time she stopped.

She felt a slight tap on her shoulder. A tall thin man in an army jacket was holding out his hand to her, looking down at Jordan's bag. She smiled. She stuffed her hand into her jeans hoping she'd left at least a buck in her pocket from her tips at the Dream Time. She hadn't. But she did find a quarter.

"Sorry, sir, this is all I've got today," she said to him, looking into his cloudy brown eyes. She noticed his long black ponytail matted with leaves, and Jordan figured he'd spent the night at the park. The man shrugged his shoulders, looked down the street, and took her quarter. Then he mumbled, "A quarter? Well, you take what you can get these days." And he shuffled toward another woman in a dark green suit, put out his hand, and nodded his head. The woman hurried by. The homeless man turned invisible.

For the second time that day, Jordan found a prayer forming on her lips. She shook her head at the strangeness of it. She didn't have time to think too much about it, though, as she moved quickly out of the way. Two rows of first graders marched past her, two teachers at the front of the lines and two at the back. Another field trip, Jordan thought, and waved at the children as they fidgeted by. They were like a miniature United Nations—a black-skinned boy walking next to a boy with bushy red hair, an Arab girl with a scarf on her head and her arm around the shoulder of a Puerto Rican girl, and four Asian boys and girls skipping next to white, brown, and blonde children.

New York was a postcard of the whole world.

A few blocks later she saw the sign for the Stage Bite Theater Group, took a deep breath, and knocked on the door. No answer. Jordan pushed the door to see if it would open and poked her head into what was obviously a small lobby for a busy theater. Black-and-white head shots of actors were tacked to the walls next to blown-up newspaper reviews of recent shows. A few old, red velvet chairs were placed in the middle of the lobby.

"Hello?" Jordan called out, hoping that a trace of Mississippi could not be heard in her voice. She walked toward two black doors that she guessed led to the theater and pushed them open. As she did, a short pretty woman with a long blonde ponytail almost collided with Jordan. The woman was wearing faded blue jeans, pointy black cowboy boots, and a long-sleeved red shirt with snap buttons on the wrists. She was probably around fifteen years older than Jordan and looked like she'd be more comfortable on a horse ranch in Texas than at an alternative theater in New York's Village. Jordan put out her hand to introduce herself.

"Hi, I'm Jordan Riddle. Could you tell me where I might find Danny Clark?"

The woman shook Jordan's hand emphatically. "That would be me. *You're* Vinnie's student?" Both women seemed surprised by the other. Apparently Vinnie had forgotten to tell either that they would be meeting a woman at the Stage Bite. Jordan assumed Danny was a male, and Danny assumed the same about Jordan. Not that it mattered. It was just a surprise to find a woman director and a woman playwright in the male-dominated theater business.

Jordan laughed. "Well, it's an honor, Ms. Clark."

"Danny. Hey, we've got to help each other as much as we can."

Her face crinkled into dozens of laugh lines, and Jordan liked her instantly. They sat down in two of the theater seats to talk. A bulky young man with spiked orange hair was hammering a set on the stage down in front of them while two women were arranging furniture for what looked like a dining room.

"Whatcha got for me? Vinnie probably told you what we're looking for, right?" Danny was relaxed in the cushioned seat, her legs crossed, and her boot knocking lightly the chair in front of her. Jordan nodded. She knew that Danny's company was wanting a new show to premiere in the next months, one that was consistent with their season. The play they had hoped to do around the holidays fell through when they couldn't get production permission. The Stage Bite was the type of theater that challenged the status quo; it was realistic but contemporary, creative but with some commercial appeal. Jordan pushed her glasses back to her eyes, pulled her shoulders up, and gave Danny her pitch.

"Right. My play, *Windfall,* is the story of a Catholic woman who falls in love with a man who's an atheist. Set in New York in the 1930s, it becomes a choice of loves."

Danny's boot stopped kicking the chair in front of her. "A religious piece? At the Stage Bite? In the Village?" Her face formed a serious smirk when Jordan interjected.

"Aren't all plays religious? Good drama is always about the conflict of beliefs in human character, right? I wouldn't call *Windfall* a religious drama as much as a human one," Jordan said.

143

The smirk disappeared entirely from Danny's face, and her eyes widened a bit as she looked back at Jordan. "Well, well. A purist. Good for you. Tell me more." Danny glanced toward the set and back to Jordan.

"Strong lead. Tamara is a devout activist determined to change the world—until she falls in love with someone who won't believe the world is worth changing or that God exists," Jordan said. "She realizes she's got to choose who she'll love more—the guy or God—and of course that decision ends up changing *her* world."

Danny's eyes were moving from Jordan's face to the set and back again, as if she were already imagining how to stage the story she'd just heard.

"Leave me your script and I'll call you."

Jordan pulled the manuscript from her bag. "Well, I just happen to have it right here."

A light laugh bubbled out of the sides of Jordan's mouth as she handed it to Danny. Thankfully, the western-looking director chuckled too.

"Better yet, let's bring in the company Saturday after next, say at eleven for a cold reading. How about if we let them decide? That's usually how we function around here. How many do we need?"

"Small cast—another selling point, I might add—three women and three men," Jordan said.

"Well, we just happen to have a company of three women and

three men. Could be your lucky day." Danny stood up and led Jordan up the aisle and back to the lobby. Both women were smiling. When they stopped at the door, Jordan turned and put out her hand again to the woman. They shook.

"Thanks so much for your time, Danny. I'll look forward to hearing what you think," Jordan said, pulling her bag up higher on her shoulder.

"That's a good sign. I'll look forward to telling you what I think. I'm sure Vinnie's prepared you well." Her eyes were soft as she said this, open and sincere.

"He has. He's a great teacher," Jordan said.

"Where you from anyway?" Danny blurted out.

"It's that obvious? Mississippi. You?" Jordan said, pointing to Danny's boots.

"Where do you think? New Jersey, of course!" Danny laughed at her own joke, and again Jordan knew she liked this woman. They nodded at each other as one went back into the theater and the other walked onto the street.

When Jordan looked up above the buildings, she couldn't see a single cloud. The fall blueness had filled the sky again. She kept walking north, found the subway a few blocks up, and waited for a train. She had to switch trains at Times Square, but she didn't mind. It gave her a chance to watch the people again.

After browsing through the drama section for a few hours at the Lincoln Center Bookstore, Jordan arrived at the Dream Time Tavern about twenty minutes before she was supposed to start working. Jack was in the kitchen with his skipper hat on, chopping lettuce and onions and singing along to the radio. When Jordan walked in, he looked up. Then he turned the radio down.

"The famous playwright," he teased. His eyes were sparkling tonight, and Jordan hoped it wasn't because he had been sampling any new Australian wines. Maybe Jack was simply in a good mood.

"Got a reading slated at a theater in the Village, Jack. Could be a good sign," Jordan said as she tied on her apron. She leaned over and tightened her shoelaces. It felt good to stretch her hamstrings.

"Oh, now, see, you're not gonna quit on me, are you, mate?" Jack stopped chopping and was looking at each part of Jordan's face. She still felt slightly embarrassed being around him after her panic attack, but he had been gentle with her since she'd come back. In fact, she realized he hadn't once brought up that night except to ask how she was feeling.

"No worries, mate. You're stuck with me for a while," Jordan said. She smiled at him and he smiled back. She noticed his jaw was clean-shaven tonight. It was firm and strong, slightly tanned, and his nose was long, the kind that almost touched the top of his mouth and made him look like a Roman soldier. Jack was exactly five years older than Jordan. Both had April birthdays, and last year they decided to celebrate all month long at the Tavern with silly pranks and party hats. Even though Jack was her boss, Jordan considered him a friend as well. If she had to work in a restaurant in this city until she could write for a living, she was glad to work for someone she respected.

He walked over to the door where she stood, and as he did she could smell the faint scent of his aftershave. It wasn't too strong, just light and airy and nice. Jordan had never noticed the scent before. Jack picked up a bucket of potatoes, and the muscle in his forearm bulged. Her boss, Jordan suddenly noticed, was getting handsome. Maybe he had a girlfriend after all, and she grinned at the idea.

She began setting the tables when he walked out into the dining room. No other waiters had arrived by this time, and Jordan still hadn't changed into her flower shirt. She thought Jack was going to tell her to get into uniform, so she stopped what she was doing, set down her spoons, and looked up at him, waiting. His eyes were serious.

"Uh...," Jack swallowed, and Jordan could see his Adam's apple moving up and down. She'd never seen her boss nervous, so she wondered if something was suddenly wrong.

"Everything okay, Jack?" Jordan asked. He angled his head as he looked at her. Then he looked down, and Jordan wasn't sure if he was looking at the carpet to see if it was clean enough or if he was thinking about how to say something important. She coughed.

She saw his shoulders lift toward the ceiling and heard his long whistle of a sigh. She shifted her weight onto her left leg and grabbed the top of the chair, still waiting. The lights were dim and the candles had already been lit at the tables for the evening crowd. Jordan took off her glasses and polished them.

The room was silent.

And as if nothing had just happened, Jack waved his hand at the woman standing before him.

"Don't forget the specials, Jordan," he said as he turned around and pushed the swinging doors back to the kitchen. Jordan watched him disappear. She shrugged her shoulders and began setting the tables again. She had no idea what that exchange—or lack of exchange—was about, but she realized one thing: Jack had never called her anything but "mate." Until tonight.

It was a slow dinner crowd, and since she was the first waitress in, she was the first to get to go home. Jack avoided eye contact with her when he told her she was off for the evening, so Jordan asked him again if everything was all right. He said he just had a lot on his mind but everything was fine. He took off his cap and held it at his side as she punched the time clock, patted him on the shoulder, and walked out.

"G'day, mate," Jordan said. "See you tomorrow." Jack forced a smile and watched her walk out of the kitchen and the front door of the Tavern. When he couldn't see her anymore, he put his cap on, poured himself a half pint, and sat down at the bar.

When Jordan arrived in the entryway of her apartment building, she found a letter from her mama. She opened it and read as she climbed the steps to her studio. Her mama was coming to visit over Thanksgiving, that is, if the doctor said it was okay, which he probably would if she kept the slower pace like she had been. She wrote how she'd always wanted to spend Thanksgiving in New York, to see the Macy's parade in person, and this was as good a year as any. Jordan stopped at the fourth floor to take in her mother's words. She carefully folded the letter and put it into her bag.

By the time she reached the fifth floor, she did not stop in front of her door. Instead, she knocked on the door across the hall to see if Barry was home. She had to find out how his audition went.

He opened the door slowly. His face dropped toward hers, his shoulders sagged. Jordan felt discouraged for her friend, but she had to find out anyway.

"So how did it go?" She stared at Barry's face, hoping something, anything good had happened for him that day.

"Well, I just got off the phone with the director." Barry's voice was somber and despairing. He did not look up at his neighbor.

"Ah, Barry. I'm sorry," Jordan whispered.

"Wrong!" he shouted. "I got the part! We start rehearsals next week, and the show opens a week after Christmas!"

Jordan punched her friend in the arm for teasing her. Then she grabbed his hands, and they skipped around their hall like children on a playground. They laughed and yelled so that the neighbor in 5D opened his door and told them to keep it down.

So they celebrated in Jordan's apartment, sipping champagne from coffee mugs as they sat on Jordan's couch. Underneath her family photograph. She glanced at her father in the picture and decided to offer a toast.

"To theater," Jordan said. Barry clinked her mug with his.

"To theater," he said, his face wide with energy. Barry raised his mug in the air and proceeded to swallow the entire cup of champagne. Jordan laughed at her friend, took a sip, and felt the sparkling drink glide down the back of her throat while her father watched from the wall.

EIGHT

Peter took the last piece of Mrs. Mowery's apple strudel out of the oven. He placed it on a tray with a glass of orange juice, a cup of coffee, and a small honey jar and took it to his wife. Jeanie didn't seem to be getting much stronger since she'd come home from the hospital, and he was worried, despite what the doctors said. They'd have the test results back soon and would be able to do more then, though, of course, they told Peter they didn't think it was serious. In the meantime Jeanie's best hope was rest.

When Peter walked into their bedroom, Jeanie pulled herself up against the pillows and brushed her hair back with her hand. She reached for the coffee, dropping a few spoonfuls of honey into the mug and stirring it slowly. The tray felt heavy on her lap, but she said nothing. Jeanie sipped the coffee, set it back on the tray, and leaned her head against the top of the pillow. She was still so tired. Everyone had told her and Peter that after a week she would be feeling like her old self; nights, though, were difficult to sleep through, and Peter struggled to make her comfortable. Her muscles ached. Her mind wandered. They were both weary.

She watched Peter as he stood in front of the closet and reached for his yellow-and-green tie, the one Jordan had sent him for Christmas two years ago. Though they hadn't shared a word in four years, Jordan still remembered her father during the holidays. One time on the phone she'd told Jeanie it felt too strange sending only one gift to her parents during the holiday season, even if he didn't acknowledge her.

"She feels guilty," Peter said to his wife as he unwrapped the present from his daughter. He stared for several seconds at the gift—a tie one year, a Yankees cap another—and when Jeanie wasn't looking, he'd rub his fingers across it, like he used to do with Jordan's forehead when she was a little girl, as if that would connect him to his daughter for a second. But the glittery Christmas gift was a dark hole inside, and Peter knew if he stayed too long touching it he might not be able to climb out. So he'd shrug his shoulders at the box and grab another from under the Christmas tree for his wife. He had to move on.

"I like it when you wear her tie," Jeanie spoke softly from the bed while Peter stood in front of their dresser mirror. He straightened the tie firmly around his neck and buttoned the collar on his shirt. He picked up his comb and ordered the thick auburn hair back on his head.

"This isn't 'her' tie. I bought this last month on sale at Dixon's," Peter said. His wife didn't seem to hear him.

"It makes me feel like you two are together again, like we are all a—"

Her husband whirled around so suddenly it startled her. "How do I look?" Peter asked in a low raspy voice that he sometimes used to get her to laugh. He stood above her with his arms out to his side, tilted his head to the right, and allowed a slight whistle of air to escape the sides of his mouth. Then he turned slowly in a circle until he faced her again. Jeanie nodded at him, lifting her right hand to form an O with her index finger and thumb, signaling her approval.

"Jordan would love seeing you wear that," she said, her eyes faraway and misty.

Peter sighed.

His wife was still so pale, he thought as he looked at her, her frame so fragile. He hated seeing her like this, let alone hearing her exert energy on matters she couldn't control—like their daughter. But she wasn't well, he told himself as he collected every speck of patience he could find, hoping that would help in her recovery.

"Get some rest, hon," Peter whispered to her as he leaned into her ear. He looked down into her small cloudy eyes—which were fixed on his—and ran his thumb along her chin and cheek. He kissed her forehead and moved down to her lips before turning toward the door.

"She's graduating from college soon, you know," her voice dreamy. "What a day that will be!" Peter looked at the woman on the bed.

"I'll call you in a little while to make sure you're all right. Try to finish your breakfast, okay?" Peter was gentle in his words and Jeanie nodded toward him.

She heard the front door shut behind him and the car start in the driveway. Jeanie squeezed the handles on the tray, her wrists shaking from the weight of it, and lifted it off her lap and onto Peter's side of the bed. The pillows slipped below her shoulders, inviting Jeanie into a tense but easier place: sleep. It was somewhere she wanted to go more and more these days.

The last of Mrs. Mowery's apple strudel was cold again.

The Saturday morning air was wet and drizzly, smearing the windshield between patches of clarity as Peter drove out of Jackson. He turned onto Lynch Street—named not for the dreadful violence of Mississippi's history but after a local military hero—and passed the Jackson State campus, dozens of small wooden homes with only a few trees and bushes in the yards, and a few housing projects.

West Jackson was considered by some of Second Baptist's older members to be the "bad" part of town, a term that always bothered Peter when it dropped out of their mouths, a term that he thought said more about his parishioners than it did West Jackson. What, after all, could make a place bad if not the people who lived there? And as far as he could tell, the folks in West Jackson were hard-working, low- or middle-income families—like Miss Mary's—who cared about their children and neighbors. The crime rate was no different here than in north Jackson where most of Second Baptist's families lived, though admittedly the houses were smaller and some buildings were abandoned or boarded up.

What his members really meant by bad was that West Jackson was starkly different from their own community because it was predominantly African American, and the difference made them afraid enough to give the neighborhood a label—bad—so as not to have to encounter it. In fact, except for Sundays when they'd drive to downtown Jackson for church, most of the folks at Second Baptist spent the rest of the week in the safe, largely white, cul-de-sacs and malls of north Jackson. The Riddles' old house was only a few streets away from the church within the city limits and, therefore, in between the two worlds.

Peter's knuckles stiffened on the steering wheel as he thought about his congregation. Almost every day gave him a reason to wonder how long it might take them to catch up with the rest of the country when it came to race relations. He exhaled a long stream of frustration and shook his head while he passed a semi on the highway. How ridiculous, he thought, to judge others simply because they were different. Granted, he was glad for the challenge and the opportunities he'd been given with this group of folks, but he could not help but wonder when people might embrace, celebrate even, a culture different from their own.

Like he'd experienced in Fiji. He hadn't known much about island life when he first accepted the call to help a church build an orphanage. In fact, Peter felt self-conscious about his white skin and American ways when he and his young family first arrived. But the Fijian pastors he worked with quickly taught him about their culture, about greetings and roles and bartering at the markets. They didn't seem to care what he looked like; they simply invited him into the mission. Their friendship was the support and bridge he'd needed as a missionary.

"Lord have mercy," Peter muttered into the emptiness of his car.

"Old habits die hard," Dr. Stately had said whenever Peter brought up the subject. Considering all the racial residue of their southern past, Dr. Stately believed it would be a slow process before they moved forward, but that they would get there. Eventually.

"We have to be patient in the ministry and consistent in our message, Pete," the senior pastor told him one morning over breakfast. "After all, yeast takes both time and hard work to get kneaded into the bread."

Dr. Stately's words hung in Peter's ear as if he were sitting in the passenger seat beside him. Sometimes Peter thought the issue should be more central to their work in ministry, more prominent on their agenda. He had wanted to make racial diversity a priority—perhaps when he had his own church—but these days he had to admit it was enough just to stay focused on what was already on his schedule, especially since Jeanie got sick.

The fields were gray and sparse along Highway 18 out of the city. Peter was gripped by their dreariness, an all too familiar feeling. With his windshield wipers keeping a steady beat against the rain, he cracked the window in his car and inhaled a fresh fill of country air. But his lungs felt stale.

That knowing ache suddenly pierced the top of his shoulders. He pressed his neck with his thumb over and over and tried to relax. It didn't help that his stomach—and his soul—felt empty. Maybe it would go away by the time he arrived for the service. Maybe the sun would break through.

After another twenty minutes or so, he pulled into the parking lot of the Mississippi State Correctional Facility and slowed down as he approached the security booth.

"Hey Johnny. Nice weather we're having, huh?" Peter said, grinning as he rolled down his window.

The guard's uniform was slightly darker than his skin. He never seemed particularly glad to see Peter, though he didn't seem unhappy either. Johnny stood up from the skinny metal chair, rotated his neck like he was just waking up in the morning, and yawned. He peered toward the sky's grayness from under the bill of his baseball cap as if Peter's comment had just registered in his head. Eventually he looked back at the driver in the car.

"I reckon. The chaplain said you'd be coming," Johnny mumbled. Peter supposed he was around the same age as the tall lean man who was now staring into the backseat of his car. Johnny's face never changed expressions, even when Peter tried to make him laugh. For as long as Peter had been coming to the prison to help with chapel services, the guard's disposition never changed. Mystery lined his eyes and few words ever formed on his lips. Yet he was the type of man who seemed born with authority, and anyone who knew him most likely did what he told them. Peter did too.

Johnny handed Peter a parking pass to put on his dashboard and waved him through to the lot just inside the prison's entrance. As Peter found a spot, he looked in his rearview mirror and saw Johnny still watching him. Peter's tongue scraped the top of his dry mouth, letting out a quiet clicking sound barely audible against the beat of the wipers. Usually, he could warm up to just about anyone he talked with, but Johnny was hard work. Maybe working at the prison had squeezed out most of his emotions. Maybe he resented Peter's white skin and religious charity. He didn't want to second-guess the man, but Peter wished their interactions were a little easier.

The sky's mist was still thick, so Peter grabbed a folded *Tribune* from the backseat, held it over his head, and hurried across the parking lot toward the entrance. A scrappy roof that needed a paint job hung over the sidewalk, and Peter ducked underneath it. He reached into his pocket for a quarter, dropped it in the pay phone that hung on the wall as a symbol of the last formal connection to the free outside world before entering the maximum-security unit, and called Jeanie.

The phone rang once, twice, a third, and fourth time. Peter tapped the edge of the receiver with his ring finger. Finally, a groggy Jeanie answered, and Peter knew immediately he had interrupted her sleep.

"Sorry, hon, just wanted to see how you were and let you know I'm here," Peter's voice now was pastoral, firm and confident, hoping it might infuse his wife with a bit of strength.

"Is James with you? He's not here at the house." Jeanie's words were hazy, delirious, and the sound of their son's name was a sudden fog he was not prepared for this afternoon.

Peter glanced out at the wet parking lot and pushed his glasses back on his nose.

"Go back to sleep, hon," he told his wife. "I'll call you when I'm on my way home."

He hung up the phone and pushed her comment out of his head at the same time he realized he'd left his Bible in the car. Again, he held the newspaper over his head, darted back across the lot, and grabbed the brown leather book from the front seat. While he ran back toward the sidewalk, he noticed Johnny again standing at his security booth, hands on both hips, watching him. Peter raised the Bible into the air and feigned laughter. When he was out of the rain, he shook his head from side to side and reached for the thick metal handle that led him inside the prison.

Chaplain Drinkwater was waiting for Peter in the lobby—if it could be called that—and rose from the bench in the corner where he'd been reading the *West Jackson News*. He was a wide man with thick black glasses and no hair on his head or jaw. The chaplain was an energetic man who loved many things in life, but high on his list was southern food: ham hocks, greens, fried okra, pimento cheese, catfish, and grits. The sum of his love showed in the width of his body, poured into designer suits and starched shirts every time Peter saw him. He was a handsome heavy man who always seemed happy.

Peter extended his hand to the chaplain when he saw him. The chaplain brushed it aside and instead wrapped his big arms around Peter, laughing and jostling at the same time he was calling to Peter, "Heymybrother!" as if it were one word. Chaplain Drinkwater's face was rich with generational pride; he was from a long line of preachers. The first he knew of were slaves on the cotton farm that used to be on these same dozen acres where the prison now stood. Once he'd told Peter that Drinkwaters—a name his great-grand-daddy and great-uncle had given themselves after the war rather than keep their owner's name—had always been on this land. So it must have been "God's will" he was here today doing work for "our other brothers still trapped in slavery." His sincerity of purpose had won Peter over the minute they met at Second Baptist's pastors' conference six years ago, and he'd been coming to help the chaplain with services ever since.

The two men walked through the metal detector into a locked area where three guards met them. The shorter of the guards pointed to Peter's arms and legs, and Peter obliged by stretching out his hands and moving apart his feet. The guard bent over Peter's ankles, patted them, and worked his way up to his shoulders and wrists.

"Routine procedure," he told Peter each time he came, though he'd never seen anyone else frisked.

He emptied his pockets, dropping his car keys, wallet, and pens into a plastic bucket, signed a visitor's form, and tore off the back copy, which he then placed under his wallet. Another guard clipped a laminated visitor's ID to Peter's breast pocket and waved him and Chaplain Drinkwater through another set of massive steel doors, which closed behind them with an echoing clang. The two pastors were escorted down a windowless hall by the guards, around a corner, and into a room with florescent lights, fifty or so folding chairs, and a thin wooden podium in the front that had a cross painted on it. A few inmates, ushered by guards, shuffled in and waved toward Peter. He tossed his hand in the air to greet them.

Soon the chairs were filled with a few dozen black and brown men wearing bright orange jumpsuits. Chaplain Drinkwater walked toward the podium and called the service to order. With a smile as wide as his presence, he welcomed the men to Saturday worship, asked them to stand, and led them in the Lord's Prayer. A few men called out the names of various hymns and the chaplain began each with a hum and a clap. From "The Old Rugged Cross" to "Great Is Thy Faithfulness" to the standard "Amazing Grace," the twenty or so men sounded more like a hundred as they pounded out each song a cappella and swayed back and forth in unified rhythm.

Peter looked around the room and noticed he was the only white man present. The reality didn't bother him so much as it humbled him; he felt deep in his bones that this was God's work and these were God's people. It was a privilege to be here no matter what color his skin was, and he felt a tinge of gratitude rise out of his belly, surprising him and filling his eyes for a moment.

It had been a long time since he felt *this* feeling, any feeling for that matter, and he hoped it would crowd out the empty ache he'd had in his chest and shoulders when he came in—at least for the time being. Peter breathed in the emotion of the room and clung to it.

When it came time for him to preach, Peter strolled from the front row and thanked Chaplain Drinkwater for his leadership, who laughed at Peter while handing stacks of Bibles to the men in each row. Peter asked Ernie, an older inmate, to stand and read from the first chapter of Paul's letter to Timothy.

Ernie nodded at Peter, rose slowly from his seat, and began in a slow baritone voice: "Here is a trustworthy saying that deserves full acceptance: Christ Jesus came into the world to save sinners—of whom I am the worst. But for that very reason I was shown mercy so that in me, the worst of sinners, Christ Jesus might display his unlimited patience as an example for those who would believe on him and receive eternal life." Ernie's reading was punctuated with a series of amens from other inmates and, of course, Chaplain Drinkwater. When he closed the Bible, Ernie raised his arms to the inmates around him like he was thanking them for their support and sat back down.

For the next thirty minutes, Peter preached about how everyone in this room had broken his relationship with God on a regular basis, but that the mercy of Christ Jesus was available to "even the worst of us. After all," Peter said, "if someone as holy as the apostle Paul recognized himself as a sinner, then surely each of us can too." Peter's hands gripped the sides of the podium, and he leaned forward as he looked at each man sitting before him.

"Admitting our sin leads us to God's grace and favor and makes us examples to those around us," Peter belted the words, and the men echoed them. "God's grace and favor," they responded.

"I know it isn't easy to confess your wrongdoings, and Lord knows there's plenty that distracts you from the straight and narrow.

But God is good and able to give each of you a new start if only you would come to him." The words flowed easily from Peter's lips. Dr. Stately had trained him well.

"God is good. And able," the men shouted as some of their hands raised toward heaven while others waved at Peter's words. More amens and "That's right" rang across the room. The man next to Ernie stood to his feet, pointed at Peter, laughed, and shook his head in agreement with the preacher before sitting back down. And before anyone was ready for their time to finish, Chaplain Drinkwater saw the crowd of guards forming at the back of the room, looked at his watch, and announced that the chapel service was ending.

He joined Peter at the podium, motioned for the men to stand, and prayed over them with a holy appeal loud enough to rouse the entire prison. His final plea moved smoothly into the first line of the hymn, "What a Friend We Have in Jesus," and again the singing sounded more like a church choir than a group of convicted criminals.

When the guards began to escort the inmates back to their cells, Peter moved toward the door where they would exit. He reached for each man's hand as they walked out, shook them firmly, and watched as they dissolved behind a wall of black uniforms.

When Ernie reached him, he stopped inches from Peter. His

eyes became sharp and soft at the same time. He took Peter's hand in his, and Peter felt the rough callous skin of a man who'd worked hard all his life and should not have ended up in a place like this.

"That was a fine word, Preach, fine word," he was shaking his head in rhythm with his hand until suddenly, as if a judge had just passed sentenced in his head, he stopped, leaned his face into Peter's, and spoke.

"I think it'd a'been a whole lot better, Preach, if *you* believed what you said."

The words slugged Peter. Ernie nodded his head, opened his eyes real wide, and took back his hand as the guards prodded him down the hall with the others. Peter's eyes stayed on Ernie, who glanced back once, nodded again to prove his point, and then was lost in the sea of orange and black uniforms.

Chaplain Drinkwater was folding chairs and leaning them against the wall as Peter joined him.

"Another good sermon, brother. Your messages are getting stronger each time you preach, you know. Before you know it you're going to have your own church," Chaplain Drinkwater smiled as he leaned a chair against the wall. "How about some lunch?"

"I'd love to, Chaplain, but"—Peter paused—"uh, my wife's not feeling so well." His palms suddenly felt sticky and moist, and he had to use both hands to pick up a chair. The ache in his neck returned, shooting through to the bottom of his skull.

Chaplain Drinkwater stopped what he was doing when he heard the tension in Peter's voice and moved toward the assistant pastor from Second Baptist. He put a strong hand on Peter's arm, shut his eyes tight, and bowed his head forward. Then he pleaded with God to heal Peter's wife, to look after her as she rested, and to minister to her family while she recovered.

Peter kept his eyes open. He stared at the chaplain's face as he prayed and hoped God was listening.

The rain had stopped when Peter walked outside the locked facility and across to his car. Chaplain Drinkwater waved from the door and disappeared back into the prison. As Peter glanced toward the sky, he noticed a few shreds of sunlight trying to break through the clouds and felt a cool gust of wind blow across his face. October in Mississippi was Peter's favorite time of year, always had been. Not too humid, not too cold.

He put his key in the ignition and backed out of the parking space. When he slowed down to the security booth, Johnny was staring hard at him. Peter breathed and reached for the parking permit from the dashboard.

"Looks like you got us some decent weather after all, Johnny," Peter tried to make light of the situation as he handed the paper to the tall expressionless man outside his window. "That was right kind of you, sir. The rain was getting to me, you know?" Peter tossed the words lightly toward the guard.

Johnny's face stayed somber, his eyes fixed on Peter. He took the parking permit from the pastor, walked inside the booth, and placed it in a file. Peter saw him write something down before he walked back out to the car. He looked down at Peter and stood silently as if he were waiting for something.

"Okay, then, Johnny, I reckon I'll see you week after next," Peter said. The guard was still staring at him. "You know you're welcome anytime at Second Baptist?" Peter said, figuring he might as well invite the man to church. He had nothing to lose.

"It's my boy," Johnny mumbled. Peter was surprised by the words, and he thought he saw the guard's eyes well up as he spoke. Then again, it might have been the glare of the sun fighting the clouds as they moved overhead.

" 'Scuse me, Johnny?" Peter rolled his window all the way down so he could hear the man.

"I think he's in trouble, Pastor. I want you to visit him," Johnny said the words as if he were directing Peter where to park his car. He reached into his front pocket, pulled out the small piece of paper, and handed it to the white man in the car. Then he brushed his hands over the gun in his holster and back into his pockets.

"That's his address. He's at Jackson State, but he's messin' up,

Pastor. He won't listen to his daddy no more, you know how it is," Johnny said in a low serious tone, his eyes still on Peter.

Yes, Peter knew exactly how it was. He gripped the steering wheel tighter.

"Anyway, I thought maybe you could help. I'm not a religious man, but I don't want my boy to, well, end up here." They were the most words Peter had ever heard come out of Johnny's mouth since he'd known him. He read aloud the address on the paper, *2505 Lynch Street #15,* and pinched the frame of his glasses with his fingers, adjusting them on his face.

"That's on my way home. I'll stop by and see what I can do, okay? Don't know if I can be of much help, Johnny, but I can at least pay him a visit," Peter spoke firmly and nodded his head at the guard.

"Appreciate it. Can't do much with kids these days," Johnny said. He turned back toward the booth, walked inside, and sat down on the metal frame chair. He raised his hand slowly to Peter and then lowered it, still watching the white pastor who came for Saturday worship services. And he nodded his head slowly to show Peter he was obliged.

As Peter drove toward Jackson, he realized he'd forgotten to call Jeanie. He'd find a phone at Jackson State and would call her from there. A drizzle smeared the windshield again, and Peter turned on the wipers. He repeated Johnny's words, "Can't do much with kids these days," and was startled by the sound of his voice echoing in the car. He flipped the radio on so he could hear something else, anything else.

By the time he turned onto Lynch Street, Peter couldn't remember passing the cornfields or the country roads or anything else on his usual drive. His forehead wrinkled several lines across it and his shoulders felt tight. He pulled into an apartment complex across the street from the campus where there was a phone booth on the corner.

Before he got out of the car, though, Peter thumbed through his Day-Timer to make sure he was on track for the day. Jimmy had youth group at the church that night, which he didn't need to go to, but he was responsible for Sunday setup and adult classes the next morning. His sister was coming for a visit sometime over the weekend to check on Jeanie, and he was supposed to stop by the Jitney Jungle on his way home. They'd been out of everything for a few days; Jeanie had been too weak to make it to the store, and his schedule had been too full. Thank God for neighbors like Mrs. Mowery.

A tiny gust of wind brushed Peter's head as he walked toward the phone. He dropped a quarter in and dialed the number. Three young black men walked by Peter and glanced at his strange presence before they entered the apartment building. The phone on the other end rang once, twice.

"Hello, Riddles' residence," Cynthia Sue picked up.

"Hey Cynthia!" his voice strained, tense from the thought of inmates and sickness and city streets. He wasn't sure if it would break when he heard the familiarity of his sister's voice. As he cradled the phone between his ear and his shoulder, Peter took off his glasses and rubbed his eyes.

"Where you been, little brother?" Cynthia Sue was cheery; she could always read her brother when he had too much going on.

"At the prison with Chaplain Drinkwater. How's Jeanie?" Peter put his glasses back on.

"Fast asleep. Earlier, though, she was a bit, well, it was like she wasn't really there."

"I know, Cynthia. I know."

"I'm worried, Peter. The doctor called and said you should call him as soon as you get home. See you soon?"

Peter told his sister he had to make a few stops before he'd be there. His mouth was dry again and he was hungry; he hadn't eaten since last night. He'd hoped Jeanie had finished the breakfast he took her. He hung up the phone, pulled the address Johnny had written from his pocket, and went looking for apartment number fifteen.

No one answered the door when Peter knocked the first time. He threw his knuckles forcefully against the wood a second time and secretly hoped Johnny's son was not home. He wasn't sure he had the energy to talk with some troubled kid who, according to his father, wasn't headed in a very good direction.

God knew he hadn't been able to help his own daughter.

The door swung open, interrupting Peter's internal debate and reminding him of his purpose. A taller and younger version of Johnny stood before him; except for the bulky red Bulls sweatshirt and baggy jeans, Peter was amazed at how much this young man looked like the guard at the prison. He extended his hand, introduced himself, and told him his daddy had asked him to stop by to see if he was okay. Peter scratched the back of his head and waited for a response.

He got none. Johnny's son had the same expressionless face as his father. He looked at Peter's shoes, then back at his face, and simply shook his head as if he were annoyed that his father had sent a white man to check on him. Peter decided to push it.

"Well, are you?" he said.

"Am I what?" Johnny's son sounded just like him.

"Are you okay? That's all I want to know," Peter stared gently into the face across from him and caught the boy's attention with his intensity. Silence lingered between them for a few seconds until finally the young man shrugged his shoulders and looked down the hall. Peter took a pen from his shirt pocket and a piece of paper from his wallet, scribbled his name, phone number, and tomorrow's hours for church services and handed it to the boy.

"Call if you need anything. Anything. And feel free to come by Second Baptist," Peter's voice had found the pastoral confidence he used for moments like these. He smiled at Johnny's son and walked back down the hall. He heard the door slam behind him.

At least he could tell Johnny he tried.

Peter did a quick run through the Jitney Jungle, buying milk, bread, coffee, oranges, and vegetables. He dropped the groceries in the backseat and drove home. Cynthia Sue's car was in the driveway, and Peter pulled in behind it. Once again the rain had let up, and Cynthia appeared at the car. She grabbed two grocery bags from the car and hurried up the steps. Peter joined her in the kitchen with the rest.

She sensed his tension and his weariness.

"So you might be wondering just how the art world in Alabama is doing these days," Cynthia's sarcasm was thick, and Peter had to laugh. "I thought so. Good thing I'm here to tell you the latest." But as she emptied the grocery bags and was about to bombard him with cultural gossip, the phone rang.

"Saved by the bell," Peter announced. Cynthia put her fists on her hips, rolled her eyes, and waited.

It was Dr. Hollander. He'd just gotten Jeanie's test results back.

Peter turned his back to his sister as he asked the doctor for the information. He heard a long heavy breath on the other end.

"It's not as good as we thought, Peter. We think it's cancer, but we've caught it early. How about if you both come in first thing Monday morning, and we'll talk about treatment options, okay?"

The doctor's words were dark windy roads Peter was not ready to travel. Instead, he hung up the phone, shook his head at his sister, and walked into his bedroom. He leaned over and kissed his wife's cheek. Then he took off his yellow-and-green tie and tossed it in the closet.

NINE

The nasal announcement bounced out of the answering machine and around the walls of the studio apartment. Jordan rolled over in her bed, batting away the sound like it was a mosquito in her ear. She groaned and pulled the blankets over her head.

"...and if you *are* interested in this position today, Miss Riddle, please call me immediately at Temps Plus Agency. Again, this is Marjorie Smithson, and my number is..." When the voice finally registered in Jordan's sleepy head, something jolted through her blood, kicking her backside out of bed and dumping her onto the floor. It had been more than two weeks since the temp agency had called, and after a busy weekend of champagne celebrations with Barry over his new job, a concert at St. John's with Sister Leslie, and three shifts at the Dream Time, her body craved sleep this Monday morning. But money had always been a strong motivation for starving artists, so Jordan grabbed the phone and tried to sound coherent.

"Yes, um, sorry, Marjorie… Good morning to you too. Okay. What—now, where is it again?" She scribbled the name and address of the corporation on the nearest thing to her—an envelope from the phone company—and stared at it while the nasal voice gave her final directions. Since Jordan grabbed the phone instead of her glasses, the lines and letters were fuzzy, and her eyes bulged trying to read them. She hoped she'd be able to make sense of her notes in an hour.

The shower took longer than usual to warm up, so Jordan ironed her skirt while she waited. She needed a cup of coffee— herbal tea was a little too timid this morning—but she didn't have time to make a pot. Instead, she poured herself a cup that had been sitting in the coffeemaker since yesterday and hoped the office where she was going would have a decent brew. Tomorrow the final payment for Vinnie's workshop was due, and an extra day of temp work meant she'd just about cover the $225 she still owed. She added up in her head what she had saved already—$125— with how much she'd make today—$75—and what she'd need to earn in tips tonight at the Tavern—$25. Even though Monday nights at the Tavern were usually slow, Jordan thought she could just about make it.

Maybe her decision to schedule chats with God was a good one after all. Today's job certainly seemed to drop from heaven.

The water still wasn't hot, so Jordan pretended she was back in Fiji—where they rarely had hot showers—held her breath, and stuck her head under the faucet. Then she wrapped her hair in a towel, pulled on her blouse and skirt, and swallowed the last of her cold coffee. She often thought her family's time on the Pacific island had provided her with a survival kit for living in New York City. On mornings like this, for instance, the old plumbing in her building didn't work as it should, just like it often didn't in their Fijian house. Or the few times she was in a car driving through New York's streets reminded Jordan of the times she sat in her parents' Datsun as they drove across the island, swerving around potholes and unpredictable drivers. And the run-down corner delis—or bodegas as native New Yorkers called them—often took Jordan to the markets of Fiji where you were never quite sure which food had started growing things because it had been there so long. Though her family had gone to the tropical island as Baptist missionaries, and Jordan had come to New York as a playwright, she long believed the two places—and purposes—had a lot in common.

Tragedy was also no stranger to either.

Move on, she told herself. *Let him go.* Today was a new day and this was a different place.

She walked over to her dresser and pulled open the top drawer. One thing she never had to do in Fiji was cram her legs into a ridiculous pair of pantyhose. As she sat on the edge of her couch,

Jordan gathered the delicate material into an open ball, stretched it with both hands so that it was wide enough for her foot, and pulled the elastic fabric up her leg. Her skin felt squished underneath. When the lower part of her body had finally wiggled its way into the twin stockings, Jordan yanked up the waist and brushed down her skirt. She shook her head at the absurdity of such a ritual.

"A *man* invented these!" she said aloud to the image in the mirror.

As she combed out her hair, Jordan decided she would go with the full-blown urban businesswoman look. Why not? She was going to have to suffer in the nylons anyway, so she might as well go all out. She spread black mascara through her lashes, ran a soft pink brush of blush across her cheeks, and reached for her red wire-frame glasses. Then she pinched the back of her favorite dangling earrings—the pair she bought last summer at a street fair on East Seventy-second—needled them into her earlobes, and reached for the jacket that matched her skirt. Her toes dropped into the black pumps that made her two inches taller every time she wore them. And before turning slowly in a circle in front of the mirror, she dabbed pale red lipstick on her lips.

Jordan stared at her reflection. She turned around again, propped back her shoulders, sucked in her stomach, and ironed out the last of the wrinkles in her skirt with her hand. She cocked an eyebrow at herself, searching for the face of a professional woman.

But her lungs could not hold the fib long before a squeak of silly air spilled from her mouth. Her shoulders sagged. Her stomach relaxed. No matter how much makeup she used or how firm she stood, Jordan knew she could not mask her identity. She was an artist, not a businesswoman; a playwright, not a yuppie. She shook her head at the woman across from her and laughed. Besides, as soon as she opened her mouth to answer a phone or ask a question, everyone would know she was a southern girl in a northern city. No one in the corporate world of capitalism took her too seriously once they heard her Mississippi accent.

She *had* to be one of those creative types, they'd tease, in search of "the dream," not the dollar.

No apologies. If Jordan had promised herself anything since leaving home, it was that she would be herself no matter what pressures New York life might throw on her. That included these times when the great skyscrapers of economic elitism needed her to fill in for the day—*and* wear nylons. So she pushed her hair around on her head and threw a final look at the mirror. It would have to do.

Jordan tossed her jeans and flower-print shirt—which she was suddenly quite thankful for—into her bag for work tonight and hurried out of her apartment. The door slammed on the latch. Before she could finish turning the second lock, she heard the phone ring inside her apartment. She rolled her eyes and suddenly heard another woman's voice fill her apartment—her aunt's.

She punched the door back and ran toward the phone. Cynthia Sue was midsentence when Jordan picked up.

"Auntie Cyn! Hey! I was just on my way out the door."

"Glad I caught you, hon. On your way to fame and fortune, no doubt?" Her aunt's voice was better than hot coffee in sending Jordan off into the day. Though she wasn't supposed to have favorites, Jordan had long designated Auntie Cyn her number one relative. After all, she was the one person who, from the start, supported her decision to move here.

No one would deny, of course, that Jordan's aunt was as different from her daddy as north is from south, and Jordan always admired her because of it. While Jordan's father rarely said a word without some reference to Jesus or the Lord, her aunt seemed to respect religion for others, even if it didn't interest her. And she didn't mind saying so. But ask her for the shirt off her back, and she'd give you the key to her closet.

Jordan secretly believed Cynthia Sue acted more like a Christian than some folks she'd grown up with at Second Baptist. She'd run back into her apartment anytime if it meant getting a phone call from her aunt.

Even if it was not good news.

"It's your mama, hon," Aunt Cyn's words turned tense.

Jordan squeezed the corner of the counter to find her balance and centered her gaze on the woman in the photograph above her couch. Then she waited.

"I'm gonna tell you straight, hon, because I think you should know. The doctors are pretty sure it's cancer, but it looks like they've caught it early enough to keep us from worrying."

"Wait. Just last week Mama was fine; tired yes, but fine all the same," Jordan said. "What happened? What do you mean, cancer?" An uneasy sting slid down Jordan's throat. She swallowed it before asking for more details and closed her eyes while she pressed the phone to her ear. The southern rhythm of her aunt's careful voice steadied Jordan's legs and heart rate.

"She and your daddy are going in this morning to talk with Dr. Hollander about treatment, but like I said, they caught it good and early."

Jordan's aunt continued talking about her mother, the kindness of their neighbors, the medical advances in dealing with this kind of thing, and two minutes more of other related subjects that Jordan could not decipher. The word *cancer* stayed lodged in Jordan's ears, clogging any other words or sentences or paragraphs her aunt offered.

Finally, Aunt Cyn's familiar voice pulled Jordan back. She told her niece she'd call later to give her any update, but as far as she could tell, her mama was still planning her trip to New York for Thanksgiving. It just wasn't time to worry.

"A little somethin' like this is *not* going to stop your mama from seeing her baby girl, you know." Cynthia was singing a lullaby now, and Jordan felt cradled in its calm.

"Should I call the travel agent?"

"No need to do that, as least for now," Aunt Cynthia said. "I promise I'll let you know when—and if—you need to come home, okay?"

Jordan leaned against the counter for support when she hung up the phone. A chill shot through her bones, but she was not cold. She thought of her mother—in the classroom with her fourth grade students, in the kitchen cooking dinner, on the beach rubbing suntan lotion on her brother's shoulders, at the store buying Jordan's favorite ice cream—and she slammed her fist on the sink. Why her? Her mama had been so generous, so selfless. This was not what was supposed to happen.

The sky in her memory instantly turned overcast, and Jordan was standing next to her parents near a small tombstone. The cemetery was no bigger than a country garden with patches of brown grass strewn across the square. Full heavy tears fell from her mother's eyes, her shoulders shook. Jordan and her father stood on opposite sides of the small, brown-haired woman, their arms around her waist to hold her up. The emotion, the rain, the death of the place weighed on them like boulders—it was an image Jordan had never been able to sweep out of her mind since they'd returned to Mississippi and since she'd come to New York.

She was thirteen years old, standing next to her parents at her brother's grave. In the rain. On an island. In the middle of the Pacific.

James was gone.

Jordan pressed the back of her neck with her thumb and glanced again at her professional reflection in the mirror. She was twenty-eight years old now—no longer a child—and her brother's funeral was a long time ago, long enough, she reasoned with herself, to lose its power over her. Whenever anxiety came at her, though, the memory at the graveyard crowded her mind. Jordan wanted it to stop.

She reached for the phone and dialed one of the few New York phone numbers she knew by heart. Sister Leslie answered, and Jordan spit the words out as if she had just swallowed a mouthful of salt water from the sea: *her mother—cancer—doctor's appointment today—treatment—please pray.*

"Can I meet you at the poet's corner?" Sister Leslie asked. Jordan shook her head at both the question and the inconvenience of her temp job—as if the nun could see her response. She regretted telling the agency she'd come in at all today.

"Give me the address of your office and I'll meet you for lunch, okay?" the Episcopalian nun pressed Jordan. Jordan saw the envelope with the address on the table and rolled her eyes at her carelessness for having left it behind.

If Auntie Cyn hadn't called, she'd be on the subway by now, realizing she had no idea where she was going.

Jordan smacked her forehead with her palm as punishment, read Sister Leslie the address, and stuffed the envelope into her jacket pocket. As she was about to hang up the telephone, she heard the soft, sure faith of her friend on the other end: "I will be praying, Jordan. God be with you."

By 8:35 a.m. Jordan was on the number 6 train heading uptown. She was due on the sixteenth floor of Thirty-eighth and Madison Avenue by nine o'clock, and she wondered if she'd be on time, though she didn't really care if she wasn't. The man across from her sipped hot coffee from a blue paper cup he'd gotten at a deli. Jordan stared at the cup, bothered that she might have to go without caffeine for the morning, but more worried at what her mama might hear in a few hours from their doctor. Auntie Cyn had said they caught it early. Sister Leslie said she'd be praying. Maybe God *was* with her.

The morning moved slowly for Jordan, though most of the people around her seemed like frenzied robots controlled by some remote gadget from the boss's office. She managed to find a pathetic cup of coffee in the break room and tried to concentrate whenever someone asked her to run off copies of official-looking documents or find a name and address in the database. But the weight of the news about her mother's health made all the paper pushing and phone calling and office hopping seem to Jordan as ridiculous as pantyhose.

Lunchtime could not have come soon enough. Jordan scrambled for the elevator and pushed back her glasses close to her eyes. When she emerged onto Madison Avenue, she could not help but look toward the sky—autumn blueness surprised her. Jordan offered it her first authentic smile of the day. No clouds sat above the high-rise buildings, but the October air was unusually damp. Jordan buttoned her jacket. She breathed out slowly as she joined the crowded sidewalk going south.

Sister Leslie was sitting at a corner table in the restaurant, immersed in a wide book that filled the table. Her head hung over the pages and her fingers pinched the edge, ready to flip the paper as the story moved ahead. Jordan could not remember a time when her friend was *not* reading some book that was as thick and heavy as tree limbs. *The Brother's Karamazov* one time, *Les Misérables* another, and an anthology of English poetry still another. Sister Leslie called these her theology books; they helped her understand both God and humans, and she couldn't imagine life without them.

"A little light reading, Sister? As usual?" Jordan joked as she pulled the chair from behind the table and sat down. Sister Leslie tossed her head up and studied Jordan's face like she was leaving one world and entering another. She was. Books did that.

"*Great Expectations,*" Sister Leslie said as she tapped the words on the page with her index finger and shook her head. "Dickens was amazing." She paused to savor a literary morsel before closing the book and nodding toward Jordan. "How *are* you?"

Before Jordan could answer, a nervous waiter in black trousers, a wrinkled white shirt, and black bow tie approached their table, handing menus to both women and staring mostly at Sister Leslie's habit as if he were feeling guilty about something. His eyes darted back and forth while he announced he'd be back in a few minutes to take their orders. He stared at Sister Leslie again, spun around, and hurried toward the kitchen.

"What power you have over men," Jordan dropped the line across the table with as much emotion as a subway conductor announcing the next stop. The pink in Sister Leslie's cheeks got pinker at the comment, so she picked up her menu and slapped Jordan's arm with it. The women slipped into girlhood giggles until the anxious waiter reappeared, still staring at the nun. The poor man's face could not relax.

"I think I'll be decadent and order a cheeseburger supreme and fries," Sister Leslie told him, staring over her menu at the waiter as normally as she could. "And a chocolate milkshake. Please." She shut the menu like she had the Dickens novel and handed it to the man, who by now was all but wiggling out of his skin. He scribbled down her order and flipped his head at Jordan.

"I better be good. Chef salad, please," she said.

"Okey-doke, burger and fries, and chef salad," his voice cracked as he read his notepad. "Oh, and a chocolate shake, right?"

The women offered him a unified "Right!" before he spun around again and rushed to the kitchen. Jordan tossed a "Don't you never mind" wave after him, hoping it might help calm his attitude. She picked up her glass of water and drank in the change of setting. It was nice to have lunch with a friend, even if it meant encountering another member of New York's ongoing cast of quirky characters—like their waiter.

"I'm okay. A little tired and probably more worried than I should be," Jordan looked away and toward the other diners. She gathered her hair off her neck and held it up behind her head for a minute or two before letting it fall on her shoulders. Out of nowhere a quiet tear dropped down her cheek. She used her napkin to erase the mascara stain it left on her face.

Sister Leslie took a sip of water and set down her glass. She moved the salt and pepper shakers into the corner of the table like they were pawns on a chessboard. The busy buzz of café chatter hung in the background.

"My grandmother was diagnosed with cancer two years ago, and do you know what?" Sister Leslie leaned toward Jordan as she spoke. "She baked a coffeecake for me last month when I visited her in Connecticut. Each day is a gift, Jordan."

"And there are no guarantees, are there, Sister?" Jordan's eyes pierced her friend's. She felt the emotion of her words rise in her stomach. Her eyebrows pressed forward at the nun. The corners of Sister Leslie's lips turned slightly upward, but she did not let go of Jordan's gaze.

"Only one. God's faithfulness. That's guaranteed," she said softly. Her words were an anchor for Jordan's drifting soul. Sister Leslie let the truth of the moment linger between them before she asked Jordan for details about her mother's health. Though the reality was not easy to face, Jordan said aloud the fear that filled her mind all morning: her mama had a disease that killed. Yes, they'd found it early. Yes, it was likely to be treatable so that life could go back to normal—whatever normal was. But it was cancer nonetheless. And that six-letter word was as frightening to Jordan as a tropical storm. Both were capable of killing people she loved.

As if on cue the anxious waiter appeared at their table, hands full of salad, a burger and fries, and shakes. He set down the burger and fries in front of Jordan and the salad he gave to Sister Leslie. The women looked at each other, smiled, and said nothing. Both were given chocolate shakes. With a final stare at the black habit, the waiter nodded and turned to another table of customers to take their order. Thankful for the comic relief, Jordan picked up the plate in front of her and traded it for Sister Leslie's salad.

And for the next twenty minutes or so they talked about everything but Jordan's mama: the characters in her play, the possibility at the Stage Bite Theater, St. John's new poetry series, greasy cheeseburgers, thick versus thin milkshakes, the autumn colors in Central Park. Neither plate had a speck of food left on it when the busboy cleared the table. Jordan leaned back in her chair and plopped her hands on her lap like they were too heavy to lift. Sister Leslie reached into her bag on the floor and pulled out her wallet and a folded piece of white paper.

"My treat today," she announced to Jordan who was about to protest until the nun raised her hand and her eyebrow. There was no debate. Jordan bowed her head and thanked Sister Leslie.

"I thought of you this morning, Jordan, when I read this poem." The nun unfolded the piece of paper. The words on it were in blue ink, written in Sister Leslie's large loopy handwriting. She picked up the corners, shook the paper, and cleared her throat. Then she recited:

> "He grew up before him like a tender shoot,
> and like a root out of dry ground.
> He had no beauty or majesty to attract us to him,
> nothing in his appearance that we should desire him.
> He was despised and rejected by men,
> a man of sorrows, and familiar with suffering.
> Like one from whom men hide their faces
> he was despised, and we esteemed him not."

Sister Leslie stopped reading as the man in the white shirt set down the bill. She handed him a credit card as she looked up at him. A quick smile broke on his face, like he'd just been relieved of his guilt. He scooped up the bill and announced that he'd be right back. She returned to the poem:

> *"Surely he took up our infirmities*
> *   and carried our sorrows,*
> *yet we considered him stricken by God,*
> *   smitten by him, and afflicted.*
> *But he was pierced for our transgressions,*
> *   he was crushed for our iniquities;*
> *the punishment that brought us peace was upon*
> *   him..."*

The waiter placed a carbon copy of the receipt on the table with her plastic card and a black pen beside it. He told the two women to have a nice day and adjusted his bow tie as he walked to the kitchen. Jordan watched him before turning her attention back to the reading of the poem.

> *"and by his wounds we are healed....*
> *After the suffering of his soul,*
> *   he will see the light of life and be satisfied;*
> *by his knowledge my righteous servant will justify many,*
> *   and he will bear their iniquities."*

Sister Leslie folded the paper carefully into four smaller squares and handed it to Jordan. Jordan was silent. She pushed her jaw forward like she was chewing on the words she'd just heard and stared into her friend's soft face before opening the page and studying the poem again.

"The poet Isaiah, chapter 53. I thought it might help a little right now," the nun's kindness was a gift for Jordan. She reached across the table and squeezed Sister Leslie's hand at the same time a thank you dropped quietly from her mouth. Slowly she folded the poem into one smaller square and tucked it into her bag.

White clouds had moved over the city since Jordan had walked into the café. In the middle of the busy sidewalk, she hugged Sister Leslie good-bye, thanked her again for lunch, and wandered back up Madison Avenue toward her temp job. The afternoon went by about as slowly as the morning, but at least Jordan felt somewhat fortified from her lunch with Sister Leslie. Whenever there was a lull in the work, Jordan would read a few lines from the paper her friend had given her; she liked the rhythm of the words and the reminder of Isaiah's promise: *a man of sorrows, and familiar with suffering.* Jordan let the description settle into her mind.

After the suffering of his soul, he will see the light of life and be satisfied. She wanted to believe it would be so.

By five o'clock she zipped the verses safely in the pocket of her bag and walked toward the elevator. She was due at the Dream Time at 5:30 and rushed to catch the crosstown bus before skipping down into the subway to get a train uptown. At 5:32 Jordan reached for the door of the Tavern, waved to the bartender, and ran to the ladies room to throw on her uniform. The jeans were a monumental improvement over the pantyhose.

As Jordan pushed back the kitchen door, Jack was standing perfectly still. Again his chin was smooth, his eyes lit with some spark of hope, and Jordan couldn't help but wonder if her boss had been smitten by some New York beauty. He looked at Jordan like he was waking up from a dream, brushed his hair back under his cap, and let a small grin form on his face before he looked away.

"G'day, uh, Jordan," he said to her, his voice light but tentative. His eyes moved toward hers. "You look tired."

"Thanks, Jack. Nice to see you too."

"We've got a big theater crowd coming in tonight. I figured you'd want to cover them. Am I right?"

"That depends. If it's a group of *working* actors who like to leave big tips, well, of course you're right," Jordan was tying on her apron as she waited for Jack's response. She yawned. The weariness of the day *was* catching up with her. Jack walked over to the tablet by the phone and read his notes.

"A group from some new show that opened this weekend on Broadway but has Mondays off. I guess that's a good sign, yeah?"

Jordan said it was a real good sign. By the time she finished setting up the back room for the group, five actors entered the Tavern. One of the waiters pointed them to the small room off of the bar and divided by two long tables. Jordan was pouring water into short glasses when another group walked in: three women and a man with perfect black hair. The last person she expected to see tonight was Vinnie.

He wore a light blue tie over his black denim shirt. Jordan saw Vinnie—and the three young actresses surrounding him—before he saw her. His arm was around the waist of one, and he led her to a seat, pulled out the chair, and helped her sit down. By the time he sat beside her, he noticed Jordan walking over.

"Hello, love," Vinnie said as he rose to greet her. "What a nice surprise!" He leaned across and kissed Jordan's cheek like they were old friends.

"One of my most promising playwrights, Jordan Riddle," Vinnie announced to his colleagues. "Remember her name because you'll be reading her plays before you know it." They all looked up at Jordan and smiled.

"That is if I make enough tonight to pay for Vinnie's workshop!"

The crowd laughed and returned to their conversations. Jordan stood staring at her playwriting mentor for a few seconds before she remembered she was supposed to be working. She handed out menus, poured more water, and took drink orders—including

Vinnie's, who asked for a double martini. Suddenly, the top of Jordan's mouth turned dry, and her tongue clicked against it like she was searching for water. A sharp pain shot in her neck. Jordan's feet were heavy. She wanted to keep from looking at Vinnie, but she couldn't.

"G'day, mates. Lots of good specials tonight," Jack was leaning over the table, welcoming the group to the Dream Time Tavern and rescuing his star waitress. His firm Australian accent slapped Jordan into work mode again, and she was at the bar placing drink orders in seconds. By the time she came back, her tray filled with glasses, Jack was still talking with his customers.

"Now the Dream Time is the aboriginal story of creation." He was pointing to the mural beyond the tables. He told the story of the dance and mimicked the sounds from the didgeridoo while each person around the table listened carefully as if Jack was their director at rehearsal. Jordan noticed Vinnie's perfect head nodding at Jack's story, indicating he was following every detail as he always did.

When Jordan set down his martini, Vinnie put his hand on her shoulder, pulled her in close, and whispered in her ear, "Thanks, love. And congratulations on the Stage Bite. You'll do great there." Jordan could smell Vinnie's cologne—reminding her of the subtle scent of evergreen—and she felt a small fire in her cheeks. He let go of her shoulder and picked up his glass like he didn't notice Jordan's embarrassment. She moved to the woman next to Vinnie and set a glass of red wine in front of her, though she was not conscious of the act. Vinnie's voice was still rolling around her head.

Jack's eyes shot from his waitress to the drinks and back again to the auburn hair that by now was across the Tavern. He told the folks to drink up and said they'd be right back to take everyone's dinner order.

He caught her at the salad refrigerator.

"You okay, mate?"

" 'Course I'm okay. Why wouldn't I be okay?"

"You seemed a little jittery back there, that's all." Jack's eyes clung to hers. The spark had gone away, Jordan saw, and instead she was looking into the serious face of a businessman concerned for his employee and his customers. She took off her glasses and rubbed her eyes.

"Maybe I am a little more tired than I thought. I'll be okay, Jack." He raised his shoulders and lowered them before returning to the kitchen. Halfway there, though, Jack stopped, turned his head back to Jordan, and studied her features like he would a painting.

"You let me know if it's too much, okay?" They both knew he was referring to the panic attack, and his words formed a long tunnel between them that no one in the Tavern was a part of. Jordan pushed away the memory of the night she'd seen her brother's face and nodded at her boss. Yes, she would let him know.

—∿∿—

The next few hours revolved around Bush Burgers, cups of coffee, and theater talk between Jordan and the actors. And Vinnie. She skipped between the kitchen, the bar, and the back room like she was the tiny round object in a pinball machine. The temp job seemed a long time ago; her aunt's words, though, stayed close. She could not shake the news of her mama.

By nine o'clock most of the cast had left the Dream Time, with only a few women still circled around Jordan's mentor. They sipped coffee before Jordan dropped the bill in the middle of the table. She was surprised when Vinnie picked it up, handed her his credit card, and returned to his conversation, which apparently had to do with the scene he'd helped fix for the show's playwright and producer just a few days ago. Jordan wondered if it was the same production that had forced him to cut short their diner meeting.

"None of my business," Jordan whispered while she cleared off the dirty plates and carted them back to the kitchen. Her legs were aching again but not as much as her shoulders. When she set down the dishes, she swirled her head in a circle, working out her neck muscles. She'd go for a jog in the park tomorrow—that would help.

She grabbed the counter and closed her eyes. Her mother's face filled her mind. She saw a frail brown-haired woman lying on a hospital bed, her skin the color of chalk and her eyes vacant. A nurse was pulling up the sheet toward her mother's head when Jordan felt a bitter sting slide down the back of her throat. A low whisper brushed her ear: *stricken by God, smitten by him, and afflicted.*

She forced her eyes open and was relieved to see a counter of food-stained plates, knives, and forks in front of her. The knuckles on her hands had turned white from gripping the edge of the counter, so Jordan relaxed them, found a fresh breath of air, and let her lungs gently pull it in. When she turned around, Jack was staring at her.

"Why don't you finish up the group and call it a night?"

His words took twenty pounds off her back, and she tossed him a slight grin as she hurried back out to the table. She was surprised to see Vinnie sitting by himself, drinking the last bit of coffee and loosening his tie.

"Something's wrong, love. I've seen it on your face all night." He set the mug down and leaned back in his chair, ready to listen. A small burst of adrenaline shot through Jordan's blood, and suddenly she felt more awake than she had all night. She handed Vinnie back his credit card and bill, and gathered the remaining dishes from the table.

"Just tired. Thankfully, my boss just told me I could go home when I finish up here."

Vinnie looked around the empty table, smoothed back his hair with his first two fingers, and smiled.

"Looks like you're done then." His eyes filled with empathy. While he finished his coffee, Vinnie watched Jordan wipe off the table and reset it for the next party. She thanked him for coming into the tavern and told him she'd see him in a few days at class.

By the time Jordan had counted her tips—forty-three dollars—found her coat, and said good-night to Jack, Vinnie was waiting at the door. He offered to carry her bag and held open the door for Jordan. Outside on the sidewalk Vinnie pointed to the moon above the skyline off in the distance. As Jordan glanced toward it, she noticed Jack standing in the doorway, watching them.

"I'm concerned about you getting home safely," Vinnie said. And without waiting for a response from Jordan, he threw up his hand and flagged a yellow cab as it was passing. It pulled over to the corner, and Jordan felt Vinnie's gentle hand on her shoulder for the second time that night. He was guiding her to the car.

The two settled into the backseat of the taxi, and Jordan told the driver her address in the Village. Though she rarely could afford a cab ride, Jordan always enjoyed them when she could. It gave her a chance to pass through the city above ground rather than beneath it, taking in different sights and perspectives that she otherwise wouldn't see. Tonight she felt strangely calmed by the streets beyond the window as well as the presence of the man beside her.

The lights of Broadway bounced off of Vinnie's face as they passed through Times Square, making him look a few years younger than he probably was—which was still older than Jordan. He was pointing out a few theaters to her where he'd been working and restaurants he loved or hated. When they pulled to a stoplight at Thirty-sixth Street, Jordan turned to him suddenly.

"It's my mother. Found out this morning she has cancer."

A small compassionate sigh sifted through Vinnie. He put her hand in his.

"See? I knew something was wrong. I'm so sorry, love."

The light turned green and the cab wove in and out of cars and buses as it headed downtown. When they turned onto Jordan's street, she pointed to her building and reached into her bag to find her wallet. But Vinnie was already handing the cab driver a twenty, telling him to keep the change, and opening the door for Jordan. The taxi pulled away from the curb, and the two stood silently on the street.

"You want to talk about it?" Vinnie stood a few inches from Jordan, his eyes pressed toward her.

"You want a cup of tea?" Jordan was surprised at the invitation that dropped out of her mouth. She suddenly realized Barry was the only man who had ever come over to her apartment before now. But this was Vinnie, the man who was breathing life into her dreams and who cared about her career.

"Would love one if you're up for it," Vinnie said still standing next to Jordan. His shoulders straightened as he rested his hands in the pockets of his leather coat. He was so sure of himself, so confident, Jordan thought. It was nice to be with someone who was clearly certain of why he was on this planet.

When they finally got to the fifth-floor apartment, Jordan glanced across at Barry's door and wondered if he was home. She put the keys in the locks and turned both. Once inside, Jordan dropped her bag on a chair by the door and went to the stove. She got distracted, though, by the blinking light on her answering machine, pressed the button, and waited, fully expecting to hear her aunt's southern accent updating her on her mother's condition.

Instead, she—and Vinnie—heard the upbeat voice of an off-Broadway director.

"Hi, Jordan. It's Danny at the Stage Bite. Just finished reading *Windfall* and wanted to let you know, well, yes, it needs a little work, but I feel really good about it. Congratulations on a solid play. We'll see you on Saturday for the reading. No need to call back. Just wanted you to know."

Vinnie tossed his arms out to the side and shook his head, delighted by the message they'd just heard. His was the face of an admiring coach watching the object of his devotion.

"I knew they'd be a good fit, love. That's great news." He walked across the small apartment and grabbed Jordan. She smelled the soft aroma of his cologne again and felt his wiry frame around hers. He rubbed the blades of her shoulders as he held her, and Jordan hugged him back.

When he released her, his hands moved to her elbows and he

stood in front of Jordan, still shaking his head at her accomplishment. Jordan laughed nervously and walked toward the stove to turn the teakettle on. At the same time, Vinnie noticed the photo of her family.

"Tell me about your family."

He might as well have pulled his finger from the wall of a dam. All that Jordan carried with her throughout the day came charging out of her in tears and coughs and memories. As much as she tried to fight the emotions from spilling out in front of Vinnie, she was simply too tired from the day and too weary from the possibility that she might lose her mother. She wanted to tell him.

She wanted an older man to understand. Her father never had, and now all of Jordan ached for some acceptance.

Vinnie brought Jordan over to the couch, sat her down, and pulled her head to his chest as she cried. His hand slid gently across her hair as he held her. And Jordan stayed close to him, letting go of the weariness and worry she'd carried through the day. But she did not let go of Vinnie.

Even when the teakettle whistled.

TEN

The morning sun was streaming through the clouds, but for Peter Riddle it might as well have been midnight. He stared at the road ahead of him, driving unconsciously to Dr. Hollander's office and listening to Jeanie's soft humming in the passenger seat beside him. For as long as Peter could remember, a quiet moving melody formed in the back of his wife's throat and followed her wherever she went: "Twinkle, Twinkle, Little Star" when their children were small; "Hark! The Herald Angels Sing" during the holidays; and so many hymns in-between that Peter could never list them all. This morning it was, "His Eye Is on the Sparrow," and as Peter drove he wondered how his wife could find a song at all.

"No matter what he says, Peter, I'm still planning on visiting Jordan for Thanksgiving." The force in Jeanie's voice was so sudden that Peter yanked the steering wheel to the right as if he were swerving to miss a stray dog. To avoid the traffic lights in town, Peter had automatically taken the highway to their doctor's office in north Jackson. After what he just heard, he was thankful few other cars were around this Monday morning.

"I think it's too soon to decide that, hon." Peter's knuckles formed tiny bumps on the top of the steering wheel. His grip tightened and his eyebrows creased forward. He glanced for a second at his wife and then focused back on the lane in front of him. Jeanie stopped humming.

"I've already decided," she said. "I might never have this chance again and I'm taking it."

Silence hung in the car. Peter's hands felt sweaty as he heard only the buzz of the car. Jeanie was quiet. He suddenly recalled another time in their life together that songs did not swirl around his wife: at the cemetery in Fiji. Except for a few furtive sobs, Jeanie was so silent that day that Peter's ears almost ached. The heaviness of *that* quiet could only mean one thing: death. It was as if *not* hearing Jeanie hum made the loss of their son a thunderous reality for Peter. When their boy died her songs disappeared.

Until one Saturday afternoon a few weeks later. While sipping coffee at the kitchen table, Jeanie started humming again. Just like that. Peter noticed as he was packing their books and photos in the living room. After the tragedy they had decided they could no longer call the island their home, and though they didn't know what they would do once they left, they knew they could not stay.

Only two weeks after the coffin was in the ground, they began shipping back their belongings. Jordan was boxing the books in her bedroom, and Jeanie had been wrapping glasses and plates, when all of a sudden Peter heard a faint little song floating from the kitchen.

When he came into the room, he saw her sitting at the table, her fingers wrapped around a mug and her eyes following the steam off of the cup as if an answer was hidden inside. And she was humming. Not loud and full like she had only weeks before. But humming nonetheless.

Peter recognized it as a hymn they had sung in Bible college but couldn't quite remember it. He walked over to his wife, put his hand on her shoulder, and stood above her. Jeanie just hummed and stared. She never said a word in response. Instead, she finished the hymn, rose from the table, and continued packing. Peter wanted to ask her what she had been thinking, how she was feeling, but the questions choked his own soul; he had no idea how he was going to cope, let alone help his wife through this. So he pushed back his glasses—more out of habit than because they had slipped down his nose—and walked back into the living room.

From that point on, the absence of their son became a secret place Jeanie retreated to often with her humming, never with words. Somehow, it seemed to Peter, Jeanie had recovered her melodies simply to avoid their encounter with hell. It was true what people said: something inside a parent is destroyed the day he buries his child. And whenever Peter tried to talk about what had happened, Jeanie avoided the conversation and entered into a song. She would not confront it. She would not. Peter, on the other hand, could not let it go. His son's death was in the air he breathed. Every day.

"I don't ask for much, Peter. But I *am* going to New York. To visit *our* daughter." Jeanie's determination broke the silence this morning and Peter's thinking, which was a good thing, because he had begun to feel the sharp empty ache of regrets in his chest. He knew they would only distract him from what they were about to do. He was also about to pass the exit ramp. Again he yanked the steering wheel over to the right and pulled the car off the highway and into north Jackson. When they'd stopped at a red light, Peter felt Jeanie's eyes.

"Okay, Jeanie, okay. Whatever you want."

Peter shrugged his shoulders as he reached for her hand. He wanted to bring it up to his face, gently brush it with his lips, but Jeanie pulled it back from him. She was still looking at Peter, and he knew from the faraway glaze on her eyes that she had gone to *that* place. Even when the light turned green and he focused back on his driving, Jeanie was nowhere near Jackson, Mississippi.

The doctor's office was as gray and stale as it had been since the day Peter brought young Jordan for her first checkup. Dr. Hollander cared deeply about his patients but not too much about decorating, so his office walls held the same Norman Rockwell prints he'd put up when he first opened for business thirtysome years ago.

"Nothing special," he liked to tell people. "If we made this place any fancier, well, people might never want to get healthy." Besides, if he kept it just comfortable enough, he figured he could maintain his fees even after the insurance industry took over healthcare. The cushions on the waiting-room chairs had been reupholstered once or twice, and he had managed to update some of the equipment and computers, but otherwise the doctor's office was, in a word, useful. If he hadn't been a doctor, Peter thought they might have been good friends. Both men seemed to care more about how things worked than how they looked.

The doctor met Jeanie and Peter at the door and invited them back to the windowless room he called his workplace. Yellowed diplomas lined the wall above his desk, and a calendar from Jackson Hardware was tacked above the light switch. Both Riddles shook their heads when Dr. Hollander asked if they wanted coffee.

"Okay, ya'll, let's get to it." The doctor was pushing papers around his desk like he was looking for instructions. His bushy white hair, which was brushed to the side, matched his mustache and eyebrows. He settled on a piece of paper, picked it up, and just as quickly put it down as he looked at the Riddles. Jeanie yawned like she was waking up from the place she'd just visited.

"Jeanie, you've got a tumor on your right breast, which we're pretty sure is cancerous. The anemia associated with it might be what's making you so tired and faint all the time." Dr. Hollander's lips pushed out, then in, like he hadn't quite decided on the next sentence. He folded his hands together on top of the desk. "But it also could have been that you've been working too dadgum hard. Either way, at least it got you in here. I think you missed your checkup last year, right?"

Peter shot a look at his wife. This was news to him. He'd thought his wife had followed through with her annual exams.

"Too many other things to do. Besides I've felt fine." Jeanie stared at her shoes.

"Hear it all the time. I'm just glad you came in when you did because the MRI showed a solid tumor. Doesn't look like it's too big yet, but we need to schedule you for a biopsy soon enough to know for sure what to do next."

Dr. Hollander picked up a red pen and a calendar from his desk. He began scrolling down the dates to see where there were empty spaces. Peter watched him, his muscles frozen by the revelation that just exploded in his ears.

"How 'bout week after next, November 11?"

Peter shook his head to force the blood to circulate in his body. "Wait a minute, Doctor. Are you sure about this?" Peter held up his hand to slow down the discussion. He looked at his wife, who still had not changed the focus of her attention, and back at the white-haired man across from him.

"I can show you the x-rays if you like, Peter."

"Shouldn't we get a second opinion or something before we schedule anything? X-rays have been wrong before, you know." Peter's foot tapped beneath him. The temperature in the room suddenly felt like it was ninety-five degrees plus humidity. Moisture appeared on Peter's forehead and the skin underneath his arms was wet.

Dr. Hollander put down his pen. He leaned back in his chair and put both hands behind his neck so his elbows stuck out like a bow tie. He blinked his eyes a few times, pushed out his lips from under his mustache, and waited.

"He's right, Peter," Jeanie said as emotionless as the walls in the room, her eyes still downward. As Peter began to challenge her, Jeanie cut him off.

"I found the lump myself a few weeks ago."

His eyes moved all over her face. "Why didn't you say something?" Peter's voice turned soft. His wife looked so small.

"When? I've hardly seen you this week."

Despite the heat in the room, a chill shot through every vertebra on Peter's spine and every rib in his chest. He wondered if his heart would pound out of his body. He was cold, very cold. He wished with all his being there was a window in the room to look out of, a place he could see beyond this office. He cleared his throat and felt all the saliva dry up at the back of his mouth. The tempo of his foot picked up speed.

"Could we make it sooner, Doctor? I'm planning a trip to New York at the end of the month."

"And you want to feel well enough to enjoy the place. 'Course you do, Jeanie." Dr. Hollander grabbed his pen again and deliberated over the calendar. "Earliest I've got is the sixth. We'd need you in the night before, but because it's a pretty typical procedure, I reckon you'd be up and around soon enough."

Jeanie was reaching in her purse for her pocket calendar. She sighed, took out a pen, and wrote *biopsy surgery* in the square marked with a six. When she folded the calendar and returned it to her purse, she looked up again at Peter as if she had just jotted down a grocery list.

He tried but could not find the depth he'd seen in her eyes the first time he met her.

Somehow Peter discovered the low pastoral voice he used in the pulpit.

"Will the surgery be…enough to beat this?" he asked. The doctor sighed, pushed a few more papers around his desk while considering his response, and then leaned back again in his chair.

"That's a good question. Just depends on what the biopsy says, what size, what stage. Once we know that we'll know what's next— chemo, radiation, drug treatment. Or nothin'." The air in the office was heavy. The only sound they heard was the tapping of Peter's foot.

"But let's worry about that when we get there, okay? In the meantime, Jeanie, take it easy."

"What about my fourth graders?"

"I reckon they'll be okay with a substitute for a little bit, right? Don't want you to push it, you hear?" Dr. Hollander rose from behind the desk and stood over the couple. Jeanie picked up her purse and walked out the door. Peter started to follow, but Dr. Hollander pulled his elbow back into his office.

"Listen, Peter. Jeanie's not the only one working too hard. I know you're not fond of this place, but it wouldn't hurt you to schedule an appointment sometime. If you're not healthy, you're not going to do her or anyone else much good, are you?" Dr. Hollander poked out his thumb after Jeanie.

Peter's chest filled up.

"Thanks for your concern, Doctor." Peter nodded, shook the physician's hand as if he were greeting a parishioner after a Sunday morning service, and walked out into the parking lot. Jeanie was already sitting in the car. Humming.

The drive home seemed longer than the drive to Dr. Hollander's office. Though Peter was in the vocation of offering words of comfort to people in need, he couldn't think of any to give his wife right now. His mind went blank each time he tried to speak. Instead, they stared in thick silence at the road ahead of them as they drove back to downtown Jackson.

When they pulled off the highway and into the Capitol neighborhood, Peter noticed the sign in front of the Mississippi Stage Auditorium announcing its upcoming show. In big black letters the theater company advertised: "Our Most Popular Revival: Tennessee Williams's *The Glass Menagerie*." He looked away from the sign and back toward the whirl of buildings, houses, and trees. The last thing he needed was to be reminded of the silliness of *that*.

"That was the first play Jordan ever saw." Jeanie's words startled him. She had not said a word since they left the doctor's office, and she rarely reminisced about Jordan's history with the theater. As much as he loved his sister, Peter often regretted allowing Cynthia Sue to take his daughter to the auditorium fifteen years ago. His grip on the steering wheel tightened.

"Now, hon, don't let one more thing upset you." Peter tried to be gentle with his wife.

"Upset *me?!* You're the one who's never liked the idea of Jordan going to the theater. I thought it might be good for her after losing her bro—"

Jeanie could not finish the sentence. She put her face into her hands and began to cry. Peter pulled the car over and reached across to his wife. She buried her wet face in his chest and wept.

"My baby, my baby." Jeanie mumbled into Peter's shirt. But he shook his head and stroked her hair, whispering to her not to worry.

"We'll make it through this, Jeanie. We will." He spoke quietly into her ear. Then Jeanie pulled her head up suddenly, moved back across the seat, and pierced his soul with her eyes. She wiped her cheeks.

"I'm not so sure anymore, Peter. It wasn't supposed to be like this." Jeanie's lips quivered. But her eyes, those topaz eyes Peter had fallen in love with, showed him something he had never seen before in his wife: resignation. That alarmed him more than the news they had just heard from Dr. Hollander. If Jeanie gave up, he wasn't sure what he would do.

"We were not supposed to lose our son. And now you want to lose our daughter, too?" The volume in her voice rose and fire filled her eyes. Peter tried to caress her face with his hand and put his fingers onto her lips as if she should not talk like this, but she slapped them away. He wanted to pull her close to him, to feel her heart beat against his, to know that she was still with him, near him, a part of him. But with every movement he made toward her, Jeanie batted him away. Her face went again to *that* place, and she grabbed the armrest, clinging to it like it was her solace.

After a long silent minute, she was humming again.

When they pulled into the driveway, Mrs. Mowery was at the mailbox in front of her house. She waved at the Riddles, but only Peter waved back. Once inside, Jeanie walked into the kitchen and put on the teakettle. She began to clean up the breakfast dishes with a fury as she waited for the water to boil.

"Since I've got the day off, I'm finally going to get some things done around here."

"Hon, the doctor wanted you to take it easy."

"Haven't swept this floor since God knows when. And the kids have piles of clothes to wash. I better get to it."

"Jeanie, the kids—"

"Then I need to get the bathrooms scrubbed," she said while still picking up the dishes. The whistle of the teakettle seemed to startle her. She reached for it and caught her balance as she grabbed the corner of the counter. "First, maybe I'll take a quick nap."

"That's a good idea," Peter whispered as he carried her tea into the bedroom. He grabbed his coat and tie, remembered his long list of work ahead of him that day, including sermon preparation for the upcoming weeks he would be filling in for Dr. Stately. He had also promised Miss Mary he'd stop by the senior center tonight to see if he could lend a hand to their fund-raising event.

"Would you like to come with me later today to see Miss Mary?" he asked. But Jeanie sipped her tea and stared out the window. Peter put another pillow behind his wife, leaned in to kiss her cheek, and looked again into her eyes. She was not there. This woman was a tired soul who looked only familiar to Peter.

"Okay, well, we'll talk later." Peter glanced again at his wife, who now was raising her hand to wave good-bye, but he knew they wouldn't talk later. Not really.

Peter pulled into the church parking lot within ten minutes. A handful of gray clouds streaked across the October sky as Peter walked across the parking lot. He sighed when he discovered a stack of memos waiting for him. As he sorted through them, he walked down the hall to Dr. Stately's office and knocked on the door. The reverend would know what to do about Jeanie's situation.

No answer. "Hmm," Peter grunted. He knocked again. No response. Peter rubbed the back of his neck, glanced at his watch, and turned around.

"Any idea when Dr. Stately'll be in, Loretta?" Peter stood above the secretary's desk. She stopped typing, removed her cat-framed glasses, and looked up at Peter.

"Well, good morning to you, too, Pastor." She tossed him a wide grin that was traced with scarlet red lipstick. Peter smiled and nodded back.

"No idea. Haven't heard a peep all mornin'. Lord knows he's got a stack of memos bigger'n yours waitin' for him." Loretta looked at the papers in Peter's hand before she focused back on her typing. The senior pastor had been gone more than usual lately, Peter thought as he watched Loretta's fingers jump across the keyboard, rescheduling meetings with him and the other staff regularly. Maybe he really was starting to think about retiring. Maybe he was considering his options. What would that mean for Peter?

"You okay there?" Loretta looked up at the assistant pastor, whose mind had gone several directions since they spoke, though his body had not moved from her desk. Her voice brought him back to his many tasks for the day.

"Fine," he threw the word out—like Jeanie had—and walked into his office.

The brown leather-bound Bible his wife had given him when he first came to work at Second Baptist sat prominently on the edge of his desk. He looked forward to dissecting the scriptures and pushing around words like pieces of a puzzle. The intellectual stimulation still fed his enthusiasm for his work in spite of what was—or was not—happening in his heart.

Pastor Peter Riddle sat down, grabbed a yellow notepad and a pencil, and flipped through the Old Testament like he was looking through the phone book for a friend's name. This series was an opportunity for Peter to raise some important social issues with the congregation again, and he wanted to take advantage of it. For three Sundays in a row he could address the need for the church to be more involved in the community, trying to move them beyond the comfortable confines of their southern faith and into a place where they could make a real difference. Peter shook his head at the challenge.

When he arrived at Isaiah 58, the focus of his sermons, Peter sat back in his chair, admiring the text. He pushed his glasses up on his nose and read aloud the fourteen verses so he could hear the sound of his voice teasing out the meaning of each. When he finished he scribbled down the dividing points where he would begin and end his three sermons. From verses one to five the first week he would explore how mere religiosity displeases God. He'd use verses six to ten the second week to discuss what real Christian faith looks like in caring for the outcast. And in the final sermon, he'd use verses eleven to fourteen to show how God rewards those who are obedient. During each service he'd read the entire chapter so the people could hear Isaiah's call to action in context. He might even invite Chaplain Drinkwater to say a few words about their work at the prison to give the sermon a practical application they otherwise might not understand.

For the next few hours Peter wrote. He copied the verses, jotted down points he wanted to make, inserted stories and quotes to bring life to the message, and thumbed through commentaries from his shelf to give him more insight on the chapter. Sometimes as he wrote, the words came so furiously his hand could not keep up with his head, which was why Peter liked using a pencil when he wrote out his sermons, just in case he needed to go back and erase something to make it stronger, clearer, sharper.

He stretched out his fingers to relax them, then cupped them into a fist again before stretching them one more time. He picked up his pencil and tore off the filled yellow paper, put it on top of a pile to his right, and dove into the blank page in front of him. And he kept writing. Carefully. Wildly. Thoughtfully. In spite of all the responsibilities he took on as a pastor, these were the moments when he felt the most connected to what he thought he wanted to do and certainly the times he felt the most alive. Maybe the only times.

Finally, he put down the pencil and picked up the pile of paper. He combed his fingers through his hair, stood up, and walked around his office reading the sermon aloud as if his congregation was sitting before him. Peter stopped after certain points to scribble in a word or erase a sentence. When he finished the last paragraph, he looked out the window and saw the lights in the parking lot had come up. The sunlight was gone. Peter realized he'd been studying and writing all day.

Peter picked up the phone and called his wife. Jeanie's voice was tired but awake enough to tell him she'd finished cleaning most of the house but did not want to go back to her fourth graders tomorrow. She had called for a substitute already. A half-chuckle came over the phone, and Peter recognized it as the laugh Jeanie used whenever she was trying to make him happy, whenever she did not feel comfortable with the attention on her.

"Last chance to visit the seniors with me," Peter teased her.

"Did you pick up James from baseball practice?"

Peter went quiet. He stared at her picture on his desk and waited.

"What time are you coming home?" her voice returned.

"Shouldn't be too late. I'll bring you some dinner from Captain Billy's, okay?"

The night air was brisk by the time Peter got in his car. Before he turned the ignition, he laid his glasses on the seat beside him and gave his eyes a hard rub with his palms. He was tired. The fullness of the last few weeks with Jeanie had worn him down. Even his morning jogs were not enough to keep up his energy. He remembered Dr. Hollander's challenge to schedule an appointment and considered it as he massaged the skin around his eyes and cheeks. Then he put his glasses back on and drove toward the Cherry Blossom Center.

When Peter turned onto Elm Street and slowed to a stop at the red light, he saw a tall, thin black man with dirty baggy jeans standing in the streetlight, waiting at the bus stop. Peter looked closer at his face and knew he had seen it before. He pulled the car over toward the young man, leaned across, and opened the passenger door.

Johnny's son leaned over to peer in at the driver. When he saw it was Peter, he hesitated.

"I'm going through downtown toward Jackson State if you want a lift."

The mirror image of the prison's security guard accepted the offer and got into the car. The smell of cigarette smoke and beer hung around him like a cloud, signaling to Peter where his passenger had just been. He cracked a window for some fresh air.

"You doin' okay?" Peter put the car in drive and pulled back into the street. The young Johnny just stared ahead of him. He unzipped his sweatshirt (which looked like it hadn't been washed in weeks), leaned back in the seat, and closed his eyes. The streetlights bounced across his brown face like the moon on water, and

Peter saw his skin was smooth, young. He wondered if he had ever shaved.

"Glad to hear it. I need to make a quick stop, just so you know." Peter glanced at the young man, who opened an eye for a second as if he were bothered by the intrusion and shut it just as quickly.

"Thought you were going to come see me at the church sometime. Your daddy seems to think—"

"My daddy ain't your business. Or mine." His voice was short. Anger rode along the top of it.

Peter's mouth felt dry. This was too familiar.

"Is that right? Well, he seems to care about how you're doin'." Peter turned the steering wheel into Captain Billy's and pulled up to the takeout window. "You hungry?"

It was the first time Peter had seen the vulnerability of his passenger, who opened his eyes, noticed where they were, and shrugged his shoulders. Peter interpreted that as a yes, so when Billy asked the pastor for his order, Peter told him three supreme dinners. He reached in his wallet and handed Billy a twenty-dollar bill.

The silence and the cigarette smoke were thick in the car as the two men—one white, one black—waited for their dinners. The evening sky cast strange shadows across the road. Peter turned on the radio, heard the static of a station he couldn't quite get, and turned the knob off. He tapped the dashboard in a two-four rhythm with his fingers.

"How you know him, anyway?" Johnny's son sounded just like his father.

"I help out with the worship services at the prison. Your daddy's been tellin' me where to go for years." Peter offered the young man a smile, hoping the line would ease the tension. It did not.

Billy came to the window carrying three white paper sacks with a red chicken printed on the outside. Peter handed one to the young man beside him and set the other two in the backseat. He waved to his friend as he pulled off and saw from his rearview mirror that Billy was looking out the drive-through window at the car, trying to figure out who Peter had with him.

Apparently the boy *was* hungry because he tackled his sandwich and slaw as soon as they were in his hands. By the time they pulled into the apartment complex by Jackson State, he'd all but inhaled the meal. Peter pulled the car over to let him out, but Johnny's son did not move. It seemed like he was looking for some word in his head.

"Don't tell him you seen me…like this." Johnny's son mumbled the words while he zipped up his sweatshirt.

"If that's what you want." Peter grabbed a business card from his wallet and handed it to the young man. "In case you need something, okay?" The two men nodded, and the younger climbed from the car, slammed the door, and strolled toward his apartment.

Peter watched him walk into the night. He could not help but wonder if some other father might be helping his own child as she

Jo Kadlecek

struggled with God knows what in that city. He took off his glasses, breathed on them, and wiped them on a napkin he'd retrieved from the Captain Billy bag before he started driving again.

A few blocks later he pulled into the Cherry Blossom Center. All the lights in the building were on, and Peter glanced at his watch while he walked in the doors. He would not stay long. He'd promised Jeanie.

Miss Mary smothered him with her usual hug when she met him at the door. She grabbed his hand and pulled him to the back community room where a makeshift stage had been set. Chairs were lined in wide rows in front of it, and the room buzzed with music, laughter, and a director's commands. Energetic white-haired men and women came and went on the stage, singing or telling jokes. Miss Mary sat Peter down in the front row as her body settled into the chair beside him.

Peter's stomach growled. He watched the performers dance across the stage in front of him, felt the elbow of Miss Mary nudge him with "Watch this!" instructions, and listened to the noises of rehearsal bounce in and out of his ears. The muscles in his shoulders tightened, the spotlights hurt his eyes. He wanted to be supportive of this but the taste in his mouth suddenly soured.

He looked up and saw thirteen-year-old Jordan's face in front of him, her lips moving with the passion of an evangelist about how fantastic the show was. She'd just come back from the Mississippi Stage Auditorium, and uncontrolled enthusiasm jumped out of her eyes, her mouth, her arms, her face. His daughter was alive.

"I found what I want to do for the rest of my life, Daddy. Aren't you happy?" She was skipping around the living room, stopping only long enough to look at him, then twirling around and walking back and forth across the room, pretending to be one of the characters in the play. He thought it was a phase. He thought she would grow out of it.

The force of Miss Mary's slap on his back was all he needed to remind him where he was. She was laughing at the scene in front of them, but he was in his home some fourteen years before, still trying to work through what he'd done wrong as a parent.

Suddenly, Peter stood to his feet, looked down at Miss Mary beside him, and put his hand on her shoulder.

"Sorry, Mary, I've got to, uh, get home." And the next thing he knew, Peter was behind the steering wheel again, driving like a young husband whose wife was expecting. By the time he pulled into the driveway, he wasn't even sure he'd stopped at any red lights. He reached behind him for their dinner and hurried into the bedroom.

Jeanie looked up at him from her magazine, startled to see him coming home so early. The color under her eyes looked darker to

Peter as he set the dinner on the bed. He leaned into Jeanie's face to kiss her, but she pulled away. So he dug their sandwiches out of the sacks.

Jeanie stared at her food as she settled back into the pillows.

Peter did not have time to ask her how she was feeling. Just as he sat on the edge of the bed, sandwich in hand, the phone rang. He sighed, smiled at his wife before getting back up, and walked into the kitchen to answer.

It was Loretta. Calling from Second Baptist. Her voice was shaking.

"Hey Pastor. It's Dr. Stately. Can you get down here right away?"

Her question was cut off as Peter hung up the phone, picked up his keys, and ran out the front door, hollering to Jeanie that he was on his way to the church.

ELEVEN

Jordan kept her eyes closed as she leaned against Vinnie. The tears had stopped, but she did not want to leave the gentle refuge of this place. She listened to the long slow breaths of the man who held her and felt his fingers follow the strands of her hair to the ends. The radiator heat of the old apartment building made it warm in her studio, but Jordan did not want to move.

She smelled the faint aroma of cologne, but it was not Vinnie's. It was her daddy's. They were standing beside the casket at her brother's funeral, arm in arm, rocking in grief and confusion and darkness. She was twelve years old, and Jordan felt her father's tears in her own; his shoulders shivered around her like they were never going to stop. He was so weak, so far away from his usual certainty and strength, and at that moment Jordan felt safer with him than she ever had. She breathed in her daddy's frailty like it was fresh air on a sunny morning. It carried her through the nightmare.

Jo Kadlecek

But that was a long time ago. Now her daddy was strong again. Impenetrable.

Jordan opened her eyes. She saw Vinnie lean back a few inches from her and felt him lift her chin with his thumb. She was startled by the look in his eyes, for somehow the face of her mentor had changed into one she had not seen in him before. She trembled, and her hands moistened.

Vinnie whispered a single word into her ear. "Relax." But Jordan could not. She felt his thumbs push into the top of her shoulders, down her spine, and into her shoulder blades.

A paralyzing chill replaced the warmth of the apartment, as if winter had just dropped around Jordan. Vinnie pulled himself off of the couch, stood over her for a second, and plopped down behind her back where he began to massage her neck and shoulders. She shut her eyes.

Her arms went limp. Vinnie slowly moved his right hand down her arm, reached for her hand, and spread out her fingers with his, still rubbing the muscles.

"Love, it's okay… What's this?"

Jordan's eyes popped open.

"What's what?"

"This…tattoo? I've never noticed…"

She turned her head and glanced down at her elbow. Vinnie held it in his hands.

"Bells."

"I see that. Do they mean something?"

"Uh, only that I'm a rebellious child."

"Or a gifted artist whose work is about to ring in a new generation of theater." His voice was dramatic and proclaimed the words with such resonance it was difficult not to believe him. Her eyes slid closed again.

"Now where were we?" he whispered, moving his hands back up her spine, pushing the sides of each vertebra, pressing the muscles around them.

"There. That's where you were," Jordan said. Her body was completely loose now, though her mind was racing. She was not sure who this man was in her apartment, how strange this scenario seemed to her, but she could not ignore how good both his hands and his words felt. She was so tired. Every bone and muscle in her body depleted from the events of the past few days.

She resigned herself to this place in the middle of her couch, weighed down by the variety of emotions whirling through her. She did not have the energy to sort through what was happening and decided that this was merely as it seemed: an innocent back massage.

Vinnie chuckled, and she felt his breath on the back of her neck. She reconsidered what was happening.

"Stop." The word was barely audible.

"How does that feel?" Vinnie teased the words into Jordan's ears. She wanted to admit that it felt good, great even, and probably would have, except the phone rang. Jordan slid out from under

Vinnie's hands and across the floor to answer. He turned slowly toward her, smiled, and waited.

"Hi Jack. Yes, I made it home all right. Why?" Jordan pushed the hair off of her ear as she gripped the receiver close. She glanced up to see Vinnie lean his head back on the edge of the couch and close his eyes. She looked out the window as she listened.

"Is that theater guy still with you, Jordan?"

"How'd you know?" Jordan squinted toward the curtains.

"I saw you get in the cab. Thought I'd call," Jack's voice was different over the phone, or maybe everything was different tonight, Jordan thought. "You need anything?"

"Uh, sure. I mean, I don't think so. I'm fine, thanks for asking. I'll talk with you soon, okay?" She hung up the phone. Vinnie opened his eyes and patted the seat beside him.

"I used to do this for a living, before theater, you know."

"Do what?" Jordan stared at him.

"Help people relax. Massage therapy, they call it." He looked up at her wide brown eyes. She felt an emotion rise in her lungs and the tension in her limbs throb. He was such a handsome man, but now the features on his face—which once she admired like a girl does her idol—seemed more difficult to read. In spite of the relief she felt from letting go of her worry, Jordan suddenly regretted asking Vinnie up for a cup of tea. She felt her cheeks flush when she thought of having cried in his arms.

Vinnie reached for her hand, but she did not move. He smiled.

"If you're not comfortable, love, that's fine."

She put her hand on his shoulder, signaling for him to wait, and stepped into the bathroom. She shut the door behind her and told Vinnie she'd be right out. She looked into the mirror as she heard him in her apartment, turning on some music, humming along to Aretha. Her face was so young, she realized. And so... unfamiliar tonight. She splashed some water across her cheeks, dried them, and pushed back her hair. Then she opened the door.

"You look beautiful, love," Vinnie said, his voice low and sure as it had always been to Jordan. "I'm glad the Stage Bite worked out." Vinnie was getting comfortable on the couch, but his statement caught her off guard.

"What do you mean? About the Stage Bite?" She blinked at Vinnie several times just to make sure she was seeing—and hearing—right.

"That I'm thrilled for you, that's all." Vinnie was loosening his shoelaces. Jordan watched him as he untied them, but she did not move. Vinnie smoothed his hair with his hand, leaned back on the cushions, and looked again at Jordan's tattoo.

She smiled at him and shook her head, trying to believe Vinnie's support. Then her lungs drew in a full breath of her dream to become a playwright. She closed her eyes and imagined a packed audience in a theater, coming to see her play, waiting for the curtain to go up on the best new drama to hit Broadway in years. The image was what she'd clung to these past few years when the city got hard and the money short. She had told herself she would do whatever it took to get there, and now she was facing a battle she had never considered part of the fight.

She felt Vinnie's breath near her face again.

"Are you all right?" his voice was soft and smooth sliding over her emotions. She opened her eyes and looked into his face, trembling at his presence. Something in her wanted to pull that perfect chin to hers, to bring his body close to hers. She reached up and put her hand on his cheek, tracing her finger down across his lips. She leaned her mouth into Vinnie's, and just before she felt his soft flesh, a hard knock on the door pushed them both off balance.

"Jordan, it's me, Jack."

Jordan dropped her head against Vinnie's chest, sighed, and then moved to the door. She heard Vinnie let go of a long breath as if he were exhaling from a cigarette. She glanced over her shoulder at his smile as she turned the bolts and yanked the doorknob toward her.

"G'day, mate." He still had on his skipper's cap, but Jack had at least taken off his apron. His feet were moving back and forth and his shoulders rolling sideways like he was ready to enter a boxing ring. Jack peered over Jordan's shoulder into her living room.

"Mind if I come in?" And without waiting for an answer, Jack walked into her studio apartment, which suddenly seemed a lot smaller than usual to Jordan. She stood at the door without closing it, a mixture of shame and relief shooting through her blood like lead.

Vinnie leaned against the counter, his arms stretched out while his hands rested on the edges. He tilted his head at Jack, grinned, and glanced toward Jordan.

"G'day," Jack said, marching in and standing a few feet in front of Vinnie, his back to Jordan.

"Nice to see you again, Jack."

Jack shifted his weight, careful to keep the anger and energy in his belly from erupting through his fists. His eyes were fixed on Vinnie, but he directed his next words toward the woman who stood behind him.

"Jordan, sorry to barge in on you like this, but after last week's, uh, event, I was a little worried…"

"Uh, well, Jack, no need. No need to worry."

Vinnie chuckled the type of laugh you'd hear from a leading man in a drama, but he was the only one who laughed. The short silence that followed vibrated off the walls and around the room, Jordan looking at the floor in the hallway, Jack glaring at Vinnie, Vinnie smiling at Jordan.

Then as if on cue in a comedy, Barry darted up the stairs and hollered, "Hey beautiful!" to Jordan at the door before he ran into her apartment. When he saw Vinnie and Jack, he stopped like he'd just collided with a truck. His eyes grew wide, bouncing from

Vinnie's confident smile to Jack's glare to Jordan's eyes, which by now were closed, her head hanging and shaking back and forth in disbelief. The tension was heavy. She rubbed her eyes with her index fingers.

Barry cleared his throat, rolled his eyes, and put one hand on his hip while the other pointed from Vinnie to Jack and back again.

"You have *got* to tell me your secret, Jordan. Not one but two gorgeous men in your apartment?" It was just the sugar Jordan needed to take the sourness out of the moment. Her eyes shot around the room, but she was too surprised by Barry's comment to look at any one face. She snickered like she did on the subway at her friend's jokes, and her shoulders began to twitch as she tried to stifle the laughter. She could feel her feet again.

"Yes, um, Vinnie, this is my neighbor and friend Barry. And Barry, you remember my boss, Jack." Jordan still could not focus on any of the three men in her apartment nor could she let go of the doorknob.

"Pleasure," Vinnie said smoothly.

"Hey guys. I just saw a great show in SoHo tonight—fabulous, you have *got* to go—but now it looks like I'm in for a double feature!" Barry was helping himself to a cup of tea, digging through Jordan's cupboards until he found his favorite mug, tea bag, and honey. As he waited for the water to get hot, he found his spot on the couch like an audience member being seated in the front row. He patted his knees expectantly and grinned.

Vinnie pushed out his chin, deliberating, and ran the palm of his hand slowly above his ear and down to his neck.

"Ah, another fan of the theater." He nodded to Barry, who grinned and blushed.

"It's such a rush to meet you, live and in person." Barry's voice grew. "I mean, you're famous!"

Vinnie coughed, placing his fist politely over his mouth as he did. He walked to the couch to shake Barry's hand, smiled, and turned toward Jordan as if Jack was not standing beside him.

"Well, love, I think I'll be going now."

"Good idea," Jack said.

"I'm, uh, sorry, Vinnie," Jordan whispered.

"Ah! But what about the show?" Barry asked, the corners of his mouth turning downward in disappointment. Vinnie shrugged his shoulders, brushed quickly past the protective Aussie, and stopped in front of Jordan. He kissed her cheek, patted her elbow, and walked down the stairs of the building.

Jordan ran her palm across the same cheek Vinnie just kissed. She rubbed it, gathered her hair off her neck, and let it fall, letting go of a short but full breath of air as she did. Jack was staring at her when she finally shut the door, his gaze gentle and full of respect.

"You okay?" he asked softly. Something in his voice drew Jordan; she stared back at him and saw that same look in his eyes she'd seen at the Dream Time. She noticed something different in his face. It was rough but etched with compassion. Confusion spread across hers.

"Yeah, fine. I told you there was no need to worry," Jordan answered. And as if it occurred to her for the first time, she asked him, "What are you doing here anyway?"

"I caught a cab right after you pulled off and called from the corner," he looked away from Jordan as he said this. "I don't know what got into me like that…"

"You don't follow all your waitresses home, do you?" Barry asked, teasing him. "Because if you do I'm thinking of applying." Barry laughed at his own joke as Jordan tried not to. But Jack wasn't so sure about it. Instead, he looked down at his shoes.

"I could tell on the phone something wasn't quite right," he said.

"Maybe. Maybe not. But, Jack, you shouldn't have come over, I mean, I can handle…" A slight pink colored her cheeks as she suddenly understood what Jack had done. He glanced up at her, then back at his shoes. Both stood in the awkwardness of the moment, not sure what to do next.

"Well, girl, it's a good thing you have friends…like us!" Barry jumped from the couch, threw his arms into a victory sign above his head, and pulled Jordan and Jack by the neck into a huddle. Their three skulls clunked together. Then Barry laughed and snorted and slapped their backs like players on a football team.

After the humor subsided Jack stepped away from the two. He glanced at his watch, took off his cap, pushed back his thick brown hair, and put the cap back on. He rubbed his eyes with his thumb and index finger like he was looking for the right thing to say. Barry went to the counter, dipped his tea bag up and down in his mug, and squirted another teaspoon of honey into the cup.

"Listen, Jordan, with all due respect, that guy's no good for you." Jack's eyes reflected now the authority of her boss, and Jordan felt like she'd just served a wrong order at the Tavern.

"*That guy* is my playwriting mentor. That's it. I owe him a lot."

"Is that what he was doing here, sugar? Collecting?" Barry raised his eyebrows as he tossed the question out like it was the most obvious one in the world. Jack waited for Jordan to answer. She shifted her weight and looked back at Barry, considering the sting of his words.

"No! I mean, well...honestly, I don't really know," she glanced toward the couch, then back at the men standing in her apartment. "It's been kind of a rough day."

Her boss looked at her with eyes that said he wanted to help but didn't quite know how. She had never seen Jack more serious or more sincere than the way he looked right now. They stared at each other for a long minute, eyes locked, and Jordan knew something had just changed in their relationship. Her shoulders suddenly felt lighter than they had all day, and whatever she felt when Vinnie was here now seemed to fade by Jack's silent proclamation of loyalty.

"It's late. I need to get going." Jack nodded to both friends, opened the door, and walked into the hallway. Jordan watched him leave and followed him to the door. She saw the top of his head as he was going down the stairs.

"Jack…see you later." He stopped when he heard this, looked up at Jordan, and smiled. That look in his eyes returned, and Jordan knew without a doubt it was directed at her.

"He's right, you know," Barry was mumbling as Jordan came back into the apartment. "Vinnie might know his theater, but so do you, Jordan Riddle. How much longer are you going to take those crazy workshops of his?" Jordan settled onto her couch, listening to Barry spend the next twenty minutes lecturing her on how talented she was as a playwright, how it was time to jump out on her own and become more strategic with her work. She nodded at her friend and pulled a blanket up over her legs. She knew he was right. She knew, too, that her lame little prayer tonight had been heard.

The next days passed quickly for Jordan as she worked on scenes from her play for the Stage Bite reading. She had decided to save any extra money she earned for when her mama came to visit rather than pay for tuition in the playwriting workshop. That meant she said yes to every temp job that came her way and every extra shift Jack offered at the Tavern.

As she thought about that night with Vinnie, she felt pulled between deep affection and utter embarrassment. He'd taught her so much about the craft and art of writing a play and been so tender with her when she'd released her worry about her mother, but she was confused about what to think of him. Instead, she decided to avoid him altogether for a while, which meant no more afternoon workshops, at least until she could come to terms with what had happened. Jordan shook her head in disbelief each time she thought about it—about him—and didn't know anymore which category to put him in.

Still, she could not help but wonder if Jack's intervention that night had in fact hurt her chances for working in the theater. If she had offended Vinnie, she worried her dream was in danger. And that was the second most terrifying thing in her life right now, after her mother's health. Though she'd questioned many things about the past five years of her time in New York, Jordan had always felt confident about pursuing her art, that it was the right thing to do. She thought she had made the best choices about her plays, but with the haunting aftertaste of the strange night with Vinnie and Jack, she was second-guessing even her ability to write.

Saturday morning she woke up in a sweat, anxious about the reading at the Stage Bite Theater that afternoon as well as her mother's health. Surgery had been scheduled for the day after tomorrow, and Jordan was tense about that. She'd fallen asleep on her couch in the wrong position, and this morning her neck and shoulders were stiff and achy. She pulled herself from a quick shower, gobbled down a bagel, and put copies of the final play revisions in her bag.

As she dug through the pocket of her bag, she noticed a piece of paper folded neatly on the bottom: the poem Sister Leslie had given her last week at lunch.

Jordan grabbed it, unfolded it, and reread the passage from Isaiah, out loud:

> *"Surely he took up our infirmities*
> *and carried our sorrows,*
> *yet we considered him stricken by God,*
> *smitten by him, and afflicted.*
> *But he was pierced for our transgressions,*
> *he was crushed for our iniquities;*
> *the punishment that brought us peace was upon him,*
> *and by his wounds we are healed."*

Jordan felt desperate and needy, and hoped the Almighty didn't mind her saying so. As she finished washing her dishes, she asked for his help in the day, to take her art and let it be something everyone was happy with, something that showed a little of his creativity and, mostly, redemption. Jordan even surprised herself when she began praying for the actors coming to the reading that afternoon, for Danny and Jack and Barry, even Vinnie. Mostly, she pleaded for the very best to happen with her play, whatever that was.

Then Jordan apologized for inviting Vinnie up to her apartment. And while she finished brushing her hair, she looked in the mirror and told herself that she did not want to be a playwright, would not continue the career, if it meant forgetting who she was.

She walked toward the door but stopped again at the family photograph above the couch. It reminded her of all the times when she was young—on the beach in Fiji, in the streets of the market, around the supper table. In almost each place, her daddy would look them in the eye, point upward, and tell Jordan and her brother, "Always remember who you belong to. It's him, not me, who's gonna be with you all the time. Remember that, okay?"

She recalled the sound of her daddy's voice, the song of his words, even the look on his face whenever he'd remind them, and suddenly, Jordan was surprised again. Instead of feeling angry at him or nervous about her play, she felt relaxed, ready even.

She picked up her bag, threw it over her shoulder, and left for the theater.

TWELVE

A half-dozen cars were parked around the entrance of Second Baptist when Peter pulled into the parking lot. Bubbles of sweat trickled down his forehead, staining his glasses like bugs on a windshield. Peter felt his nerves pierce the top of his shoulders as he turned off the ignition and got out of the car. He swallowed hard, hesitating before opening the door to the church.

As he did he shut his eyes and saw a black sky circling over the sea. Sand whipped around the beach, and the ocean climbed into whitecaps that exploded in the air. In every direction Peter looked, chaos flew past him. People were running, screaming, falling. Knocked down. Turned over. Swept away. Lost.

It was happening again. The world was a greedy fire of water, dragging everything he loved toward it, and Peter felt like there was not one drop of it he could control.

He popped open his eyes and sucked in the Mississippi air to remind himself where he was. The taste was firm. Peter took off his glasses and wiped them carefully with a tissue he found in his pocket. The effort forced him to think about something else, about magnolias in bloom and fried catfish, about Jitney Jungle grocery stores and Jackson Baptist Bible College. About places where he belonged, not places where he was different. He had believed that this was where he and his family could come back to life. Where familiarity and routine would keep them safe and protected. Where the mission of Second Baptist could offer him purpose and responsibility. Dr. Stately had seen to it.

Dr. Stately. The sting in Peter's eyes reminded him why he had returned to the church tonight. Panic had filled Loretta's voice. He had to be here. He didn't have any choice but to leave Jeanie alone. Again.

The door slammed into Peter's shoulder with a force that did not match the size of the woman who pushed it. Loretta was clearly upset; she'd been waiting for Peter to arrive since the phone call, pacing the church's long corridor. As soon as she saw him at the door, she shoved it open and yanked him in.

"He's in here. Deacons and Jimmy are here too. It's not good, Pastor." Loretta's face was pale, her eyes somber. "It's not good."

She ushered him down the hall, past the many photos of church-sponsored missionaries that hung on the wall and through the lobby. Stacks of welcome brochures on the visitors' table spilled over as the two whirled by. Finally, Peter and Loretta were in the sanctuary, hurrying down the aisle to the front row where seven men sat across from one white-haired senior pastor.

Dr. Stately's eyes were cloudy; little dots of pink colored his cheeks. He wobbled as he leaned against the end of the hardwood pew, his legs stretched out in front of him. When Peter sat down beside the others, he could not keep from staring at his elder. A hundred question marks hung over his head. As the deacons shifted nervously against the pews, Jimmy cleared his throat like he was ready to make announcements at youth group, except there was nothing youthful about his disposition tonight.

"Peter, we've got a little problem," Jimmy spoke as any southern gentleman would—politely and around the issue.

"Ah, let's just get right to it, Jimmy," Dr. Stately's voice shook as he looked up at the people who were staring at him. Something was missing from his face, Peter noticed. Those were the same lines around his eyes, nose, and mouth, but his face seemed empty, vacant even, lifeless, as if someone had drained the person out of the body, only the body kept moving. Dr. Stately placed his palms on his lap and studied them.

"All right then. We're asking Dr. Stately to step down from the pulpit. Effective immediately." Jimmy's words were a gust of sand whipping across Peter's ears. Few things through the years had been solid ground for Peter more than Dr. Stately's leadership, and now a gale was knocking his feet out from under him. He looked from

Dr. Stately to Jimmy to Loretta and back again, trying to make sense of what he just heard. He shook his head and gripped the edge of the pew with both hands as if to keep himself from tipping over.

Jimmy read his face. "Peter, we wanted to talk with you about it, but with all you're dealing with at home, with the family, well, we hoped it wouldn't come to this."

Peter's eyes burned again. His throat filled with sorrow, rage, and fear all at once when he heard the mention of his family. Then he swallowed each emotion and buried them someplace deep. He felt the blood in his fingers pinch his skin.

"Hal's been comin' across a bunch of inconsistencies in various funds, specifically the senior pastor's, so when we tried to ask him about it, well, you know as well as anyone how hard it's been lately to nail down two minutes with Dr. Stately, except for Wednesday staff meetings!" The deacons nodded with Jimmy's accusation. Jimmy pulled off his baseball cap and placed it across his lap. "Now Hal's the pickiest accountant we've had in years, all due respect. You know, as well as I do, he don't get much wrong. So we decided to wait for the pastor tonight to ask him what was goin' on, and when Loretta went into his office to get him, well, she saw him fixin' the books."

"With my own eyes," Loretta mumbled, as if she still couldn't believe what she'd witnessed. Peter looked above Jimmy's head like the sentences he had just spoken were still hanging in the air. Stealing? Were these people accusing the most faithful senior minister

in the state of Mississippi of embezzling funds from the congregation of Second Baptist? No. Peter shook his head again and told
himself this was not happening. It could not be happening.

"There must be some mistake," Peter said, his eyebrows pushed
forward like arrows. He pulled his glasses closer to his eyes, desperate to see more clearly.

"No, Peter, it's not a mistake." Dr. Stately's words matched his
face, vacant. "I was getting bored with the ministry and thought I
could…"

"Bored? Since when was church work supposed to entertain
you?" Peter hurled the words at his boss as a volcano of anger
rumbled in his gut. His foot snapped out of control, and his forehead was hot and sweaty again. If Loretta had not been sitting
between them, Peter might have jumped across the aisle and
grabbed Dr. Stately by the throat. He felt betrayed.

"I just wanted a new challenge, I guess, so I thought I'd see if
I could win a little money." The senior reverend's voice was quiet
and listless. He continued to stare at his hands. "Never thought it'd
get the best of me."

"Right before you got here, Peter, Dr. Stately was telling us he'd
been spending a little too much time at the casinos on the Gulf
Coast. Guess they were a little more, uh, interesting than life in
Jackson." As Jimmy explained the ugly details of Dr. Stately's gambling habit—which had apparently been going on for the past ten
months—Loretta began to sniffle. She dabbed her nose and eyes

with an old white hanky, and Peter watched as one of the leaders put his arm on her shoulder to console her. Peter's tongue scraped the roof of his mouth and found nothing but dry heat. He trembled.

"How? How did this happen?" Peter said to no one in particular. And the silence that followed his question lingered over them. No one moved. No one answered Peter's question. No one tried to ease the pain. His foot tapped furiously.

Finally, one of the deacons—Bobby Simpson, a reserved, balding man around Peter's age—interrupted the heavy quiet with a soft cough.

"The question now for us, folks, is whether we should call the police." There was a gentle prodding in Bobby's voice, a calm authority that everyone in the room took seriously, including the senior pastor, because he moved his focus from his palms to Bobby's eyes.

Peter, however, looked down at his own fingers and noticed they'd turned white. He let go of the pew, rubbed his chin to make sure he could still feel his skin, and confirmed to himself that he was actually awake, that he really had just heard someone put "police" and "Dr. Stately" in the same sentence.

"That feels a little premature, y'all," Jimmy said. "What if we give Dr. Stately a chance to return the money, to make up the difference?"

"All right. But I don't think it's a good idea for him to serve as senior pastor anymore," Bobby said.

Heads nodded in consensus until the silence covered them

again. The small group stared at the man who had been their spiritual leader longer than any of them could remember. No one in the room believed they would ever be having this meeting. One of the lights in the back of the sanctuary flickered on and off. They waited.

"I'll step down. Call it an early retirement, if that suits y'all," Dr. Stately's voice quivered with a hint of defensiveness and embarrassment. Certainly, *he* never thought this night would come. The elder minister paused before he spoke again. "And I will return all that I took, plus interest."

"I'd say that needs to happen real soon," Peter blurted out. The words weighed them both down, and for a second their eyes locked. A terrible knowing passed between the two men, as if the language of weariness and emptiness and misery was all they had left between them. But it was a language they both knew painfully well, and in an eerie way, Peter suddenly felt closer to his mentor than he ever had.

Both had misplaced their faith and were feeling the consequences.

In spite of this odd camaraderie, Peter's anger toward Dr. Stately had not subsided. Far from it. In fact, the storm kept coming, and Peter felt it slap his jaw, shaking his neck and his shoulders.

Bobby spoke again. "Okay. I think we're makin' a little progress.

'Course, we've got this problem now of being a church without a pastor." He scratched the base of his skull as he spoke.

"That's what assistant pastors are for, to fill in or step up when the senior—" Jimmy stopped himself. "Anyway, I reckon that's why you're here, Peter, to step up." And before Peter was cognizant of the conversation taking place around him—his head still reeling from the chaos of the moment—the deacons nominated, voted, and passed the motion that Peter Riddle would be the interim senior pastor of Second Baptist Church of Jackson. His status would be temporary until the congregation could vote him in officially.

Effective immediately.

This was hardly the way Peter dreamed of getting his own church. He'd always assumed he would receive a call from some little church in the Mississippi Delta or maybe even one across town. Dr. Stately would stay at Second Baptist only until some young version of himself, fresh out of seminary, came along.

Tonight, though, Peter's dreams and beliefs had been slung across the state of Mississippi and splattered in a heap on the floor in front of him, all in a matter of minutes. Each aspect of the night was a punch in his stomach, and all he had left now was a pile of pain he did not want to confront. Peter could not—would not—believe he'd been destined for *this*.

Certainly, God's jokes on him had lost their humor long ago. As far as Peter was concerned, God had lost track of him altogether.

Peter's muscles throbbed. A few deacons gathered around Dr.

Stately, shut their eyes, and laid their hands on his shoulders, praying that "the minister would consider seriously the steps he'd taken and return to the Good Shepherd."

Peter folded his arms across his chest, shook his head, and felt a bitter sting slide down his throat as he watched. He knew the deacons would expect him to join the intercession, but nothing in his being—or his bones—could move him from the pew. He was disgusted. And he wasn't exactly sure what the source of such disgust was: Dr. Stately or God himself.

What he was sure about was that prayer seemed like a monumental waste of time right now. God had obviously not heard his pleas before—first his son, then his daughter, now Jeanie. And if Dr. Stately had allowed himself to be reduced to this desperate place, Peter hadn't the slightest interest in talking with God on his account. The man had made his choices. Peter was too angry to pray.

Instead, he picked up a hymnal and heaved it against the wall.

Loretta stopped sniffling, and the deacons stopped praying when they heard the sharp crack of the book against the wall. Jimmy stood up. Bobby followed.

"Y'all can go ahead and pray all you want. But I doubt it'll make a lick of difference. The man's going to do what he damn well wants to." Peter was on his feet, pointing at Dr. Stately, flames in his voice. "How's that from your *new* senior pastor!" He was breathing hard now, shoulders heaving up and down while his glasses slipped off the ridge of his nose. When Peter stared at the stunned faces in front of him, he wondered what in the world he was doing here.

He shook his head in disgust again at Dr. Stately, at the people in front of him, at the church where they stood. But Dr. Stately merely sighed and looked at the hymnal on the floor. Then he looked up at Peter, and for a long and heavy moment he smiled. Peter blinked. It was a knowing smile, one that understood flying hymnals and exasperated words. It was a smile of jealousy even, as if Dr. Stately had long ago wanted to throw something across the sanctuary but never had. Peter shivered.

He turned around, walked up the aisle, and was just about to push open the door when he heard a sound from the front of the sanctuary echoing across the pews.

"This is the time, Peter. This is for you."

Peter spun around to the faces down front. They were staring at Dr. Stately, who was standing up now and looking toward Peter. There was no smile on his face any longer. Instead his eyes were serious and charged.

"Be careful, Peter. I never meant any..." Dr. Stately's words faded into a slow and reticent voice, one that was vastly different from the one Peter had just heard.

Peter felt his heart pick up speed as he looked around the sanctuary, the lights shining in the colors of the windows and across the top of the organ. He saw the thick wooden cross that hung behind the pulpit, and his eyes followed it up and down, side to side. He swallowed as he stared and felt his fists relax at his hips. And for the first time in a long time, Peter's shoulders suddenly did not ache.

The night air brushed Peter's face as he got into his car. He drove into the darkness, too tired to feel angry anymore, too tired to feel anything, but not tired enough to go home and fall asleep. He wanted someone to talk with. Jeanie had long ago stopped listening to him, and she would not be awake by now anyway. He was not about to disturb her. He thought about calling Chaplain Drinkwater, but since it was after 11:00 p.m., he knew it was too late.

Instead, he decided just to drive. He turned the corner onto Lynch Street and went past Jackson State. He thought of Johnny's son and wondered how he was. He drove past the Bible college, into downtown, and around by the Capitol, thinking nothing in particular but feeling every emotion associated with each site he passed. He wanted to remember anything familiar.

A few blocks beyond the Mississippi Stage Auditorium, Peter pulled into the parking lot of the Eudora Welty Public Library and turned off the car. It wasn't a conscious decision to come here; he just did. He rolled down the window and felt the October chill drift across his cheeks. He stared up at the entrance to the library—the streetlights casting soft shadows across the windows—and Peter remembered all the times he'd driven Jordan here. As a teenager she loved to come to the library, check out anthologies of dramas and biographies of playwrights, wander through the Mississippi Writers Room, or read the magazines on New York City. Peter never understood his daughter's infatuation with the theater, but he could never deny the joy in her eyes after she'd read a play or attended a musical that came to town. It was a love he never got used to, one that did not fit in his world. He always wanted it to go away.

Tonight Peter did not want to think about Jordan, though he could not stop it either. After all, it was Jordan who had first betrayed him when she moved to New York four years ago, just as Dr. Stately had tonight. Even Jeanie's illness felt like a betrayal, another slug in the stomach, until finally the beating was too much.

Peter began to cry. He set his glasses on the seat beside him, pulled his hands to his face, and could not stop the emotion of the night, the pain of his days, from colliding into a million sobs and heaves. He groaned and wept and shook in the darkness of the Mississippi night, his car a strange refuge from the onslaught of piercing memories. Faces shot across his mind: his son's tanned skin that last day Peter saw him at the beach; Jeanie's pale cheeks in the hospital last week; Cynthia Sue's stern eyes in the kitchen;

Dr. Stately's defensive gaze in the sanctuary; even the stoic glare of Johnny, the security guard at the prison. They all floated quickly past, like spirits hurrying through a house said to be haunted. And with each image Peter wept, hard and raw and present, the volcano finally spewing out of his eyes and into his hands.

When Jordan's auburn hair appeared in his memory, though, outlining her full soft smile, Peter's sobs began to wane, his shoulders steadied. It was as if the face of his daughter offered him something he needed most in this outpouring but never expected to find—relief—and to his own astonishment, he accepted. It surprised him. Instead of feeling angry, Peter was simply exhausted. He wanted nothing more than to go home and climb into bed.

"This is the time, Peter. This is for you."

Peter thought about the words he heard in the sanctuary but did not have the energy to make sense of them. Instead, he tucked them away in his head and hoped they would settle into some semblance of meaning down the road.

He took a handkerchief from his pocket and wiped his eyes and nose. Then he pulled the car out of the parking lot. The air from the open window dried his face as he drove. Jackson's streets seemed darker and slower than usual, but Peter was glad for it. By the time he pulled into his driveway, his eyelids were heavy and his heart empty. But this was a different kind of empty from the sunken aches he'd felt for so long. This was the emptiness of surrender, the hollow drum of resignation. Somehow, Peter knew he would sleep better tonight than he had in months, maybe years.

And he did.

Over coffee the next morning, he recalled for his wife the details of the previous night: the discovery of Dr. Stately's gambling problem, the deacons' dismissal, Peter's instant promotion, even the drive through Jackson. Peter did not, however, tell his wife about how he wept and wailed in the library parking lot. Jeanie's face looked whiter than usual, Peter thought, and he wasn't sure she could handle it. He poured her another cup of coffee and asked how she was feeling.

"Like a hurricane just went through my house," she said, her voice chilled with familiar terror. With that Jeanie began to hum, to wander off to that place where life was anywhere but here. She stared out the window. Peter slid his hand under hers and tried to prod her back into their kitchen, but she yanked it away. She hummed louder, closing her eyes to listen to whatever melody was floating through the air. Peter did not recognize this hymn; he barely recognized his wife in these moments.

Then, like she was walking through a magic mirror, Jeanie suddenly appeared again, grinning at her husband and clearing the breakfast dishes.

"Are you driving me to school this morning?" she asked as if nothing had just happened. Peter tilted his head at her, trying to understand the trip she'd just taken. As she handed him the car keys, he wondered if she had heard anything he'd just told her.

"Hon, you called for a substitute, remember?"

She set down her dishes and looked at Peter.

"I did? Oh, yes. Of course, I remember. I am feeling a little tired."

"I didn't think I was going to be able to wake you this morning," Peter said.

He kissed her cheek as she climbed back into bed. "I'll finish the dishes. You take it easy," he said. But Jeanie was already asleep. He looked at her face and worried how much she was slipping away.

She'll get better, he told himself. He picked up his Day-Timer, read how full his schedule was for the day ahead, and within seconds let go of his worry for his wife, replacing it with a long list of matters concerning Second Baptist Church in Jackson.

During the following Sunday's worship service, Jimmy made the announcement to the congregation that Dr. Stately was stepping down from his position for an early retirement—though most folks already knew what had happened. Word traveled fast in Jackson and faster still in Baptist circles. Jimmy explained the voting procedures for confirming the new senior pastor—Peter Riddle—and announced it would take place at the next official congregational meeting on Wednesday, November 16, at 7:00 p.m. in the fellowship hall. Coffee and child care would be provided.

Peter stepped to the podium to preach the sermon he'd been planning to preach for weeks, the first in a series from the book of Isaiah. From the pulpit he scanned the faces of the teachers, mechanics, bankers, and farmers who'd made up Second Baptist—more or less—since he'd come back from Fiji. He saw Miss Mary smiling at him from her pew. He saw Loretta and Bobby and their families. And he saw the dozens of other families he'd talked with at one time or another for the past fifteen years. These were his people or as close as he would ever come to having some.

He did not see Jeanie. She needed to sleep this morning, she'd told him. She'd been sleeping a lot lately, mostly because she said she did not feel like doing much of anything else. He did not argue, hoping the extra rest would do her good.

He did wish, though, that she had been standing next to him when he shook the hands of these same folks as they filed out of the sanctuary and back into their routines. Several congratulated him on his new position; others simply smiled at him with south-ern politeness, conveying to Peter they'd really rather have heard Dr. Stately preaching this morning and that this new change would take a while to get used to.

Miss Mary, of course, could not have been prouder as she smothered him, her floral-print dress swaying back and forth in the motion.

"Doesn't God work in downright interestin' ways? I'm tickled pink for you, Pastor. I am. 'Course, it doesn't give you an excuse to stop visitin' us at the center, you hear?" Her laugh and her hug pushed away Peter's anxiety about his first morning as *senior* pastor, and he couldn't help but let a shy grin spread across his cheeks as Mary patted his back and went looking for a cup of coffee and a friend.

Two days later Peter drove Jeanie to the hospital for her biopsy. She hummed as she walked through the doors and would not let Peter wait with her before the surgery.

"Don't you have better things to do, Peter? I mean, it's just a routine procedure," she said coolly. "That's what Dr. Hollander said, and since you've got other things to do, you should do them. I'll be fine."

As much as he wanted to believe her, Peter wondered if she really would be fine. He hadn't spent much time at home lately because of the increased demands of his job, and now he felt helpless as Jeanie shooed him out of the waiting room.

By the time the operation was done, Peter had met with two new Sunday-school teachers, dropped off some supplies at the clinic in West Jackson, led a brief staff meeting at the church, and called Cynthia Sue about Jeanie's biopsy. Dr. Hollander greeted him at the hospital's lobby as a nurse pushed Jeanie in a wheelchair toward him.

"Couldn't have gone smoother, Peter," the doctor said. "Now we'll send it in to the cancer center in Hattiesburg for results. We'll know more then. In the meantime make sure she doesn't go back to school for a while, okay?"

"What's awhile?" Jeanie asked, rising out of the chair, her cheeks tight and the color of chalk. Peter hadn't seen her look so pale.

"Take your time. Maybe a month or so?"

"What about Thanksgiving?" Jeanie asked.

"Doubt we'll hear anything by then. If you're asking whether you can still take that trip you told me about, well, I reckon it'd be okay. As long as you don't try and pack in every dadgum tourist attraction during the whole week," Dr. Hollander warned, his face wrinkled with kindness.

Peter didn't have time to ask the doctor any other questions before Jeanie darted out the door. She sat in the passenger seat, buckled in by her seat belt, staring out the window by the time Peter caught up with her.

"How you feeling?"

"I saw him, Peter."

"Who, hon? Who'd you see?"

"James." She smiled at her husband. He dropped the car keys, picked them up, and fumbled with the ignition. She kept smiling.

Then just as quickly her tone altered. "Oh, I'm sleepy, sugar. And sore," her voice faded. "Take me home." They drove home in silence, awkward at the presence of pain, afraid of the possibilities of change.

The phone was ringing as they walked in the door. Cynthia Sue wanted to know how her favorite sister–in–law was feeling, so Peter handed her the receiver. He pulled a chair out from the kitchen table for Jeanie to sit down and made them a pot of coffee while she talked on the phone.

"A little slow but I'll be fine. I'm still planning to see Jordan for Thanksgiving."

"Well, ain't that a hoot? My editor just told me I should cover the Macy's parade for the paper. He seems to think folks in Mobile want a firsthand account—'course I happen to agree!"

"Fantastic!" Jeanie exclaimed. "But we'll surprise Jordan about your coming, okay? She'll be thrilled."

Peter looked up at Jeanie when he heard this. Cynthia Sue agreed that was the only reasonable way for both of them to sneak up there and told Jeanie she'd call the travel agent as soon as they got off the phone. After he poured two cups of coffee, Peter sat next to his wife and stared at her. He was still trying to get used to the idea that she was just coming home from the hospital because of a cancer scare, and now she was determined to leave again. To see their daughter no less.

Jeanie took a careful, slow sip and set the mug back down. "She's arranging the flights so you don't have to worry about that,

Peter." She paused, looking for something. "I don't suppose you'd want to come too?"

The coffee burned on his tongue.

"Hon, you know how crazy things have gotten at the church now. There's no way I could take time—"

"She is still your daughter."

He blinked. Things had not been great between him and Jeanie, but he'd never heard such accusation in his wife's voice.

"Jordan made her own choices. I tried to warn her—"

"Of what? Doing what she loves?" Jeanie glared at her husband. She rose from the table, grabbed a sponge from the sink, and wiped the table, though there was no mess on it to clean. Then she sat back down. Maybe the surgery had affected her more than he thought, but she would not stop.

"We already lost one child, Peter. I can't for the life of me understand why you'd want to lose another."

A tide of anger rode behind the question. He reached across the table for her hand, but it was limp, unresponsive to his. She looked at him again; her eyes ice.

"What will it take to get you two together again?"

"I've got work to do here, Jeanie. Besides, you know as well as I do, Jordan does not want to come back home…where she belongs."

"I asked you a question."

"Oh, for heaven's sake, Jeanie."

"What will it take, Peter?" She stood up again, her hands hanging desperately at her sides, her eyes filled. "Tell me. Now. What will it take?"

"How would I know? What do you want me to say? Another hurricane or some terrible storm that makes her realize she needs to come home?" Peter breathed hard at the emotion between them and pushed out his chair to rise. He gripped the edge of the kitchen table to remind him where he was, that he was *not* on the beach in the middle of a storm looking frantically for his son. He was here, in his home, in Jackson. With his wife, whose face was pale and void.

The boy's auburn hair, stained with blood, flashed in Peter's mind. Jeanie had pushed too far.

He stood up, swallowed the last of his coffee, and dropped his cup in the sink. Sweat formed above his glasses and across his eyebrows. Jeanie shook her head, sighed, and walked slowly down the hall to the bedroom. She shut the door.

Peter wiped his forehead with a tissue and at the same time noticed Jeanie's mug still on the table, full of coffee, steam rising off the edge.

THIRTEEN

A siren howled outside the theater, amid the honks and shouts of New York's street noise, but none of the actors sitting on the stage seemed to notice. They were reading aloud the last scene of Jordan Riddle's play, *Windfall*. So the only sounds they paid attention to were words and sentences and emotions from the characters they were playing.

Danny sat at the head of the long wooden table, her hair braided back into a ponytail that lined the middle of her back. The actors gathered around her like a sales team around their CEO. Small half-moon glasses rested on the edge of Danny's nose, and her eyes and brows were as focused as the lights around the stage. From a black cushioned seat in the front row only a few feet away, Jordan listened, awed by the life these human voices infused in the pages she had written, terrified *and* thrilled that they were reading her work.

There was nothing quite as exhilarating as creating a story for the stage and then watching the process of other artists absorb it, digest it, and believe it so fully that it became utterly and completely *theirs* as well. Writing was a solitary journey, but performing was very much a community exchange. It required an assortment of talents Jordan could not even hope for on her own, and she loved how it used each one's gifts to create something far bigger and far grander than any of them could have imagined alone.

This was what made the theater such a spiritual gift for her; it possessed the magical ability to transform lonely words into human connections. It explored the hard and wonderful stuff of living by inviting everyone present to participate together. Theater, Jordan had come to believe, enticed people to leave their self-absorbed existences and enter a world where they could care about someone other than themselves, where the affections and struggles and risks of another human being mattered more than their own. At least for a few hours. That was the beauty of such art; it called people out of themselves.

Danny scribbled something on the page in front of her while an attractive woman to her right uttered the last lines of the play. The woman had been reading the part of Tamara, the protagonist whose Catholic faith took her to a place where she had to choose between loving a man who believed in nothing except her or believing in a God who loved everything in her *but* the relationship she was in. The actress wiped her eye as she turned the last page. Jordan could not tell if the woman was genuinely moved or if she was still in character.

But the silence around the table confirmed the work. Heads were nodding at Danny, and "Tamara" was flipping back through the script, admiring the language and depth of the role she'd just interpreted. Jordan shifted in her seat, swallowed, and felt a ball of excitement being tossed around her stomach. A tall thin actor in his thirties pushed out his chair, stood up, and looked at Jordan.

"A helluva story. Nice to read a work that stirs things up for a change." He grinned as he spoke to Jordan. She nodded her appreciation toward him and felt the pink in her cheeks fill out. Jordan, too, stood up, if for nothing else than to get the blood circulating in her legs so she could feel her feet. The actor went backstage for a second, reappeared with a box of notebooks, and began handing them to each person around the table.

"I agree. Jordan, I'd like to talk over a few things with you, but for the most part, I think this is a play that will be good for the Stage Bite right now. Anyone object?" Danny spoke as she pushed the papers of her script into a pile. Then she picked up the pile, tapped it on the table, and placed it in the three-ring binder the actor had given her. The other actors ignored her question and did the same with their scripts, as if three-ring binders were a hand-shake between a playwright and the Stage Bite Theater Group, a contract that said they would produce this play. The rings, apparently, sealed the deal.

Jo Kadlecek

Jordan took off her glasses and breathed on them, more to release some air than to clean the lenses. This moment had been a long time coming, and it suddenly made all the workshops, the readings in her apartment, the early morning rewrites, even ushering at Broadway theaters worth the effort. A surge of gratitude rose up through her rib cage and pushed her lips upward. The dream was no longer somewhere off in the distance. It was here, now, in this small theater in New York's Village, in Jordan's favorite time of the year. Divinely placed, she was sure of it.

But with a dream's realization came the weight of responsibility; Jordan knew that, too. She had watched it enough in other playwrights to observe that one success did not qualify you as successful; it only meant you were given a rare opportunity to share your art with more than your friends in hopes that others might come to enjoy it as well. If anything, having a play produced in this city simply allowed the process of creative expression to continue. It did not end it as though it were a final product that could be marketed and sold like fast food before the masses moved on to the next fad.

Jordan gulped back the tension she felt, pushed on her glasses, and crammed her script into her bag just as another siren passed outside the theater. Danny motioned for her to join her as they walked back up the aisle, discussing a few scene changes, rehearsal dates, and publicity options. They would probably open the weekend after Thanksgiving, with final dress rehearsals the week before.

That meant they had about five weeks to build a set, learn lines, and block the scenes. Since these actors already knew each other well and were experienced with this kind of tight schedule, Danny felt confident they could pull off a successful performance of the play, one that would benefit the theater and the actors as well as the playwright and the audience.

"That's what the Stage Bite's about, after all: giving folks the kind of plays we think will make a difference, right?" Danny's question was rhetorical and when they got to the door, Jordan didn't know whether to hug the director or simply shake her hand. She opted for the latter and tried to look professional.

"I appreciate the opportunity to work with you," Jordan said, surprised at the firmness in her voice.

"Hey, it's a good piece. Vinnie'll be proud, huh?" As Danny laughed at her words, her face filled with the lines and crinkles of a lifetime of satisfaction. This was a woman who loved what she did, who was devoted to the adventure of life in the theater, knowing full well there was nothing smooth or easy about it. She pressed Jordan's shoulder and pushed open the door for her that spilled onto a crowded sidewalk.

"See ya soon, Jordan Riddle!"

As the door slammed behind her, Jordan cringed at the mention of Vinnie's name and brushed it away like a cobweb. She would not let the strange memory of her last encounter with Vinnie stain this feeling. Instead, she reached into the front pocket of her jeans, looking for a few dimes or quarters. Around the corner she found a pay phone on the wall next to a deli and pushed the coin into the slot.

"Sister Leslie? We're in! The Stage Bite is putting on *Windfall* just after Thanksgiving!" Jordan's face was full and bright as she told her friend about the reading, Danny's response, and the talent of the actors in the company. Sister Leslie screamed on the other end, just as a young mother pushed a stroller past Jordan and a teenage boy with a baseball cap turned backward walked by. Jordan smiled at them because this was a day when she wanted to smile at everyone. The mother nodded back and the boy held up his fist in solidarity as he tipped his head toward her. On the corner a cab honked at a bicycle carrier who responded by blowing the whistle he held between his teeth. Then they both sped through the intersection like they were racing, huge smiles on their faces. A group of Japanese tourists watched it all from atop the double-decker Big Apple tour bus, snapping photos and pointing at the show below them.

Jordan hung up the phone and walked toward the subway, still smiling at everyone who hurried by. As she skipped down the steps into the subway, she saw a small brown-haired woman with topaz eyes climbing up. The woman wore a black jacket and brown slacks, and Jordan could not help but think of her mother as she looked at the woman. The idea that she would be here in a few weeks was almost more excitement than she could bear on this day. Jordan planned to take her all over New York, show her every café, museum, and tourist site she had come to love. She wanted her mama's first trip to Gotham to be as thrilling and fantastic as hers had been.

Her father would no doubt be beside himself, Jordan thought.

When she arrived at the Dream Time Tavern, Jordan found Jack in his usual spot, chopping onions behind the counter in the kitchen. She came up quietly behind him—placing her fingers over her lips to tell the other cooks to keep quiet—and moved her hands over his eyes. Jack stopped the motion of his knife and laughed.

"All right, mate. It's only going to be funny if you've just won the lottery and decided to share." Jack tapped the counter with his empty hand and played along with the game.

"Better. You've just become the proud boss of one of New York's hottest new playwrights!"

"Oh, blimey, now I've got to find a new waitress, I suppose." Jack set down the knife, grabbed the hands on his eyes, and spun around to see Jordan's rich brown eyes and lashes inches from his. Neither moved. Both seemed stunned by the face across from them, frozen for a lovely minute. An entire conversation took place between the two without any words at all, a mutual understanding from one gaze to the other.

"Today's specials, Jack? Hello? What are they?" A stocky waiter had rushed in, noticed the chalkboard was blank, and insisted on knowing what to tell his customers. Jordan's face went pink as she stepped back toward the refrigerator, but Jack kept staring at her. As he did, a slight but certain sound escaped the sides of his mouth.

"You were saying, Jordan?" Jack waited to hear the rest of Jordan's news. His face, smooth and cleanly shaved, was centered on whatever might come out of Jordan's mouth as if that was the only important information of the day. The stocky waiter looked at Jordan, then at Jack. He rolled his eyes, turned around, and walked back into the restaurant.

"The Stage Bite Theater is producing my play, Jack. It opens after Thanksgiving." Jordan leaned against the gray refrigerator door. "That's all." She reached into her bag for her apron and tied it around her waist. The kitchen was hot and busy with workers coming and going, and Jordan suddenly just wanted to blend in.

"Well, it's about bloody time someone in this town recognized talent when they saw it." Jack was now standing in front of Jordan, extending his hand to her.

"Congratulations, Jordan. You deserve it." He smiled as she took his hand. They shook and held each other's hand for a little longer than usual before pulling them back to their sides. Jack's shoulders were broad and proud, and Jordan felt a small breeze slide around her cheeks, cooling her off and helping her relax. This man meant what he said to her.

"Well, I don't know if I deserve it. But thank God for small miracles!" And for the next few minutes, while she prepped the salad plates and filled the salt shakers, Jordan reviewed for Jack all that happened at the Stage Bite that afternoon. How the actors' voices had found the right tones for their characters, how Danny's vision for directing the play impressed her, how even the theater was an ideal space for this particular play. It really was a godsend, a good fit, a gift. Jordan believed that was all true.

Apparently so did Jack, because he had not moved an inch as Jordan flew around the kitchen, listening to her rattle off the events of the day, still smiling. When she finally stopped she glanced up at her boss, who reached out his fingers and cradled her wrist like it was a bouquet of flowers.

"Save me a ticket for opening night, okay?" Jack asked with a humility she hadn't seen in him before, as if attending the theater to see her play was a privilege he had never experienced but had always hoped for.

Jordan pushed on her glasses. "Sure, Jack, but what about the Dream Time?" She couldn't recall many nights when Jack was not working there.

He shrugged his shoulders like he had made the right choice, smiled again, and went back to his knife and onions. Jordan laughed at his response as she watched him, feeling even more grateful than she had after she left Danny and the actors a few hours earlier. She hurried out into the restaurant and began waiting on her customers. The night matched the goodness of the day because each table left her a twenty-percent tip. Certainly, this rated as one of Jordan's all-time best Saturdays since coming to New York. By the time she got back to her apartment, Jordan was sure she was at least three inches taller.

Taller still when the phone rang and it was Jack making sure she'd gotten home safely.

The weeks that followed were exhausting in the best possible way. Jordan would leave a morning temp job—that suddenly seemed to drop out of nowhere—hurry directly to the Stage Bite for afternoon rehearsal, and by five o'clock catch a subway uptown to the Dream Time for an evening shift. She'd collapse in her bed by midnight or 1:00 a.m. after talking on the phone with Jack—who was calling regularly—or catching up with Barry to find out how his rehearsals were going. Some mornings Jordan would get up early to fix a scene Danny had asked her for or to fit in a jog around Central Park. On the couple of days she had off, she managed to make it to the poet's corner at Saint John's for some reflection, often running into Sister Leslie, who insisted on buying her friend lunch.

Every minute of the month seemed accounted for, but to Jordan it never seemed busy. Busyness drained the passion out of people. These four weeks, though, were not busy. They were full—

brimming with the provisions, joys, and challenges Jordan needed to watch a dream spring from someplace in the future to life in the now. The process energized her.

The morning of November 21 Jordan was on the bus heading toward LaGuardia Airport. She sat next to the window, her nose almost touching the glass, watching the buildings, shops, and people change sizes and colors as the bus passed through various neighborhoods. An old Carole King song ran through her head, and she couldn't help but sing it under her breath: "I feel the earth move under my feet... I feel the sky tumbling down, tumbling down... I feel my heart start to trembling..." Then she'd glance at the pages in a novel on her lap or back out the window, and sing her song, though none could hold her attention for long. In a few minutes she'd be at the airport, waiting for her mama's plane. Jordan didn't have many visitors from out of state.

She stood beneath the flight information monitor, found the gate where the flight from Jackson would be coming in, and hurried toward it. Unfortunately, the flight was a few minutes early, and the bus had made Jordan a few minutes late, so she quickened her pace, dodging in and out of the passengers and flight attendants who filled the terminal. She was determined not to miss seeing her mother's face when she got off the plane. Though they talked on the phone once or twice a month and wrote each other letters regularly, Jordan had not seen her mother since the spring she'd flown to Mobile to visit her aunt, and her mother had come down from Jackson. That was two years ago. Jordan had been homesick for a southern spring, the smell of magnolias and cherry blossoms, and the taste of fried catfish and grits, so her aunt sent her a ticket and surprised her by bringing her mama down too. Cynthia Sue was good like that.

Her daddy never knew about that trip.

When Jordan arrived at the gate, the captains were just walking out, adjusting their caps and chatting as if that was the easiest flight they'd flown. She waited a few more minutes, looking down the empty ramp, until she realized no one was left on the plane. A tiny flicker of disappointment welled up in her eyes. She leaned over the drinking fountain, took several long sips, and collected herself. She'd go to the baggage claim; that was the backup plan. But as she stood up and dried off her face with her hand, she felt a tap on her shoulder.

" 'Scuse me, miss, you look like a nice New Yorker. Could you help out a couple of lost southern girls?"

It was Aunt Cyn. As Jordan screamed in the terminal, a security guard sitting on a stool across from the drinking fountain glanced up, then back at his newspaper like this type of interaction happened every day. Jordan grabbed her aunt with both arms and twirled her around in a circle of laughter, not letting go of her hands until she suddenly realized her mother was not with her.

Jordan stopped instantly.

"Where's my mama?"

"Freshenin' up. You know how much coffee those stewardesses pump into you!" No sooner had she said this than Jeanie appeared from behind her, a wide grin on her face. Jordan immediately saw how pale her mama looked, but she laughed again and squeezed her mother so tightly they looked liked a single human blur.

Within an hour they were sitting in a taxi crossing the Triboro Bridge, admiring the skyline of New York shining in the morning sun and talking about the flight, the surprise of Cynthia Sue, and their plans for the week. They did not stop talking until the cab driver pulled over to the corner in front of Jordan's building, ripped off a white piece of paper from the dashboard, and handed it behind him without ever turning his head. Cynthia Sue grabbed it, made a face at her niece, and laid two twenty-dollar bills in the driver's hand.

By the time they reached the top of the stairs to Jordan's apartment, Barry was just coming out of his door. His black leather bag slung over his shoulder matched his jacket, and his short dark hair stood off his head, a gelled sculpture of disarray.

"Well, look who's here! I was hoping I'd get to meet your mama before I left for work," he hollered and then hugged Jeanie like he was hugging his own mother. Jordan introduced him to her aunt as well, and he grabbed her too.

"Great to meet you both. You'll have an amazing time with this fabulous girl of yours. Gotta run—off to rehearsal." Barry kissed Jordan on the cheek and raced down the stairs. The three women laughed as they waved after him and walked into Jordan's studio.

"Welcome to my humble abode. The tour won't take long," Jordan said as she took her mother and aunt around the one-room home, pointing out where the teacups were and the towel rack above the toilet, and telling the stories of various plants, photos, and candles she'd picked up at street fairs. When they paused in front of the couch and noticed the family photo hanging behind it, no one said anything. But Jordan's mother stared hard at the four Riddles in the picture, and all the while Jordan stared at her.

"Your daddy wanted to come, hon, but he's so busy at the church as their new senior pastor," Jeanie said softly, still looking at the picture. Jordan knew he wouldn't have come if he had all the time in the world, but she decided not to challenge her mama. The light on her mother's face showed Jordan just how frail she had become. She seemed smaller, weaker even, than the last time she'd seen her. Dark pockets were wedged between her eyes and her cheeks. Jordan took her hand.

"Nice place, hon. I especially like the bathtub in the middle. Very practical." Cynthia Sue teased her niece, pulling Jordan's shoulders in close to her and lightening the mood. Jordan was about to respond when her aunt took over. "But we've got another surprise for you. Pack your bag 'cuz you're staying with us at the Waldorf, compliments of the *Mobile Beacon* and a whole truck load of press discounts!"

The three women grinned and squealed in unison, and Jordan did as she was told. Then she taped a note to Barry's door explaining her living promotion for the next week, sat in a cab for the second time that day, and twenty minutes later walked into the lobby of one of Manhattan's most posh hotels. When they saw the size of their room, all three women erupted again in laughter, falling onto the beds and kicking off their shoes. The hotel room was bigger than Jordan's apartment.

That night they sat in orchestra seats to watch the musical *Les Misérables* playing at the Helen Hayes Theater, compliments again of Auntie Cyn's press discounts. Jordan did not mind at all sitting through the performance as opposed to standing in the back with the ushers. It felt good to see a show just to enjoy it rather than usher for it. And this show certainly made her cry every time she saw it.

Jordan was curious how her mother would respond to a slice of New York's theater world. As far as she knew, this was her mama's first time to the theater, and considering how her father had always reacted to it, she wondered why she had agreed to go at all. Jordan hoped it would not be an extra weight on her mother's shoulders as she stood between her daughter and her husband. But when they went for dessert afterward at The Pink Teacup, her mama did not say much except that she thought the show was "real nice." Instead, she sipped her coffee and hummed, listening every now and then to Jordan and her aunt discuss each detail of the production, from the rotating set to the story's spiritual implications. Jordan caught her mother's eyes and saw they were misty.

"You okay, Mama?"

"Just wish your brother could have seen that. Wouldn't he have loved that story?"

Jordan and Cynthia exchanged looks while Jeanie smiled at them. Jordan hadn't heard her mother talk about James for years. Her mama's comment stunned her.

"Jeanie, you must be exhausted," Cynthia Sue said. "Let's get you to bed, okay? We'll need our energy for all the fun tomorrow."

Jeanie nodded and let her sister-in-law lead her to the street. Jordan followed behind, suddenly unsure of the week ahead.

Thanksgiving morning they woke before the sun came up, caught a subway downtown from the Waldorf, and by 7:30 a.m. had their place in front of Macy's department store on Thirty-fourth and Broadway. The famous Thanksgiving Day parade started at nine o'clock, but crowds began to gather at Herald Square and along Broadway hours before. The three women were layered with sweaters, jackets, and scarves to fight the November chill. They stood beside a father and mother with three small children at their side who were equally bundled in winter coats. Together, they shivered in the morning air and moved their feet up and down to keep warm. Jordan clapped her hands and smiled at the children.

By 9:00 a.m. the parade had begun. Floats with Broadway singers and pop stars went by, the Rockettes from Radio City Music Hall danced in front of them, and huge balloons of cartoon characters floated high above them, soaring slowly in the cold fall air. Thousands of people stood around Jordan and her mama and aunt, cheering with each performance and applauding both the performers and the workers who kept the parade moving.

When the marching band from Ole Miss High School in Oxford, Mississippi, passed in front of them, playing an upbeat version of "Swing Low, Sweet Chariot," Jordan's mama cheered and waved her arms like she'd just become the band's conductor. Jordan had never seen her mother so delighted by a song. Maybe it was the fact that it was a band from her home state, maybe it was the old Negro spiritual. But Jeanie danced and jumped around the sidewalk like it was the last time she would sing the heavenly chorus. Jordan and her auntie joined in the small-town enthusiasm, partly because they were surprised at Jeanie's public display of emotion, and partly because moving around kept them warm.

Cynthia Sue shrugged her shoulders at Jordan and turned up her own version of a jig to the swing tunes. The children beside them giggled when they saw this and immediately imitated her. Jordan laughed and shouted and shook her head in awe at another of New York's divine moments. Here, in the middle of Manhattan, twenty thousand people watched a Thanksgiving Day parade and two Mississippi women twice her age were dancing with Latino children in the street! Where else but New York City could she witness such an event?

When the band finished its song, Jeanie, Cynthia, the children, and Jordan hollered and whistled with a volume that would have made the entire state of Mississippi proud. They slapped each other's backs like they had won a great victory and chuckled until their faces ached. Another float with *Sesame Street* characters was passing, and the parents beside them quickly pointed their children's attention back on the parade.

"I'm going to get us some hot chocolate," Jordan yelled to her mother and auntie, who nodded their heads and went back to watching Big Bird. Jordan elbowed her way through the crowd, smiling and excusing herself, until she found a corner deli open. She waited in line for the drinks, put them in a bag, and made her way back into the masses of thankful watchers.

Back in front of Macy's, she pushed her way through a few crowds to the spot where they'd been standing. Her mama was not there. Jordan stepped around fathers, dodged children, and walked in a circle in front of the store until she finally found the family they'd been standing next to. But she still did not see her mother. Anywhere.

Panic punched the inside of her stomach. She looked over people, around faces, past floats and bands and clowns. She could not find her. She did not see her aunt anywhere either. Jordan's pulse shot out of her coat and the sky went dark. Around and around she turned, dizzy from the search, terrified by the whirl of chaos blowing around her.

She had been here before. The day she lost her brother at the beach. The day the storm took him away.

"Help," Jordan mumbled into the frigid air. "Help, God. Help!" She was turning still; the faces around her had melted into leaves and trees thrown by a massive wind. Her face felt frozen but her arms were on fire, her eyes stinging at the motion. She reached for a breath with her lungs, but she could not find one. When she reached again, everything turned black.

Cynthia Sue's familiar face was what Jordan saw first. She was grinning at her niece, still wearing her winter scarf, still looking like she did when they'd come to the parade.

"Hey little girl. I must have just passed you. It took me forever to find the ladies' room in Macy's." She spoke calmly to Jordan, as if nothing had just happened. Jordan studied her face, her rosy skin, her perfect makeup. And she felt her aunt take something out of her hand.

"Thanks, hon. This will hit the spot." Cynthia Sue slurped the hot chocolate and stared back at the parade as a Broadway singer passed on a makeshift sleigh singing "Jingle Bell Rock." Jordan shook her head to get her bearings again. She looked up and saw the sign on Macy's department store. She looked up the street and saw a giant turkey flying in the air, an icy blue sky beyond the buildings.

"Where's Mama?" Jordan's words were crisp, panicked. Her aunt looked around and realized her sister-in-law was no longer standing next to her. She was, in fact, not anywhere close by. And then Cynthia Sue's face began to jitter. Within seconds she recovered her control.

"You scour that side; I'll stay on this side," she yelled over the noise, pointing. "We'll meet back at the hotel in exactly two hours."

Jordan nodded and listened as she heard her aunt yell to the family who'd stood beside them. They seemed to think she'd left sometime after the Mississippi band, but they weren't sure.

Jordan crossed the street and poked and pushed her way through dozens of people, stopping every five feet to observe the faces and sizes of the groups she'd just gone through. She asked police officers on the corners and vendors on the sidewalk if they'd seen a short, pale, brown-haired woman in a scarf walk by. Everyone they asked shook their head, as if the idea of noticing someone like that on a morning like this was absurd. It was.

Jordan imagined the worst. She tried to stay calm, praying the whole time, but the end result was the same: her mother was gone. She did not want to imagine a world where her mama was not here. Her father would probably blame her for this as well. And then Jordan would be absolutely alone.

Surely he took up our infirmities and carried our sorrows. She remembered the words from the verse and drank in the promise. A strange feeling of fear and calm blended over her as she walked, still looking for her mama, still wondering what in the world had happened, but somehow believing she would see her again.

By the time Jordan found her aunt in the lobby of the Waldorf, they both were frozen and confused. They hugged. As Jordan stayed in her aunt's arms, she looked across the lobby. There was her mother, sitting quietly, her head resting on the top of her hand, her eyes closed.

"Mama, where did you go? What happened?" Jordan was beside her mother now, her aunt right behind them. But Jeanie did not open her eyes. A faint little smile moved her lips, and Jordan leaned into her mother's face. She heard her humming. Her head moved slightly with the melody, and there was no mistaking the song.

"Swing Low, Sweet Chariot."

Jordan blinked. She knew her mother had been sick, but this was something altogether new to her. She glanced at her aunt, whose mascara had smeared below her eyes, and all Jordan knew to do was grab Jeanie's hand.

When she did Jeanie looked up into her daughter's face. Her smile grew.

"Your father loves you, you know that, Jordan? He just thinks he's—"

"Mama, where were you? We looked everywhere."

"Wasn't the band wonderful? I followed them down the beach. Did you hear it?" Jeanie's words had a haunted color in them, and now Jordan was afraid.

"Mama, this is New York. Today's Thanksgiving. We were at the parade." Jordan was almost shouting at her mother, kneeling beside her in the lobby of the Waldorf, hoping she could wake her out of whatever nightmare she was having. Cynthia Sue put her hand on Jordan's shoulder for support.

Jeanie closed her eyes again so they crinkled. Then she opened them slowly, as if the effort was a greater burden than keeping them shut. She sighed. She raised her shoulders, looked at her daughter, and patted her cheek.

"Gee, honey, your face is cold. You shouldn't have been at the parade so long. It's freezing out there." Jeanie stood up and hugged Jordan quickly, then let her go.

"Honestly, Jeanie Riddle, you almost made me a prayin' woman," Cynthia Sue said. "We were looking everywhere for you. Scared the daylights out of us."

"Well, I thought the plan was to come back here. Sorry."

"Mama, I thought I lost you," Jordan whispered to her mother, holding her hand and standing beside her.

"I am not always going to be around, Jordan."

"Don't say things like that."

"Well, it's true, hon. I have cancer, you know."

"You'll beat it," Cynthia said quickly, always the fighter. "The treatments these days are amazing. And they caught it in time."

Jeanie looked at her sister-in-law calmly.

"I know. But that still doesn't mean I'm going to be around forever."

The sentence was strange and soft on Jordan's ears, not at all what she was expecting to hear from her mother after thinking she'd just lost her in the city. But it was oddly comforting at the same time. She did not know how to interpret what she'd just heard, yet for some reason it gave her a bizarre sense of relief.

"Now, for heaven's sake, I'm starving. Where are we going for lunch?" Jeanie was in the revolving door, swirling out onto the street when her sister-in-law and daughter raced after her.

They spent the next three days exploring the city as tourists: strolling through The Cloisters at Fort Tryon Park in northern Manhattan—a religious exhibit of the Metropolitan Museum of Art—and window shopping on Fifth Avenue. They rode the Staten Island Ferry across New York Harbor to see the Statue of Liberty. Jordan even took them to the Dream Time Tavern for Bush Burgers and Kangaroo Pie—and to meet Jack.

"G'day, mate," he said as he brought out their orders. "Pleasure to meet you. And welcome to the Dream Time."

"Nice to meet you," Jeanie said, observing each move he made.

"Have you been enjoying New York?" he asked while setting down a plate.

"Sure have. Say something else, Jack," Cynthia Sue teased him. "What an accent! You're a lucky girl, Jordan!"

Jordan's eyes widened at her aunt in disbelief.

"What? What did I say wrong, sugar?"

"No, I'm the lucky one," Jack interjected, setting down their drinks. He smiled at Jordan.

"See there, hon, that proves my point!" Cynthia said. They all laughed at the exchange. Jeanie watched him hurry back to the kitchen and nodded at her daughter. Jordan felt relieved by her mother's approval, but she still couldn't stop worrying about her. She'd wanted to talk with her about the biopsy, about the treatments and the recovery strategies, about how she was feeling, but every time she tried, her mama seemed far away. It was clear that she was happy as a tourist and did not want to think about anything else. So Jordan asked her aunt to snap as many photographs of them as she had the patience for, including one at the Dream Time. With Jack.

As they were leaving the Tavern, Jack turned to Jordan and pulled a punch she did not anticipate.

"So, Jordan, you have invited your mother and aunt to the dress rehearsal of your play, right?" He beamed at her, then raised his eyebrows toward the older women.

"This is the first I've heard of it, hon," Cynthia Sue said. Jordan was suddenly nervous.

"Well, it's the last night you're here and—"

"And what?" her mother said sternly.

"And I just wasn't sure you'd want to come. I mean, for all I know you think my playwriting is some silly hobby, and I'm just a—"

"She's a talented woman, ladies. I plan on going and hope you will too," Jack said, standing firmly between them. Jordan's palms went moist as she waited, anxious at what she might hear. A horn honked out on the street.

"Couldn't imagine a better way to end our trip, could you, Jeanie?" Cynthia Sue turned to her sister-in-law. Jeanie hesitated, looked up into Jordan's face, and her eyes filled. Indecision ran across her mama's face, as if going might breach some covenant she'd made with her husband, but not going would hurt her only living child.

"I'd do anything to see you and your daddy come together again, hon. You know that. Anything."

No one moved. Jeanie paused and gazed at the face of her child. Jordan felt Jack's hand on her back to steady her.

"It's my work, Mama, and I love it. It's who I am. And I don't think he'll ever accept that," Jordan said, feeling a small fire in her throat as the noise of the Tavern suddenly grew behind her.

"He just raised you to be different. He's always thought you could do more than—"

"I think I'm doing exactly what I'm supposed to do. In fact, I'm more sure about this than I ever have been. And if Daddy doesn't think so, well, I can't make him understand." Jordan's voice was full and firm, a song of conviction slipped around each syllable. She pulled Jack's hand from behind her and held it in hers. Tight. Jeanie walked inches from her daughter's face and looked steady into it.

"You sound just like he did…a long time ago." A fragile smile formed on Jeanie's lips. "He won't like it, and I don't understand it, but"—Jordan watched her mama's face turn pink—"I'll be right behind your aunt. And your friend Jack."

Jeanie kissed Jordan's cheek, turned around, and walked out onto the busy street. "Y'all comin'?" she asked. "I've got to go buy a new dress!"

Cynthia Sue and Jordan ran after her. Jack waved from the window before turning back to the kitchen.

FOURTEEN

The phone had not stopped ringing since Peter was sworn in as senior pastor of Second Baptist. A few men called to congratulate him on his new pastoral responsibilities. Some mothers called for advice about their children. Most people called, though, simply wanting to make sense of the reverend's sudden decision to "retire early." Peter spoke as little as possible of Dr. Stately's gambling problem; he was struggling to understand it himself. Still, as folks pressed him, wanting to know the details behind their pastor's announcement, Peter grew more and more thankful the deacons had kept him unaware of the circumstances. Now there was little he could say.

"Just pray for him," Peter told each parishioner who asked. He said it not because he particularly believed in prayer these days, but because that's what people expected to hear from a senior pastor. After all, they expected their church leader to guide them through all the terrible turbulence that entered their lives. When the boss came down hard on them at work, for instance, the pastor's job was to encourage them to press on. When the children were sick, he visited, and when a marriage got rocky, he provided the tools to work it out. He was more than a man who spoke from the pulpit each Sunday morning. Around here a senior pastor was the model of Christian virtue and endurance, stronger than most in spiritual discipline and insight, taller in stature than anyone who walked through the door, and closer to Jesus as a result. People listened to his voice, believed what he said, and did what he told them. Because Dr. Stately had been such a pastor, he sat high on the pedestal of church leadership, so high that a fall was long and painful.

Maybe folks expected too much. Maybe Peter did too.

Peter returned the receiver to its cradle, rubbed his temples, and sighed. He jotted a name on a yellow pad of paper, keeping track of each church member he had spoken with over the past week and writing a few notes beside the name to help him remember their conversation. No sooner had he set down his pencil than the phone rang again. Peter shut his eyes tight, breathed, and shook his head, as if that would make it stop ringing. For as long as he could remember he had wanted the role of shepherding a church, but he was not sure this was what he had in mind. It rang again. He picked up the phone but kept his eyes shut as he answered.

"Peter?"

The sound of Dr. Stately's voice on the other end jolted Peter in his chair. He popped open his eyes and felt a hot breeze of anger and confusion blow across his face.

"It's Dr. Stately. I wanted to explain a few things."

"Not much to explain. You stole. You gambled. You resigned. What else is there?"

Silence vibrated in Peter's ear. He grabbed his pencil and drew a line from the top of the page to the bottom, adding occasional triangles or boxes at the sides. His stomach turned over as he waited. He heard Dr. Stately clear his throat.

"It's all true. I admit it. But there is still another matter."

"I don't want to know about it." The lead of Peter's pencil broke as he made a deep scratch on the paper.

"That's exactly why I'm calling. Because you haven't wanted to know about it for the past five years."

"Is that right? What exactly would that be, Dr.—?" Peter stopped himself. He could not say the name.

"I think you know."

"I didn't know a thing about your gambling. Why would I know what you're talking about now?"

"Because it's about Jordan."

Peter tossed the pencil in the trash can and pushed his glasses closer to his eyes. His toes beat up and down against the floor.

"What *about* her?"

"She's never been a bad kid, Peter. You think we don't know how she's hurt you. Listen, she might not be who you want her to be, but that doesn't mean—"

"Amazing insight, coming from you."

"You have every right to be angry with me. But hang on to this bitterness with your own flesh and blood, and it will eat you alive."

The edge of Peter's mouth throbbed as the words penetrated his skin. He was smirking, not because the words had come from Dr. Stately, the man whose chief sin had just wreaked havoc on the life of Second Baptist. Peter was smirking because he could not help it; Dr. Stately was right. Again. And he resented that.

"It's a slippery slope, Peter. It starts out innocent enough, and the next thing you know you can't let go of the damn thing. It takes over."

"You should know." Peter stood up as he spoke, the phone cord curling around his elbow.

Dr. Stately coughed. "I do know. And I've got to live with that. Just like you'll have to live with your disappointment toward Jordan. If you don't deal with it, believe me, you'll lose your church, too. And everything or everyone that's important to you."

The sunshine outside the window had left the day, and Peter could see the lights in the parking lot come up. His mouth felt dry and a ring of pressure ached around his neck.

"Well, thanks for the advice," he said. "Tell me this one thing, though. Why'd you do it?" The agony of the question had weighed him down since that night the deacons first confronted the reverend.

"I told you. I was bored."

"I heard you. I didn't buy it then and I don't now. You'd built a solid ministry for thirty years. People respected you. How could you be bored?" Peter's forehead felt hot, and a film of sweat formed across it as he waited for the answer.

Dr. Stately paused, then in the softest voice Peter had ever heard from him, he said, "The terrible irony of the church, Peter, is how lonely it is to lead. You'll see... God help you."

The sudden click and dial tone in Peter's ear jarred him. He held out the phone in front of him and glared at it as if Dr. Stately's words were still inside and he was trying to decipher them. He was not sure if it was the conversation that made him shiver or the draft from the hallway when Loretta opened the door to his office.

"Okay, Pastor, I'm outta here," Loretta said as she laid a small stack of pink memos on his desk. She'd put on her thick blue coat to protect her from the December air and the strap of her purse hung around the elbow crease of her arm. But when she glanced up at her new boss, she stopped still.

"Lord Almighty, you look like you've just seen a ghost. Everything okay, Pastor?"

Peter set down the phone, pulled out his pastor's voice, and bluffed. "Just another interesting phone call. You take care now, Loretta, ya hear?"

Loretta smiled at the lightness in Peter's recovery, patted his arm, and waved as she walked out of his office and down the hall. He watched her in the parking lot as she slid into the old station wagon she'd had for years and drove off. She'd been a faithful church secretary for nearly as long as he'd been alive, and he wondered how she was feeling in the wake of Dr. Stately's departure. As he pulled down the blinds in his window and reached for his coat, it occurred to him that he'd never thought to ask her how she felt about much of anything. Until now.

By the time Peter walked through the front door, Jeanie had macaroni and fried chicken on the table. She'd been back from New York for almost a week now, and Peter thought she seemed both lighthearted yet far away. He had hoped her trip would be a useful distraction for his wife, who had seemed distressed by the news of her health as well as her husband's new position. But he wasn't so sure the trip had been useful at all. The rings under her eyes seemed grayer and her steps slower than they were before she left. Maybe she was still recovering from a week as a tourist in the busiest city in the country. Or maybe the surgery hadn't been so easy on her body after all.

Or both.

He pulled the chair out from the table and sat down, loosening his tie and setting his glasses in his pocket. He pushed the palms of his hands around his eyes and massaged the tiredness out of them. When the smell of chicken floated past his nose, Peter stopped rubbing, picked up a drumstick, and took a bite.

"No grace?" Jeanie asked, looking blankly at her husband. Peter did not hear a trace of emotion in her voice; she was not judging him for ignoring the dinner ritual nor was she enthusiastic about talking to God. Hers was the face of a child with the flu, confused about when the medicine was coming.

Peter set down his chicken, bowed his head, and mumbled, "I'm glad for a good meal and a wife who went to the trouble of making it. Amen."

She stared at him as he spoke, waiting for him to finish his first couple of bites. She was used to waiting. After she passed him the macaroni, then the salt and pepper, Jeanie ran her index finger across her forehead, pushing back her hair and fixing its shape.

"Peter, I've been wanting to tell you, I saw one of her plays," she said as if she were talking about a sale at the Jitney Jungle.

Peter's chin was leaning over his plate, his upper body tucked in close to the table. He'd just put a forkful of macaroni in his mouth when she made her announcement, and he wasn't sure it was going to stay there when it registered with him what she'd said. He chewed quickly and swallowed.

"What do you mean, hon?" It was a day to bluff.

"Your sister and I went to a dress rehearsal of a play Jordan wrote herself. With a boyfriend of hers. The last day we were there. It was nice. He was too."

Peter took another bite of the chicken, washed it down with a sip of milk, and shrugged his shoulders at the woman across from him. He tried to smile.

"It was in Greenwich Village, at a small theater, but quite a few people came. The cast and the director seemed to think it was a good play. So did Cyn." Jeanie blinked at Peter. Her eyes shot from his glass to his knife and back to his face. She was nervous, and he hated that his daughter had made her so. He scraped some noodles onto his fork with his knife and took another bite.

Jeanie shifted in her chair. "I knew you wouldn't be happy about it."

"Then why'd you go?" Now it was Peter's voice that did not hold any emotion. He was empty, void of any direction or energy. His bones felt weary from the day, and his mind was still fighting the warning he'd heard on the phone from Dr. Stately. Though he lifted his shoulders and chest for a breath, he had more trouble finding one than keeping it.

Jeanie, however, was gaining steam. She'd pushed around the food on her plate though she never ate a bite of any of it. With a sudden gasp, she gulped an entire glass of water, slammed it on the table, and pushed her chair away.

"Why did I go? Because I had to see for myself what you've said was so evil about our daughter for the past four years."

The temperature in the kitchen suddenly felt like the hottest Mississippi summer day on record. Red blotches filled Jeanie's face.

"I never said that about—"

"Not with words. But in every other way possible, you have all but drawn an *A* on her chest, Peter Riddle, and I can't handle it much longer." She was standing up now, putting away dishes, opening the refrigerator door and slamming it shut, shoving the teakettle under the faucet before plopping it back on the stove. "I *won't* handle it."

Jeanie tossed a napkin toward the garbage but missed. Peter picked it up and dropped it in the can.

"Honestly, I don't know what's wrong with it. Just because it's not inside a church doesn't mean it's doing so much harm." She was pacing as she spoke.

"Calm down, hon. The doctor said you needed to relax more. I don't want to see you worked up over something silly like—"

"What?! You think it's silly to stop talking to your own daughter for almost five years because she chose a different life from the one you wanted for her?"

"That's not what I said."

"What if she's good at it, Peter? What if she's actually making a difference up there, reaching people who would never in a million years step into some decrepit church building filled with a bunch of gossips, gamblers, and hypocrites—like you—who get together Sunday mornings to 'praise the Lord'?" She raised her hands in the air and twirled in a circle to mock him. Fire was behind her voice, and her face was a collage of colors. When she stopped, her eyes stretched wide, frozen open, glaring not at Peter but through him and into his veins.

"I've had enough!" she screamed. Her words slugged him low and hard, knocking the breath out of him and sending him reeling. He stumbled back toward the living room and fell on the couch, feeling struck from all sides. Her cancer, Dr. Stately, this rage, their son, Jordan, all tumbled around him like shattered glass: painful, cutting, raw. He covered his head with his arms and hands and curled his legs toward his chest.

"Oh, God," he moaned. But God was surely dead to Peter. And if he were alive, he was going to great lengths to make sure it was Peter who died.

He moaned again and writhed and groaned. He felt sick and could taste his dinner coming up.

But like a cornered animal, Peter sat up straight when he heard Jeanie hurry into the living room. Her eyes were still frozen, but now they were nowhere near him. Anger did not fill them, only deep, deep sorrow. They'd gone to another land, that place where hope and joy no longer lived. Jeanie picked up her keys and pushed open the front door. Before she took another step, though, she turned toward the man on the couch.

"I'm...going...out."

She looked straight ahead and did not move.

"This is the time, Peter. This is for you."

Peter sprang off the couch, grabbed his wife, and turned her toward him.

"What did you just say?"

The question hurt her ears.

"I'm going out."

"After that. Didn't you say something else?" His grip on her wrist was tight, and she squirmed under it. She shook her head at him, coming back into the present and recognizing the living room behind him. Jeanie's topaz eyes looked up.

"No. That was all I said," her lip quivered. "I wanted to say so much more, but I...but you..." Then Jeanie flicked back her head and began to wail and scream like a mother at her child's funeral. She wept for the cancer that invaded her body, the son they'd lost at sea, the daughter who'd been estranged, and for the anger that had stolen her husband. She hurled it all into Peter's arms, mumbling about each until she melted on the floor into a terrified child who was lost in her nightmare. She could not stop shaking.

Peter cried too. Into the beautiful brown hair he had always loved as he held his wife. Somewhere over the years he'd lost his bride. How did it happen? Why had God been so absent? Why was there so much pain between them? Now they rocked against each other's bodies, quietly and somberly, until sleep finally relieved them.

Sometime in the night Peter picked up his wife, carried her to bed, and pulled the blanket up to her shoulders. The next morning, he could not remember doing it, but he could think of no other explanation when he woke up next to her on their bed.

He lifted his head from his pillow to stare at her face, swollen from the eruption of tears and still asleep as the sun came up. Her words about Jordan pierced him, and his head hurt from remembering. He swallowed, but there was nothing in his throat, so he got up and walked to the kitchen. As he tried to put the events of the previous day out of his mind, Peter gulped a glass of water. He made a pot of coffee, but all he could think about were the words thrown at him in the last twenty-four hours. Like tiny demons sitting on his shoulder, they harassed and taunted him.

It'll eat you alive.

What if she's good at it?

Lonely to lead.

Hypocrites like you.

Peter slammed his fist on the counter to drown out the noise, held on to the edge, and gasped for air. He closed his eyes and told himself this would all be over soon. One way or another they would move on and everything would be as it once was. He begged for mercy. He had to keep going.

As he drank his coffee, Peter read his daily schedule. He shook his head in dread when he saw what was scheduled for 10:00 a.m.: the appointment with Dr. Hollander to hear the results of the biopsy. The timing could not have been worse in light of all that Jeanie had endured already, but they needed to know what the next step would be for her treatment. Peter's stomach ached from the possibility that lay before them. It was likely they'd have to operate again. Or she'd have to endure chemotherapy or radiation. She was already so frail; he wasn't sure how her body would cope with so much shock to it. But maybe it would help her get better.

Maybe through the pain healing would come.

Gently, he brushed Jeanie's shoulder to wake her. She was groggy from the nightmare of the evening. Back and forth she tossed her head until finally she raised it, looked at Peter sitting above her, and listened to his voice.

"Hon, we're due at the doctor's in a few hours. Biopsy results."

She pulled her body out of the bed and walked toward the shower, taking the cup of coffee Peter had brought her. He watched her slow chalky movement, her wobbly steps, and he followed her in case she could not hold herself up. The bathroom door shut in front of him, and when Peter heard the water running, he wandered back down the hall toward the kitchen.

But he stopped when he got to Jordan's room. And for a minute he fought the impulse to open the door. When he could endure it no longer, he grabbed the doorknob and pushed it back. Peter did not enter the room. He simply looked from the doorway at the remnants his daughter left behind: the single bed, the poster of Fiji, a few high-school yearbooks. Though she had not set foot in this house in almost four years, her presence was still strong. Jeanie had insisted on leaving her room this way.

The sick feeling from the night before clogged the back of his throat, and Peter felt disgust rising from his stomach. His eyes watered, and then, as if a drawbridge were lifted in the back of his mind, he suddenly knew that the object of his disdain was not the girl who used to live here.

It was himself. He was a failure.

A father's desire for his child ached in Peter's arms. He felt it in his veins and muscles, the longing to hold his daughter again, to protect her and comfort her as he had when she was young. The room was empty, though, silent, cold, and empty. His heart was queasy. And for the first time in many years, he could not think of what to do next.

He just stared.

The creak from the bathroom door jolted Peter down the hall and into the kitchen where he placed a piece of toast on a plate for his wife. But she did not eat it once she sat down. Nor did she drink her coffee. Jeanie simply sat at the table, her face tired, her eyes empty and dark.

When they backed out of the driveway, Peter realized he'd left his Day-Timer on the table. He pulled the car back into the driveway and ran back inside. He'd forgotten to turn off the coffeepot too. He pressed his thumb against the switch, grabbed his book, and turned toward the door right when the phone rang. Peter's lungs filled with frustration, and his shoulders sagged. He picked up the receiver.

"Hey Pastor. It's Loretta."

Peter exhaled, pushed back his glasses, and pulled his shoulders back.

"Yes, Loretta?" She heard the shortness in his voice.

"Gotta young man here. Says he has to see you. Now."

"Who?"

"Says you know his daddy from the prison and told him to come by anytime he needed something." She paused. "Apparently he needs something."

"Can he come back in a few hours? I've got another appointment I was just on my way to."

"Let me check." Peter pressed the phone between his neck and shoulder as he waited for Loretta. Johnny's son. Must be in trouble or he would never have come by the church. Peter rubbed the corners of his eyes up under his glasses with his ring finger and shook his head at the timing of the boy's visit.

"Nope. Says he's gotta be somewhere else." Loretta whispered next. "Pastor, this kid seems pretty desperate. Nobody else is here right now. Maybe you better come in?"

Peter agreed, hung up, and walked back to the car, Day-Timer in hand.

"Slight change of plans," he said as he got behind the wheel. Jeanie looked straight ahead like she had anticipated this, like she was familiar with such words.

"Sort of an emergency at the church, hon. A young man whose daddy works at the prison where I go to preach." The taste had returned to his mouth. "Loretta just called, said he was kind of desperate."

The trees were bare that morning, and the sky beyond them cold and icy white. They'd driven halfway down the street before Jeanie responded.

"Of course, Peter. You've got to go. I'll drop you off and drive myself."

Peter glanced at his wife, trying to read her. Her rage from the night before was absent from her face, but something was hidden in her voice.

"Are you sure? We could reschedule with the doctor." He wasn't sure why he said this; Dr. Hollander had told Peter that his appointments were completely filled for weeks to come. He had squeezed this one in because the biopsy results came back and he didn't think it could wait.

"I'm sure. I think I'd rather be alone when I talk with the doctor." A fragile smile formed on Jeanie's lips. "If you don't mind."

She reached across the seat for his hand, a foreign gesture these past months. Her fingers were thin and chilly, but Peter was glad to feel the softness of her skin again.

Except for the distance of her humming, they drove in silence.

When they pulled into the church parking lot, he turned off the car and put his other hand on top of hers.

"You're sure about this?" He stared at her face, her eyes, her lips, trying to understand how she might be feeling. His own emotions were lame and broken, and as much as he wanted to, Peter could not interpret his wife's. She had wanted to support him in his work at the church, often coming alongside him—until recently —regardless of what it meant for her through the years.

These days, though, they stood on separate mountains, a deep valley between them.

"I'm sure," she answered. "It's the right thing to do. It's best this way." Jeanie's eyes froze again as an eerie chord echoed from the sound of her voice. Peter leaned over, turned her chin to his, and kissed her.

"I'll have Loretta or Jimmy drop me off up at the doctor's office as soon as I'm done, okay? Shouldn't take long. Then we can drive home together." Jeanie only looked at Peter as he said this, her mountain slipping farther and farther away from him.

Like she'd just heard a scream in the night, Jeanie snapped her head quickly toward the windshield of the car, serious in her gaze, and stared at something in the parking lot so intensely that Peter looked too. Nothing was there. He glanced back at her. She began to hum again.

"Jeanie, it'll be okay. I know it will." It was his best preacher's voice. He squeezed her hand until, slowly, she drew it back away from his and plopped it on her lap.

" 'Course it will." When she said this Peter gasped. Suddenly, his wife looked the same as when he first saw her in the dining hall of the Bible college: lively, soft, curious. In the short time they'd been sitting in the car, it was as if Jeanie had traveled between two worlds of possibility, caught in both, until she settled into one where happy memories were better than present realities, where pain and separation never intruded on idealism.

She smiled at her husband just as she had at that first dinner they shared together. Then she climbed out of the car, walked around to the driver's side, and waited for Peter to get out. She patted his arm and slid into the seat.

"You take good care, Peter," Jeanie said, looking up into his face before pulling away from the curb and into the street.

She waved from the window.

A battle brewed in Peter's gut as he watched her drive off, the tension of wanting to be two different men at the same time, neither of whom would fail the people he cared about, both of whom would be honest and true. He knew he was not one nor the other, and the bottom of his skull and the top of his neck ached from the war.

The December wind smacked his cheeks.

Johnny's son was not slouching in his seat. Though his long legs stretched out on the floor before him, he sat upright, his shoulders pressed against the back of the chair, and his hands moving on his thighs like they were a piano. He wore his Bulls baseball cap and the same grimy jacket Peter had last seen him in when he picked him up off the street and took him through Captain Billy's.

As soon as Peter walked in, the young man sprang to his feet. He tapped the face of his watch as he searched Peter's face.

"This is the time," he said in a low anxious voice.

The words paralyzed Peter. What did they mean? What could they mean for Johnny's son?

"Well, Pastor, I guess you've met this young man." Loretta was standing next to them, snapping him out of his frigid state. He extended his hand to the young man who shook it and then let go. Peter ushered him into his office as Loretta peered over her glasses at the two.

"What is it? What's wrong?" Peter asked.

"It happened too fast... I didn't know what to do... It was

messed up…" The words spilled out of him, blurry and strange like snow in spring, and moisture formed across his forehead.

"Slow down, Son," Peter said as he sat in his chair behind the desk. "By the way, Johnny never told me your name."

"J. J." He stood up, then sat back down again. "I'm in trouble, Preach. I was with some folks last week I shouldn't of been with and ~~saw some stuff~~ I mean, stuff, I shouldn't of seen." He licked his lips.

"What kind of stuff?" Peter put his hands behind his head so his elbows poked out. If he could appear relaxed, maybe J. J. would relax.

"Oh, man, you know what I mean. Stupid stuff. Drugs."

"Anybody hurt?"

"Naw. Just lots of folks high."

"Were you?" Peter knew it was a bold question, but he figured the son of a prison security guard could handle tough questions.

The young man paused. "No. And that's the point. It scared me enough to never want to hang with them again."

"So? Why'd you come here?"

"So I'd know the right thing to do."

Peter's heart dropped. The putrid taste of failure and fraud lined his mouth when he heard the sincerity of Johnny's son. He could not even think of the last time he'd stopped long enough to wonder what the right thing was, let alone how to do it. For fifteen years the pain of his son's death had turned his heart into a brick wall that nothing and no one could knock over. With each new disappointment or loss another brick was added. Right living for Peter was a long time ago. He laughed.

But when Peter looked up at J. J., he remembered how he had once had the same intense desire. There was a passion in him to pursue what he was made for, to discover why he was created. Like an old friend misses another, Peter missed, ached even, for that passion, and J. J. helped him realize it.

"Preach, c'mon. That's why I came here. I figured you know. Don't give me the silent trip."

"I reckon your daddy would probably know a lot more about doing right than I would, Son."

J. J. took off his hat at the mention of his father and sat up straight again. He did not look afraid when he heard this, nor did he look as angry as he had when Peter first met him. Instead, something seemed to register in his head when he heard his daddy's name, in the same way Peter had remembered his destiny when he looked at J. J.

The two men sat quietly in Peter's office, both thinking through the events and choices, faces and words they'd experienced in the last several weeks. Both stared at themselves in the mirror of their souls, humbly aware of their weaknesses, desperate for a strength that could take them in the direction they were hungry to go: to know the right thing to do.

Peter broke the silence with a question that surprised him

when he heard it drop out of his mouth. He blinked as if he were listening to a different man. "Would you like to pray, Son?"

J. J. nodded at the white pastor across from him and bowed his head, holding his cap on his knees. And for the first time since he could really remember, Peter talked with God. No bluffing or preacher's voice. Straight, truthful, sorry. Just as he was: needy and broken. And somehow, in spite of his years of wandering and bitterness, in spite of his resentment and hypocrisy, he knew he was being heard.

"Amen," J. J. said as Peter finished praying. He put his cap back on and stood up.

"Cool," he added as he shook the pastor's hand again. He nodded his head at Peter, told him he'd see him later, and then he left. Loretta passed J. J. in the doorway, smiled at him, and hurried in to see Peter.

"Would you mind driving me up to Dr. Hollander's, Loretta? Jeanie's got an appointment."

"Got the car keys right here, Pastor." He followed her to the old station wagon, but he did not see his car when they pulled in front of the doctor's office. He asked Loretta to wait while he ran in.

The musty smell of the clinic met him at the door. When he walked into the waiting room, a bell above the door jingled, signaling his entrance. The nurse looked up.

"Dr. Hollander available?" Peter did not wait for a response. He hurried down the hall toward the doctor's office, knocked, and went in. Dr. Hollander was shuffling papers into a pile on one end of the desk. When he saw Peter he stopped shuffling and waited. He did not speak.

"Where's Jeanie?"

"You just missed her." He pushed out his jaw and pulled it in again. Then he folded his arms across his belly.

"Sit down, Peter." Peter did as he was told.

"The biopsy gave us good and bad news. It is malignant, which means we're going to try surgery first to stop it from spreading. I think we can get most of it right now because we caught it early enough."

"Which news was that?" Peter pushed his glasses toward his eyes.

"Both. No one likes surgery, but the results from this type of procedure are almost always positive. She's got a really good chance of lickin' this thing, Peter, and she probably can." Dr. Hollander sat back in his chair and breathed deeply, like it had already been a long day. He took a sip of cold coffee and took his handkerchief from his pocket to wipe his mouth.

"And?"

"And what? After surgery, if it doesn't work, we look at other treatments. But that's a big *if*. She should be back to normal in no time." Dr. Hollander's white hair had fallen over his eye, and he pushed it out of the way. "Jeanie seemed okay with it. Actually, she didn't really respond with much emotion at all, which I wondered about. Didn't even schedule the surgery—she said she wanted to wait. Which I assumed meant until she talked with you."

Peter looked down at the floor. His hands felt sticky and hot, but he also felt strangely comforted, a feeling that had long been missing in his soul.

"But, Peter, we don't want to wait too long for this surgery, okay? The sooner, the better."

"Okay. Thank you, Doctor. We'll call you soon." Peter rose from his chair and extended his hand. He nodded, and as he was almost at the door, he turned toward the physician.

"Sorry I wasn't here with her."

"Well, I reckon you can't be everywhere all the time, right, Pastor? Congratulations by the way." He waived as Peter opened the door and marched down the hall out to Loretta's car.

"We just missed her. Mind if you just drop me off at home?" Peter was in the passenger's seat.

"Mind if I take the back road instead of the highway? I hate the busyness of that dadgum interstate." Peter did mind. He was anxious to get home to Jeanie. But he was also in Loretta's car.

"You're the driver."

"Oh, shoot. Look what time it is. Forget the scenic route. We'll hustle down the highway."

But they did not hustle. Or hurry. For some reason dozens of cars were backed up almost to the entrance where Peter and Loretta got on. Cars formed one lane and crawled slowly down a single road of the interstate.

"Oh, Lord, must have been an accident," Loretta said as she turned the radio knob to find some report on what had happened, but all they heard was static. Peter tapped the top of the dashboard with his fingers, then caught himself and stopped. He just wanted to be with his wife. To do the right thing.

By the time they slowed enough to where the police cars and ambulances had gathered, they saw a car crashed into the cement wall of the overpass, pressed like an accordion at the base of the bridge. The wall was thirty or so feet from the pullout lane, far from the flow of traffic and isolated in its position and function. The driver, Peter thought, must have lost control entirely. Or else driven into it like an arrow at a target. Firefighters and paramedics were trying to break open the doors to get the driver out.

"Lord have mercy. Looks like someone drove straight into that wall!" Loretta whispered.

Peter's back tightened and his lungs fought for air as they got closer to the car. He recognized it. Panic smothered his chest as his eyes locked on the back of the bumper. He started to shake.

It was *his* car.

"Stop!" he screamed to Loretta. She pulled to the shoulder of the road behind a police car, its light flashing in circles. Peter jumped out of the car. And he ran.

By the time he got close to the car, officers were putting their arms out to stop him. Someone yelled at him, but he did not understand what he heard. Another grabbed him and pulled him back toward a patrol car, keeping him in a wrestler's locked hold. His arms flailed and his body struggled to get loose, but the grip was too tight. He screamed with every ounce of life in him.

Then he looked up just as the firefighters pried open the car's front door. They reached in, then out again. They brought a stretcher close to the door and gently lay the bloody mass of human flesh on top. Brown hair hung over the side, and Peter saw every strand in the sunlight.

"NO!!"

He went limp, and the siren from the ambulance blared past him.

FIFTEEN

J ack opened the door to Jordan's apartment building for her and followed behind. The cold December temperatures outside had fallen to single digits, and the night air made it seem even colder. Tonight's performance of *Windfall*, though, was hot, according to Danny, marking a strong opening night for the Stage Bite Theater, not sold-out but close. Drama critics from three newspapers attended, and the actors delivered fine performances. This could be the break Jordan had prayed for.

Even Vinnie came, the first to his feet at the curtain call, leading the audience in Jordan's first standing ovation. She was embarrassed by both the attention and his presence.

Jack, too, had insisted on coming to the play to support her, just as he insisted on making sure she got home safely afterward. They climbed the five floors to her apartment, thawing from the cold and talking about the excitement of the evening. She offered him hot tea before he went back out into the winter night to catch the subway home.

"You'd be feeling pretty good about this show, huh, Jordan?" Jack asked as he closed the door behind him.

"I'm still amazed it happened at all. It's why I came to New York." Jordan grabbed the teakettle and two mugs at the same time. She pointed to the couch for Jack and turned the stove on under the kettle.

"Well, it succeeded in getting this tough old bloke thinking about a few new things." Jack settled against a pillow at the end of the couch and took off his gloves and coat. The apartment was warm, bordering on hot, because of the heating unit in the old building and the controlled heat that came from it. The superintendent of the apartment always kept it up high to make sure everyone was warm. Sometimes Jordan kept the window open just to let out some of the heat.

"If my play got you going even a little, well, then I'm better than I thought!" They laughed at the joke and sipped tea on the couch, awkward at the other's company but enjoying it nonetheless.

"So what's next, Jordan Riddle?" Jack turned toward Jordan as he drank some of his tea. His gaze was serious when he leaned in her direction, his arm perched across the top of the couch.

Jordan scratched the back of her head and noticed the family photo above the spot where Jack sat. She couldn't help but wonder what her daddy would think of this man. She was glad she'd taken her mama and auntie by the Dream Time for dinner last week on their visit; she'd wanted them to see the place that had helped pay her rent these past five years, but she also wanted them to meet Jack. They, of course, were enchanted.

"What's next? I don't know. Broadway maybe. London's East End. I'm not picky." The peppermint tea warmed Jordan's whole body.

"That's great for you, Jordan, but what's next for us?" Jack cleared his throat as he spoke.

"Us?"

"Us. I was wondering, I mean. If you wanted, maybe we could, uh, go...out...to dinner sometime?" Jack was drawing a little circle with his finger in the couch beside him, concentrating on it like he was creating a great work of art.

Jordan smiled.

"You mean some place besides the Dream Time?"

He laughed and nodded.

"I'd love to, Jack. I think you're one of the nicest guys I've ever met." He stopped drawing and looked up when she said this. "Next to Barry." They both laughed again. Jack let out a long, bellowing sigh of relief, as if he'd been holding in the question for weeks.

When she got up to pour some more hot water into their mugs, Jordan noticed the light on her answering machine flashing. By instinct she pressed the button.

"Hold that thought, Jack."

He grinned. But when the panic in a woman's voice filled the apartment, neither smiled for long.

"Hey Jordan. It's your auntie. Call me as soon as you get in. It's an emergency. Doesn't matter how late." Jordan felt a flutter of nerves punch her rib cage as she heard Cynthia Sue's distress. Her aunt was always calm. Always. Something was really wrong.

Another message came out.

"Hi, hon. It's me again. Call me. Soon as you can."

Jordan grabbed her phone and her address book, looked up the number on the *R* page, and dialed.

"Hey Auntie. It's me, your favorite niece." Jordan tried to infuse the optimism of the evening into her voice, forcing a smile into the phone, hoping that would make whatever was wrong, right.

Her face went white as she pressed the phone to her ear. Her eyes filled. And she struggled to hold on to the side of the table where the cord lay. Jack jumped beside her.

"I'll catch the first flight I can. I'll call you from the airport, okay? As soon as I know what flight I'm on." Jordan was shaking. "Tell her I'm coming, Auntie Cyn. Tell her I'm on my way."

She dropped the phone in its cradle and turned to Jack.

"It's...my...mama." A flood of tears exploded from Jordan's soul and into Jack's chest. He wrapped his arms around her and held her steady as she let them go. Five, maybe ten, minutes passed as she cried and shook and trembled until finally she hunted down a breath, brought it in close, and slowed down. She looked up into Jack's face. Tears lined his cheeks too.

"What do you need me to do?" he asked softly. Jordan tried to hear him.

"She's in the hospital, Jack. Lost control of the car. Intensive care. I've got to get to the airport."

"Okay, mate. You get your bag packed, and I'll call the airline and a cab. You'll be able to catch a red-eye flight tonight. Anyone else you want me to call?"

She strained to think, tossing shirts, jeans, and underwear into a bag as she flew around the apartment. Yes, Sister Leslie. Barry. Danny and the folks at the Stage Bite. Even Vinnie. Jordan wanted all of them to know. Could he please call them?

" 'Course I will," Jack said as he hung up the phone. "Flight leaves in an hour and a half," he glanced at his watch. "We better go."

The chill of the night now was deeper in Jordan's bones as she and Jack ran outside and into the cab that had pulled up to the curb. The ride was quiet and quick. Jack held Jordan's hand as they drove along, but still she trembled. Thoughts of her mama captured her mind and sucked all of her feelings toward them. She shook her head to brush off some of the fear and turned to the man beside her.

"Guess you're going to need to find a new waitress for a while, boss," Jordan said, her voice still shivering.

"No worries, mate. Don't even think about it. This is much more important than work." Then Jack reached into his pocket and grabbed a business card from the Tavern. He wrote his home phone number on the back and pushed it into her bag.

"Call as soon as you get there. So I know you're safe. And then whenever you need to. Anytime." He smiled at her. "Collect." Jordan saw that glimmer in his eyes she had noticed a month or so ago. Now she understood who it was for.

At LaGuardia Airport Jack paid the cabdriver and carried Jordan's bag after her into the terminal. She was buying her ticket at the counter and fighting back tears at the same time. He put his arm on her shoulder and leaned into her ear.

"You are the bravest person I know." The words lingered in her ear for a moment. "Don't forget to call me when you get there. Okay, Jordan?" She nodded at him. He lifted her chin and kissed her cheek. Jordan then picked up her bag and walked toward the gate.

She waved back toward Jack, who was still standing in the terminal looking after her. He raised his hand to her, bowed his head, and tipped his cap in Jordan's direction. It was a gesture that melted some of her worry and helped slow her trembling. In it she saw that Jack's care for her was a profound reminder of something greater than themselves, pointing Jordan back to the comfort and affection she'd always believed to be transcendent. God-like. Human love, she remembered, was a tiny—but certain—reflection of the Creator's. She was not alone.

The words rose up in her like a fountain: *Surely he took up our infirmities and carried our sorrows.... The punishment that brought us peace was upon him.* Her heart stilled. Her sorrows had *already* been carried. Somehow as she entered the plane to head home to Jackson—the first time since she had come to New York five years ago—Jordan knew there was a peace far beyond whatever circumstance lay ahead. She found her seat by a window, looked out, and saw the lights on the wing sparkle in the darkness. Then she closed her eyes and tried to rest.

Cynthia Sue found her at baggage claim. They held each other long after the luggage and passengers had gone from the area, sniffling and shivering and wanting the comfort of each other's arms to change the reality of Jeanie's condition. The prognosis was not good. Jordan's aunt told her that the doctors were not optimistic. The impact of the car against the overpass wall had been so great it shattered much of her body and pushed her to the edge of life. She must have been driving well over the speed limit and plowed right into the wall with disastrous force. Emergency surgery had perhaps prolonged her existence, but a coma locked away any sign of the woman they had once known.

"I told her you were coming, hon," Cynthia said as she let go of Jordan and wiped her eyes with a tissue. "I think she heard me."

"I *know* she did," Jordan murmured. She squeezed her aunt's wrist, leaned across, and kissed her on the cheek. They locked elbows and walked toward the car.

"Your daddy's been there the whole time. Hasn't gone home or to the church or anything." Cynthia glanced at Jordan as she spoke. "He's a wreck, Jordan. That's what you're walking into."

The words invaded Jordan's mind and formed a picture of her father sitting beside a hospital bed. When they had found her brother's body that day after the storm, his pulse was still beating, and the doctors at the American military base in Fiji thought they could save him. Jordan's father sat close to his son, clinging to his hand and believing the boy would get better. Young Jordan watched him from the doorway, certain her daddy could make her brother better like he did everything else then, but too young to know how close to death James really was. She had not seen her father in a hospital room since.

She took a deep breath.

The sun was just rising over Jackson, and Jordan watched the city like she did a favorite movie she'd seen over and over, observing scenes from certain places, associating particular streets with people she'd known, anticipating what was coming next as they drove toward the hospital. Most of the town was as she left it—though now it seemed smaller and slower than she remembered.

Some buildings were familiar; others had been knocked down, and Jordan felt their absence.

Except for the few physical details Cynthia Sue prepared Jordan for about her mother's condition—bruises, stitches, machines she was attached to—they drove without saying much. Jordan listened but could not imagine. When they turned down Capital Street and into the parking lot of Jackson Memorial Hospital, Jordan's stomach rose under her chest. Her palms grew wet and her throat clogged. Not only was she about to see her mother in an excruciating condition, but she would have to encounter her father in the process, a stranger whose presence—and disapproval—she felt daily.

"I'm scared, Auntie Cyn," she whispered. Her aunt reached across the seat, patted her arm, and said something Jordan had never heard come out of her mouth: "Well, sugar, I reckon this is a real good time to pray."

Jordan stared at her for a second, glanced back out the window, and, grateful for the reminder, let go of some of her fear.

On the elevator she felt the strong, slender fingers of her aunt's link in hers, and the closeness lifted her courage. When the door slid open, though, Jordan's heart went wild and her rib cage was a battlefield where emotions shot from side to side like bullets. A heavy drop of pain rolled down her cheek, the beginning of her confrontation, and she brushed the wetness with her fingers.

The hallway was stale and white, full of smells and sounds that reminded Jordan just how far away she was from New York City. She asked her aunt to wait when they passed a pay phone on the wall. Jordan dialed Jack's number collect. He was asleep but glad to hear her voice, to know the flight had gone smoothly and that she was now at the hospital.

"I'm going in to see her now. I'll call you tomorrow." Jordan hung up the phone, tired and nervous but braver for hearing Jack's voice.

Nurses huddled around stations, lights flashed above doors, and visitors walked dazed as they emerged from rooms. When she and her aunt arrived at the intensive care unit, Cynthia Sue wrote her niece's name on a form for the nurse, who looked over half-moon glasses at Jordan and nodded her head. Then she turned toward the hallway and beckoned for Jordan to follow while Auntie Cyn stood at the desk, watching and dabbing her eyes with a tissue.

Except for the red-and-white lights on the monitors and a few streaks of morning sun squeezing through the window shades, Jeanie's room was dark. Jordan stood at the doorway, the light behind her, and gasped as she saw her mama. Tubes jetted from every part of her body to IV stands and machines, her face blackened from the bruises of the impact. Jordan inhaled and entered the room, fixed on the woman lying listless on the bed.

Dried blood lined her mama's cheeks. Her eyes twitched

beneath swollen lids. Jordan leaned into her mother's ear and smelled a strange mix of rubbing alcohol and lotion.

"I'm here, Mama. It's me, Jordan. I love you." Jordan pressed her nose lightly against her mother's hair. She ran her fingers over her forehead, stroking her skin and whispering over and over how much she loved her. But her mama did not move. She did not respond at all. Her breathing was hard and cumbersome, as if stacks of weights lay on top of her lungs, and the wheezing sounds drowned out even the buzz of the machines that helped her breathe at all.

Jordan sat gently on the edge of her mama's bed and stared down into the face of the woman who just a week ago had laughed in her apartment. She picked up her cold, limp hand and covered it with both of hers, careful to keep it still and caressed. And she searched for every prayer and scripture her mama had taught her when she was a little girl, hoping they might bring her back from the faraway place she had gone, knowing it was not likely, but clinging to the possibility nonetheless.

Hers was a human faith, one that believed against reality, that somehow remained attached to the flimsy promise that anything was possible even when it was not probable.

"Jesus, please," she muttered aloud. She stared at her mother as she prayed. "Make her comfortable. Help her." Jordan's eyes watered as she spoke. She shook her head back and forth, fighting the moment but hanging on to it as well. She reached into her pocket and pulled out her glasses and the paper that Sister Leslie had given her weeks ago; it was as worn and ripped as she was. But she read it anyway, close to her mother's ear, stammering to get through each line as if her life depended on it, just in case it did.

> *"He had no beauty or majesty to attract us to him,*
>> *nothing in his appearance that we should desire him.*
> *He was despised and rejected by men,*
>> *a man of sorrows, and familiar with suffering.*
> *Like one from whom men hide their faces*
>> *he was despised, and we esteemed him not."*

She looked up at the window as a burst of sunlight escaped the sides of the shade, falling like beams across the floor. Jordan's eyes spilled onto the paper, and she brought her wrist across them to absorb the tears. She kept reading:

> *"Surely he took up our infirmities*
>> *and carried our sorrows,*
> *yet we considered him stricken by God,*
>> *smitten by him, and afflicted.*
> *But he was pierced for our transgressions,*
>> *he was crushed for our iniquities;*
> *the punishment that brought us peace was upon*
>>> *him...*

Jordan stopped, and she slowly folded the paper. She set it in Jeanie's hand, closing her fingers around it, though there was no strength or grip in them.

"Hold on to this, Mama. He went through this…pain…too." The words had barely dropped from her mouth when Jordan felt a deep and sudden relaxation seize the muscles in her shoulders. It was as if there were a cease-fire in her soul. She began to sing to her mother. "Swing low, sweet chariot… Comin' for to carry me home…"

Another voice joined her.

Her father had been sitting in the corner behind the door. He was singing too.

Startled by his voice, Jordan shot her head toward him. Startled perhaps more by the stains on his cheeks and the softness in his eyes.

He continued, "I looked over Jordan and what did I see?"

His voice collapsed when the song fell off his lips, pierced by the irony of the words and the agony of the event that had brought his daughter to this place. He stared at her, admiring her in the morning light, noticing the beauty of her mother reflected in her face. He blinked. Jordan did too. And as if a hundred pounds had been holding it down, Peter pushed his hand up into the air, shaking and trembling to get it free, until finally, when it reached the top of his shoulder, he spread out his fingers. He waved at Jordan.

His daughter's eyes filled for him.

"Hey Daddy," she whispered, exhaling a breath of fear. Then

she saw her father's broken face. "She'll be all right, Daddy. He's got her like he's got James."

When Jordan said her brother's name, Peter stood up, grabbed the back of his skull, and shook his head like he was trying to pry it off.

"I should never have let him swim alone that day… I should never have let her drive…without me…"

Jordan glanced up at him and saw another man standing in front of her. One she had not known before. This man looked like her father, but his face was tormented with doubt. It was an expression Jordan had never seen in her father. She stood up and turned away from her mother at the same time that a gust of anger and compassion collided in her heart. She pushed her glasses back on and faced her father.

"Daddy, you are not responsible for James," she said quietly.

He pushed his hands to his ears as if he could keep out the truth, but Jordan's voice squeezed in anyway.

"Or Mama."

He threw his hands down and stared at her.

"I shouldn't have let them go…"

"You let *me* go."

Peter fell back into the chair. "*You?* I didn't have a choice."

"I think that's the point, Daddy." Jordan spoke softly but surely, the voice of an artist who had just finished the last stroke on a beautiful painting.

Peter's eyes clouded. "If I had been there, I could have protected them."

"But, Daddy, *nothing* is guaranteed to us." Jordan stood directly in front of her father now. His hands trembled on his lap and his eyebrows pierced forward at the thought of what she was saying. "Except God. *He's* our guarantee. Didn't you teach me that when I was little?" Then she set her hands on top of Peter's to steady them, and he sighed as he felt his daughter's warm palm above his knuckles. He said nothing; he just stared at her fingers and tried to remember all the times they had been together, not apart. And slowly he stopped shivering.

A nurse pushed open the door, hurried across to Jeanie, and checked a thin tube that was attached to the crease in her elbow. Jordan turned toward her as Peter rose beside her. It was the same nurse who had shown Jordan to her mother's room. As she checked Jeanie's pulse, sorrow crossed her face. She glanced over her glasses again at Jordan, then at Peter.

"It's soon," she said.

"I'll get Auntie Cyn," Jordan said, turning to her father. She squeezed his hand, walked to her mother, and kissed her cheek. Then she opened the door to the hallway to find her aunt.

Peter came beside his wife. He kissed the same cheek their daughter just had and nestled into her face.

"I'm...so...sorry, Jeanie." His tears dropped on her skin.

Cynthia Sue and Jordan entered the room, pulled their chairs next to Peter's, and held each other's hands. The three of them listened to Jeanie's labored breathing grow louder and louder. Dr. Hollander came in and felt her neck and pulse. Then he put his hand atop Peter's shoulder.

"Let me know if you need anything," he said, nodding also to Jordan and Cynthia Sue before he pushed the door again and walked back out.

Not long after that, Peter bowed his head, Auntie Cyn sobbed into her hands, and Jordan leaned into her mama, kissed her cheek, and said good-bye.

Three days later, the organist at Second Baptist played "The Old Rugged Cross" and "Great Is Thy Faithfulness" as Jordan sat in the first pew, a few feet from her mother's coffin. Her aunt sat between her and her father, a tissue knotted in her fist and a black sweater around her shoulders. The December air had warmed slightly, but the church felt drafty this morning. Christmas wreaths hung on the pulpit, a strange reminder of the season and a seemingly incongruous symbol for a funeral.

Jordan was numb. She stared at the red-and-green ribbons around the evergreen ring and recalled a dozen Christmas mornings when she had pulled her mama out of bed to open presents. The colors around the lights on the Christmas tree reminded her of the colors this morning in the church: sparkling, lively, changing. There were a million things she hadn't said to the woman who loved her all these years, and now the missed opportunities felt heavy on Jordan's soul. How grateful she was, though, for their time together in New York. And for the solace her mother provided in coming to her play just two weeks ago. Now Jordan's fingers yearned for her mama's hand one more time, to hold it as they said grace for Christmas dinner or as she stumbled through the confusion of this time. But she could not touch her. Jordan hurt from the absence.

Dr. Stately stepped to the pulpit when the organist played his last note. Regardless of his current position, Peter felt he was the only one who could lead this service. He had been Jeanie's pastor as well, and even with all that happened, somehow Peter knew that Dr. Stately would be the only one who could know what to do on a morning like this, because *he* certainly didn't. These past weeks had pushed Peter into the chaos of his illusions, exhausting and depleting him and reducing him to the man he really was. He closed his eyes, hoping he would gaze on the face of his bride as she walked down the aisle toward him. Instead, he saw Jeanie's expression as she drove off from the church the day of her death, and he shivered at her distance. How much he regretted. Now all Peter wanted was a last chance to do the right thing for her. He would say good-bye to her as her husband, not as a pastor. He breathed softly at her memory and put his hand around his sister's hand.

"Dear friends, these are the moments when words are difficult to find," Dr. Stately began. He searched the faces before him, as if he were asking for their help, but no one offered him any. Silence echoed around the sanctuary. Dr. Stately glanced at Peter, but Peter's eyes were still shut.

"Our lives are full of mysteries. Tragedies come to each of us, and often all we know to do is ask why. Why do these things happen? Why do we lose that which we love? For what purpose?"

The question rang off the wall and into every eardrum present. Jordan pressed her neck against the top of the pew, straining to listen. Peter opened his eyes and looked toward the pulpit.

"I cannot presume to know the answer for any of you. Perhaps we have loved too much. Perhaps our grip on something—or someone—was too tight, so tight that we could not grab a hold of the other gifts in our lives because there was no room for them. Or perhaps God so wants our attention that he will stop at nothing to show us the intensity of his love." He paused, glancing at the coffin. "Oh, what fools we are for thinking we control our lives!"

People shifted in their pews. The flowers on top of Jeanie's casket glistened under the candlelight; their beauty seemed to glow. Dr. Stately continued.

"Our sister Jeanie Riddle cared deeply for her husband, her daughter, her family, friends, and students. In so many ways hers was a sacrificial life. But in a split second, death stole her away from us, reminding us of the frailty of our lives. We are guaranteed no days together, no relationships, no perfect health or great careers.

Yet just as Job was stripped of everything precious, or King Solomon his power, so, too, do our losses become lessons." He swallowed. Then he spoke so softly almost everyone sat forward to hear him.

"They point us to a cross, to a man so familiar with suffering that his own death became the greatest sacrifice in the history of our world. Why? For what purpose?" The question hung in the air like a banner. No one moved. "So each of us might know the *only* gift that deserves all of our devotion: him. This much I know is true."

The church was still.

Dr. Stately kept talking for a few moments before he invited others to say a few words if they wanted. But for Jordan and Peter the time simply dissolved into a kaleidoscope of sounds, colors, and shapes. Prayers and passages from the Bible, silence and songs, handshakes and tears, all held them and lost them as they wrestled between thoughts and memories, stories and meaning.

The woman who had been their only link for the past five years was gone.

They drove to the cemetery quietly, looking out the window as they passed familiar sites through Jackson. Then they stood beside each other in the morning sun, a crowd around them as they listened to Dr. Stately's last prayer. Together they threw dirt on the casket as it was laid in the ground. And as they turned to the limousine, the minister announced that Jeanie's family would take visitors back at the fellowship hall of Second Baptist.

"All are welcome," he said.

The driver pulled off slowly, and Peter stared out the window toward the faces of those who were leaving the grave: Loretta and her family, Jimmy, Miss Mary, the deacons, and some seniors from the Cherry Blossom Center. He even saw Chaplain Drinkwater walking beside Johnny as they got back into their car. His heart sagged.

But he also noticed a nun in a black-and-white habit standing beside a tall man in a leather jacket. They walked with another man back toward their car, talking together like they were old friends. They did not look familiar to him.

The drive back was much the same, with Peter, Jordan, and Cynthia Sue still dazed by what they'd just done, still stunned by their loss and what it meant for them. Their knees touched each time the driver went over a bump, and the closeness made them aware of each other's presence when they were otherwise lost in their grief. Cynthia Sue broke the silence.

"So, hon, when you heading back?"

Peter looked at his daughter. He had not considered this.

"Not sure yet," Jordan responded.

"You're going back?" Peter's emotion filled the question.

"Yes, Daddy. I have a show right now in production and—"

"I know. Your mother told me—" he stopped himself. He saw his wife's face. "She was really proud, Jordan."

"Well, she should be. It's a helluva play," Cynthia Sue beamed as she turned to her niece. "I'm proud too, sugar." She pressed Jordan's hand.

Jordan's eyes filled. Then she took off her glasses and wiped them.

Her daddy watched as she did.

The atmosphere inside the fellowship hall was vibrant, considering the occasion, and outsiders might have found it disrespectful if they did not know this was a homecoming of sorts. Sweet and magical aromas met everyone at the door as they first strolled past a table with photos of Jeanie and a guest book they could sign if they wanted. The ladies group from the church had set up a square table in the corner with a punch bowl of sweet tea. Tiny green-and-gold paper cups sat around it. Across a long table beside it were plastic plates, napkins, and dozens and dozens of casseroles, green-bean salads, black-eyed peas, corn breads, hams, turkey, and fried chicken. On a table up against the wall was another lined with homemade cookies, fruit pies, chocolate puddings, lemon cakes, and whipped cream.

Loretta and her family were first in line, followed by anyone who wandered in after them. A quiet but friendly buzz filled the air, and every now and then someone laughed aloud. Children ran back and forth under the basketball hoops, and elderly folks sat close to the tables filled with food.

Barry caught Jordan as she first walked in. They cried on each other's cheeks and shook for a few minutes. Then Barry let go and held Jordan's hands in front of her.

"I will say this: you are the *only* human on this planet who could have gotten me inside a church!" They laughed and hugged again.

"I hope it wasn't too painful, Bare," Jordan joked.

"I managed," he said. "Now hug these other friends because I need some food." Barry pushed Jordan toward Sister Leslie as he hurried toward the tables. The two women cried, too, as they rocked back and forth in their embrace.

"Thank you so much for coming, Sister," Jordan whispered. "I gave my mama your poem. It meant the world."

Sister Leslie's cheeks turned pink, then wet from her tears. She leaned into Jordan's ear.

"Anything. You need anything, and you let us know, okay?"

Jordan nodded.

"I was fascinated by your minister's sermon. I'll be back in a second, okay?" The nun strolled over to Dr. Stately, who was talking with Chaplain Drinkwater, and Jordan couldn't help but expect they were in for an interesting conversation. Before she had time to consider it, though, two firm hands came from behind her and covered her eyes. She smiled at the game.

"Hey mate," Jack whispered in her ear. She turned around, and his eyes were full and rich, gripping hers. A tiny flutter of joy jumped in her ribs. Her palms turned warm, and she hoped Jack would not grab them. He leaned in and kissed her.

"You okay?" he asked softly.

Tears slipped again from her eyes. "So glad you're here," she whispered.

Cynthia Sue appeared out of nowhere.

"Jack. It's so nice of you to come. Now talk to us in that Aussie accent of yours." Jordan's aunt grabbed his hands and swung them back and forth. Jack pulled back shyly and glanced away.

"I'm so sorry for your loss," he whispered to her. Cynthia's eyes welled as he spoke. So did Jack's. He handed her a tissue, and Jordan put her arm on her auntie's shoulder. Then she looked across the room.

She saw Barry pointing to Miss Mary's flower dress and gesturing his admiration of it to her. Mutual appreciation filled their faces. Then Miss Mary set down her plate on the table beside her and smothered him in a massive bear hold, jiggling in line behind the punch bowl.

Jordan could not help herself. She elbowed Jack and Auntie Cyn, pointed to Barry and Miss Mary, and a laughter so deep and so real erupted that people around the room might have thought it was the sound of one person echoing across the room.

Peter noticed it, too, and looked to see what had caught their attention. He saw Miss Mary's flowery love all but smashing some poor soul in a leather jacket, and for the first time in a long, long time, Peter Riddle chuckled. Then he laughed. And then he could not stop. For several moments, and in a loud bellowing sound, he laughed hard and he laughed long. Hope was returning to his bones, and a feeling he had not experienced in years shot through him: acceptance.

He walked across the room, took his daughter in his arms, and laughed and cried at the same time he held her. The feeling surprised him.

A small celebration had begun.

ACKNOWLEDGMENTS

This process has taught me two things: (1) writing fiction is really hard, and (2) without the gift of other people, of community, I would never have survived. And so I want to say thank you:

To Don Pape, friend and vice president at WaterBrook, whose prodding over the years and vision for me as a novelist really did prompt me to take the first step.

To Scotty Smith, Jo Hopping, Janet Mazur, and Bernie Sheahan, whose readings (or "hearings") of early drafts and comments made this a better story and a more enjoyable journey.

To Andrea, Sonjy, Melissa, Pamela, Daniel, Sanne, Debbie H., Jason, Katherine, and so many other amazing friends, whose support in my craft and example of integrity in theirs keeps me going.

To Vinita Hampton Wright, whose creative gifts in her novels and friendship first gave me hope for the strange and much-abused genre known as "Christian" fiction.

To scads of other authors whose works will always inspire and instruct me, some of whom I mention here from my most influential category: Flannery O'Connor, C. S. Lewis, Dorothy Sayers, Walter Wangerin Jr., Maya Angelou, Tennessee Williams, Arthur Miller, Lorraine Hansberry, Annie Dillard, Harper Lee, and Zora Neale Hurston.

To Dudley Delffs, my friend and editor at WaterBrook, whose fiction sensibilities, skillful mentoring, and gracious vision gave this story a much better life.

To my husband and partner in creative adventures, Christopher Gilbert, who dropped what he was doing to read every chapter…twice…and who still loves me. 'Tis a sweet marriage indeed that shares the love of story.

Finally, to the next generation of artists of faith, whose courage to create in the face of legalistic dogma and anemic spirituality reminds me that the hand of redemption never grows weary.

To all of the above, and to *you*, the reader, who was kind enough to read this, I'm grateful.

About the Author

Jo Kadlecek is a former waitress, soccer player, and English teacher who currently writes full time from her home on the Jersey Shore, just south of New York City. She is a frequent teacher at workshops, retreats, and conferences, and she holds a Master of Arts in communication and another in humanities.

For more information about Jo, please visit her Web site at www.lamppostmedia.net.